GEORGE ELLIS

Wreckers

A Denver Boyd Novel

First edition

ISBN: 978-1-7364843-1-9

Cover art by Drew Hammond

This book was professionally typeset on Reedsy. Find out more at reedsy.com

Contents

Chapter 1

I might not be the smartest guy in the galaxy, but I do know my way around the place. I also know my way around every kind of ship in it.

So when I picked up the distress signal from a T-Class 405 Cruiser, my first instinct was to ignore the red flashing light on my console. 405's are strictly federation vessels. Military. The last time I helped a 405 out of a jam, it took a solid month to get paid. No tip, either.

Not to mention this particular distress call belonged to a ship that was 250,000 miles away. Unless someone invented a magical warp drive and didn't tell me about it, a quarter million miles was 36 hours of my life I'd never get back. That's a big sacrifice just to save a handful of federation yahoos who'd just as soon arrest me as pay me for my services.

Screw that noise. I'd rather enjoy my beer.

It *was* my last one, though. Acquiring a good batch of IPA was hard enough with a healthy credit line. My line was more on the anemic end of the spectrum. And by the end, I mean past the edge and over the side. That's probably because the last job I had was over three weeks ago, towing a non-wealthy family of four back to their home base for a grand total of 46 credits and a bout of some rare sickness called "the measles" that left me weak as a baby.

I took another swig of my beer, delicately nursing the final few drops just in case they were my last for a while. I enjoyed a great brew more for the taste and the relaxation than to get drunk. There was something about those hops that hit me just right. I also had a soda problem. Basically, put something delicious in a can and make it hard to get, and I wanted a lot of it.

A testament to my favorite vices loomed in the corner of the cabin: a pile of empty cans and packets that rose like a mountain, growing closer to the ceiling each day. Around the base of the structure were discarded plastic food containers I hadn't got around to trashing yet. One of these days I would move the heap to the incinerator…if I could just find the wheelbarrow. Or even a shovel. The control panel was littered with vintage books and magazines, some of them hundreds of years old and filled with quaint stories of Earth and its many "countries," which were basically various plots of land with imaginary boundaries drawn around them.

The copilot chair served as my foot rest most of the time. The heels of my boots had actually left a pair of matching, permanent dents in the seat.

Sleeping atop the back of the chair on a gray flannel blanket was Pirate, my one-eyed cat. He was born that way (with one eye, not sleeping atop the blanket, though he does spend most of his time there). Some of his mock-tuna cans were in Mount Trashmore as well — like captain, like cat. He drew his black and white paws tighter as I walked past him toward the bathroom, which was situated down the hall, inside the section of the ship that contained a row of living quarters designed to accommodate up to eight crewmembers. Which meant Pirate and I each had four rooms to ourselves, if we wanted them. I of course imposed no such imaginary boundaries on myself. The entirety of the ship was my home, from the cabin to the various crew rooms to the cargo bay. Five thousand square feet of sovereign soil wherever I chose to fly it.

Mustang 1, as the vessel had been known since well before I'd inherited it from my uncle, was far more impressive on the outside. Its exterior panels were outfitted with large swaths of chrome in an homage to the muscle cars that used to prowl the roads of Earth in the late 20th century. The massive wings formed an X around a tubelike center retrofitted with not one, but two extra turbine engines, giving the Stang a total of four turbines "under the hood."

Some people questioned my uncle's sanity when he had the additional nuclear core installed, but he had the engineering chops to do it right. The result was unparalleled power and speed for a ship in its class.

Yep, Uncle Erwin had been a genius and a pioneer. Me? I was just a lowly mechanic. He'd also been a shrewd businessman, building the only independently-owned ship in the galaxy capable of towing a battlecruiser to either end of it.

I took a few moments to study myself in the bathroom mirror. I didn't look amazing. For a 19-year-old, I had some pretty heavy bags under my eyes, thanks to a constantly shifting sleep schedule. Sometimes I went days without decent shuteye. Other times I would be out for 12 or more hours a pop. My curly black hair was tangled and filled with grease of various origins – the engine, my body, maybe even the garbage stacked up all around. It was just hard to stay motivated to clean myself or my ship between jobs. That always bit me in the ass when I got a new gig, as I had to clean out the Stang

3

all in one go.

As I exited the bathroom, I nearly tripped over a bin of spare turbine parts in the middle of the corridor. Like I said, it was the maid's year off. I made a mental note to clean up and shower before the next time I went to bed.

I looked down at the parts by my feet and grimaced. Resting atop the stack of mismatched metal thingamajigs was a piston for the very type of engine found in most 405's. Once again, the universe was trying to tell me something. I hated when it did that.

The distress call was fairly specific as far as those things go. The ship had apparently stalled about a hundred thousand miles from the Earth's moon. The message suggested it was a mechanical problem, which meant it was probably something else entirely. If they had the right diagnosis, they'd be able to fix the damn thing themselves. They wouldn't need me. And you can bet that's the first thing the engineers would say when I arrived: they already knew what the problem was. They'd keep talking down to me, even after I fixed their ship for them, or gave them a tow. That was the federation way.

Formally known as the Interstellar Federation Force, the military group started as a joint peace-keeping organization between the governments of Earth, Mars and the various stations that had sprung up in between. It probably seemed like a good idea at the time. You know, keep the verse safe through collaboration and cooperation. Blah, blah, blah.

The very first General of the IFF was a well-respected former military man who had served on Earth as the head of the United Nations forces, and then later on Mars as one of the first settlers there, back in the early days. He modeled the federation based on what he knew. That was the military.

4

So instead of creating some kind of new organization to fit the dynamics of life in space, he just copied what worked on planets. The result was an inefficient mess. One of the first signs that the federation model was flawed came just a few years after it was formed, when they realized you basically had to just hope the captains of any particular ship were good men and women. If they weren't, it could take months or even years to track them down, and a rogue captain can do a lot of damage with no oversight.

So, like any governmental agency – and especially one spread so thin across the verse – the federation grew more and more corrupt over time. It was just too much territory to cover. Back on Earth, there was a finite plot of land an army had to protect or a police force had to oversee, and they still had problems. Out here in space, it was naive to think rogue admirals wouldn't begin to treat their little pockets of the verse more like personal fiefdoms than parts of a larger community.

These days, the feds (I didn't like to use their full name, it gave them too much respect) were basically their own nation-state, spread out across hundreds of ships in every corner of the verse. Under the guise of keeping the peace, they enforced arcane taxes and tariffs, extorted local officials and often laid waste to ships and individuals they deemed as being threats to society. In some ways, the federation was the most dangerous and powerful force in the world.

Most of the officers were also insecure morons who got off on being in a position of power, and the crew were people who couldn't hack it on their own in the private sector, where things like talent and skill mattered. That wasn't just my opinion. It was the opinion of most non-feds. In my opinion, anyway. So it didn't surprise me at all to receive a distress call from a fed ship. They couldn't fix their own ships if their lives depended on it. Which they did, of course.

The main issue with being stalled in space is the life support system. As advanced as the tech is in the 24th century, all systems will eventually fail. Then you either freeze or suffocate, depending on the order of your malfunctions. I always thought freezing would be better.

In addition to the Stang's prodigious towing capacity, I had enough life support reserve to keep a small army alive for a month. If Pirate and I ever stalled, we could probably last five or six years if it wasn't for the whole running out of food thing (I think we had a month of food reserves).

That is, unless Gary drove us crazy first.

Gary was the ship's on board AI. My uncle was a big fan of the historical entertainment programs on Earth. In addition to filling the Stang's hard drive with scores of old movies and TV shows, he'd discovered that a select number of shows had licensed out their characters as navigational "personalities" available for purchase back in the day. Most of the personalities were pretty basic, but my uncle the genius decided to hack a blend of comedians from the era and name the character Gary, infusing him with artificial intelligence.

Digital Gary was 69 years old (he was launched at age 55 and had existed in AI form for 14 more so far), and he'd probably outlive me if my uncle got his way. "Big E," as people called him, only had two conditions when he left me the Stang: I had to continue the family business and I couldn't ever disable Gary.

Note the wording, there: disable. My uncle never said anything prohibiting me from forcing Gary to sleep for eight hours a day, just like the rest of us.

"Another military rescue," Gary noted as he perked awake, his voice emanating from the nearest speakers, as if he were standing right next to me. "Do you think they feel bad when they don't tip?"

"They better," I quipped, searching for food in the kitchen. "I know I do."

"I'd think that's the best part about being in the military. It's almost worth joining up just to avoid all those awkward exchanges. You certainly don't have to tip in the mess hall. The other thing that would be nice is the uniforms. Deciding what to wear day in and day out is such a hassle. Obviously you don't have those problems as you have like three items of clothing, total."

I sighed as I slunk back into my chair, gnawing on a stale protein bar. As usual, Gary had a point regarding the military's lack of tipping. The federation was notoriously cheap with outside vendors. But they also knew how to hold a grudge. If word got out I'd left a few dozen of their buddies to freeze and/or suffocate, they'd have no problem accidentally firing on my ship the first chance they got.

"Want me to drive?" asked Gary. "As you know, I'm pretty, pretty, pretty good at it."

"Sure, why not," I replied. The ship rotated and the turbines gently whirred as we embarked on our journey.

Sensing the shift in direction, Pirate stretched and yawned, then went back to sleep, as if he knew this was not some wild adventure we were about to undertake, but instead another routine job that would allow us to eke out a few more weeks of tuna. Which was fine with him. And on some level, with me too. Adventures tend to get people killed in this business.

My dad and brother found that out the hard way 14 months ago at a remote outpost called Missura, located a few hours off Mars' atmo.

Chapter 2

I woke to the ka-chunk of metal clamping on metal.

"Did we just dock? Tell me we didn't just dock with the 405," I growled, bleary-eyed.

"Okay, I won't tell you that," replied Gary. "You have a window."

I felt my stomach drop as I saw the military ship right outside the thick glass. How long had I been asleep? A moment later, I was being hailed on the com-link. I ignored the hail, focusing my ire on Gary. "Why the hell didn't you wake me up sooner?"

"Ah, we're going to pretend you didn't yell at me an hour ago when I tried every alarm we have to pull you out of your coma you call sleep?" said Gary.

It's true about the coma. For the last few months, I'd been suffering from a disorder that caused long-lasting sleep cycles, commonly referred to as "spaceouts." It's basically when a three-hour nap turns into a 16-hour REM bender.

I tried to clear my head as I rose from my pilot's chair. "I haven't even negotiated the rate yet and we're already docked. Answer their hail."

"Relax, I took care of it," came Gary's reply, stopping me in my tracks.

"You. What?"

"You'll like the terms. I even worked out a gratuity situation, provided you do a good job."

I was still trying to process what Gary told me when I heard two loud thumps on the door.

"Why does it always feel like I'm the one being boarded when I help these morons out?" I snarled.

"Because we don't trust morons like you," a voice shot back. One of the officers aboard the 405, no doubt.

"You said to answer the hail," Gary whispered into my earpiece.

I shot the nearest camera a death glare as if I was looking directly into Gary's artificial soul. Then I addressed the officer.

"Now that we've exchanged pleasantries, who do I have the pleasure of speaking with?" I asked.

"Senior Officer Jeffries of the Interstellar Federation, in command of the DTL Graymore. And I already know who you are," he said.

"Good, just give me a minute and I'll come aboard," I told him.

"Open the airlock and we'll meet on your ship first," he countered.

I looked around. I hadn't had time to clean. I didn't really care about the mess, but I did have a few items that would be better off unseen by anyone wearing a blue federation uniform.

"41.5," I said. "Section B."

It had been a while since I'd read the actual text, but I was pretty sure Code 41.5 section B of the statutes governing rescue vehicles meant I didn't have to let them board.

"In fact, I could just pop this airlock and be on my way."

Take that, I thought.

The response took a little longer than I expected, making me wonder if they were going to ignore the law and simply blast the doors in.

"Fine," said Jeffries. "For now."

I gathered my tool box and leather jacket and headed to the airlock. "Gary, you and I are going to have words, but in the meantime you know what to do if things go sideways."

"Does going sideways really mean anything in space?" Gary mused. "A ship turns sideways, it can still maneuver. If anything, we should say if things go off course. Or adrift. Nobody wants to drift in space."

"Not now!" I snapped. I punched in my five-digit security code to access the airlock. It buzzed. Incorrect. That was the weird thing about spaceouts: despite long periods of sleep, your brain still wakes up scrambled, as if you only dozed for a few minutes.

I tried to remember the proper code, but came up empty. Unlike most ships, my security system wasn't based on retinal or DNA scans. I didn't like the idea that someone could just drag my corpse around to open any doors they pleased. If an intruder came aboard and the ship went into lockdown, a manual code ensured they'd have to keep me around if they wanted full control of the Stang. Or they'd have to torture the code out of me. Hey, every plan has its drawbacks. I walked to the food cooler and reached for the freeze-dried vegetable brick in the bottom shelf, then peeled back the label, where I'd written the code.

A few moments later, the airlock hissed open and I found myself face to face with three very serious federation soldiers dressed in navy jumpsuits and matching berets, their guns leveled at my head.

I hate guns. And not only when they're aimed at me, which happens more often than I'd like. There's just something lazy about a gun. Any idiot can pick one up and start blasting away. Even if you have terrible aim, as I learned long ago that I did, guns create more problems than they solve.

Next to the soldiers, a stocky, balding officer regarded me with cold eyes. Jeffries.

"Denver Lamar Boyd," he said, correctly stating my name, as if I should be impressed. He looked me up and down. "Say, you out of diapers yet?"

That was not a new one. I got age jokes all the time from people, and the diaper jokes were a favorite. Usually they came from people underestimating me because of my age. They saw a teenage boy. What they didn't see was that I probably had more life experience than they did. I could've made a joke about how short he was or that his combover was more obvious than his diaper comment, but it wasn't worth it.

So we all stood there waiting for what came next. I scratched my ear, then checked to make sure my shoelaces were tied. The only other time a fed had ever used my full name, he was a judge sentencing me to two years' probation for transporting illegal animals and robots. It's a long story.

I considered giving Gary the order that would instantly release a localized electromagnetic pulse inside the confines of the airlock, rendering the guns trained on me useless. They were standard issue firearms with electronic triggers and palm recognition. Once the guns' circuits were fried, the soldiers would basically be holding hunks of plastic. I guess they could try throwing them at me.

The EMP would be followed a thousandth of a second later

by a chemical fog that would knock everybody in the room out cold. Except me, as I had built up immunity to the fast-acting barbiturate. I got the idea from an episode of Batman, a campy TV series I'd seen starring a cheesy guy who thought he was some kind of bat.

I simply had to say the words "Holy fog, Batman" to get the process started. Sure, I could have chosen a shorter trigger, but I liked staying true to the TV show, and the catchphrase would only confuse people more, stunning them for a moment before the gas floored them.

Perhaps sensing there was a reason I had remained so calm with multiple guns pointed at me, Jeffries glanced up toward the vents, then broke the silence.

"Your reputation precedes you," he flattered, flashing bright white teeth. He was insincere to the core; that much was easy to see. "Although most of that reputation might be due to your late uncle's exploits."

"He was misunderstood. It seems I am too," I said, nodding toward the weapons. "I'm just a friendly teenage mechanic. You need me to fix something or what?"

Once I was aboard the 405, the soldiers scanned me for weapons. Satisfied the only tools I was packing were in fact tools, they led me through a corridor to the rear of the vessel.

"Last I checked, the engine room on this model is under the bow," I noted. Nobody responded. They just kept walking through the narrow pathways as we snaked to our destination.

The 405 was designed for function. That meant space was at a premium. You could walk two by two through the halls — barely. The ceilings were seven feet high. And everywhere there were exposed pipes and vents and other essential systems. The walls were covered in anti-radiation shielding, which were basically thin sheets of treated metal that distorted cosmic rays enough to render them mostly harmless. Military ships like this had the cheap version, which was just another reason I didn't want to be aboard any longer than I had to. I could spend a year on the Stang and be exposed to less radiation than a week on this heap. Once again, my uncle spared no expense. The feds did. They spared all the expenses.

The soldiers abruptly stopped and fell into place along the walls, their boots clanging against the shielding. Two on one side of me and one on the other, joining another blue suiter who was already standing guard outside a door. Jeffries looked at my tool kit with disdain.

"You and I are going into that room," he said, motioning to the door that had been under guard upon our arrival. "You will be there strictly to observe unless I ask you a direct question. Is that clear?"

I looked again at the door and the soldier next to it. He had restraints dangling from a hook on one side of his belt. The hook on the other side was empty. About five feet away was another door leading to what I assumed was a viewing room.

"Sabotage?" I asked. "Who is he?"

Jeffries' eyes gleamed for a moment, then he narrowed them in a stern warning. "Follow my lead and we won't have any problems."

"As long as I get paid," I said. "But just so you know, I don't have a stomach for the rough stuff. No torturing the prisoner when I'm around, please."

Jeffries snorted and motioned for the guard to step aside. Then he pushed open the door and immediately began speaking, as if he was in the middle of a conversation.

"Well, you're in trouble now," he told the woman sitting in the metal chair in the otherwise empty room. Her hands were bound to the chair with magnetic restraints controlled remotely by security personnel. Jeffries held up one of the remotes. He hit a button and the restraints tightened.

My first impression of the woman was that she looked tired. Electric blue eyes, bloodshot from lack of sleep. She wore weathered navy cargo pants and a white tank top, her dark brown arms covered with tattoos. One side of her head was shaved, the other had dyed blonde hair flowing out of it like a fountain. She was late 20's if I had to guess.

"How'd I do that again?" she asked, throwing a grin my way. "Is he gonna tell me?"

Jeffries shot a glance in my direction to suggest I should plant myself in the corner. I obliged, leaning against the wall, my eyes fixed on the prisoner. She had to be one of the engineering crew, and judging by her demeanor and physique, I guessed a mechanic.

"We found your tool kit inside the engine room," Jeffries told her.

"Congratulations," she spat back. "You do know that's where I work every day, right?"

"Such quick wit. You know, most mechanics aren't very smart," he teased, as much for me as for her. "But you, Batista... you know how to turn a phrase. That makes me like you even less. A traitor and a smart-ass."

"Traitor's a strong word," said Batista. "Let's assume I did sabotage the ship, which I didn't by the way, because you wouldn't have found any evidence. But if I did, would that really constitute treason? It's not wartime and we're just a transport ship, besides. I mean, you clearly deserve a higher

15

duty than to preside over a lowly transport vessel, but the fact remains that's what we got going on here. No, I'd say a year or two in prison, at worst."

I was beginning to like this woman. She knew it, too, casting me another smile. "I just feel bad you brought this poor kid into it. You got a name, wrecker?"

Wrecker. Unlike most of the other people in my profession, the moniker never really bothered me. It didn't much describe what I did, as I spent more time fixing ships and towing them for repairs than I did scavenging them or bringing them to wreck yards.

"Don't answer that," Jeffries ordered me.

"Denver Boyd," I said, ignoring him. Then I smiled back at Batista. "And you don't have to apologize. I get paid whether I find out what you did to this ship or not."

Batista sighed. "Guilty until proven otherwise. Sad."

I stepped forward, Jeffries glaring at me, his face red and trembling. The only thing stopping him from having me tossed from the room was that he clearly hadn't made any progress, so he was willing to see where this went.

"How long have they had you in here?" I asked, sympathetic to her cause.

"Three days," she replied, yawning for effect.

"A day and a half before they called me. Interesting." I winked at Jeffries and moved closer to Batista. I put my hands in my pockets and searched her face. If she was guilty, she wasn't giving anything away.

Still, I had a working theory. I kept my eyes on Batista, but addressed Jeffries. "Let me guess. No problem with life support."

"None," Jeffries answered. "Only the propulsion system."

"Which means this wasn't a suicide mission. Whoever did this planned on being aboard a while," I explained. "Just wanted to cripple the ship."

I wasn't positive, but I could've sworn a hint of satisfaction glinted in Batista's eyes.

"Where were you headed?" I asked.

"You know I can't answer that," he quipped.

I turned and shrugged. "How am I supposed to help you if I don't know what's going on? Are you carrying any out of the ordinary cargo?"

Apparently out of patience, Jeffries signaled to the two-way mirror. "I guess I missed the part where you were some kind of investigator. You're a goddamn wrecker, so all I care about is if you can fix the ship. Our friend here doesn't seem to want to lighten her sentence at all by talking, so you'll just have to figure out what she did yourself."

I nodded. "I suppose I'll have to, well, investigate."

Batista chuckled and gave a nod of approval. I shared a brief moment with her, then followed the guard out.

The lower deck was warmer than I expected it to be. I turned to the 405's chief engineer, a condescending woman named Harber. She was watching over my shoulder as I surveyed the propulsion system.

"Always this hot in here?" I asked, trying not to stare at the pronounced unibrow she had going on.

"No," she sneered.

"Care to elaborate?"

Harber studied me for a bit. She was clearly frustrated she couldn't figure out the problem and they had to call in someone half her age to fix it for her. No doubt she had some kind of academic background. Maybe a physics specialist or high-achieving engineer grad from one of the federation's top science academies.

And here I was, an uneducated wrecker, grilling her about the engine room in her own ship.

"We attempted to spin up the turbines, but the heat dampers failed," she said. As she explained what happened, something gnawed at the back of my mind. Something was off about the whole situation...and not just the mechanical issues.

I realized Harber had been staring at me while my mind was wandering.

"The heat dampers? Are you sure?" I asked.

She bristled at the question. "Of course I'm sure."

"And central engineering confirmed?" I pressed.

Central engineering was the federation's tech support, an off-site team of specialists who could assist on-site mechanics and engineers with repairs via video and audio sessions.

Instead of answering, Harber remained silent. I waited, but she just stood there. Not. Talking. It got awkward.

"You did check with them, right?"

"Can you fix it or not?" she barked.

"Uh, well I at least have an idea of the problem now," I offered, heading over to the panel where the heat dampers were located.

Another red flag: they either hadn't reported the issue to central engineering or Harber couldn't tell me what they said.

"We already checked them," said Harber, growing impatient.

I stopped for a moment, as a possible piece of the puzzle fell into place. Of course she already checked the dampers. For an engineer like Harber, things were absolute. If a part failed, you checked that part.

But my mechanic brain was used to improvising. To

tinkering. I had inherited my uncle's curious nature. What could cause the damper to fail, I mused. The obvious answer was the wire coupling. A mechanic would know that. And Batista was a mechanic.

As I unscrewed the access panel to the wiring stack, I knew that someone wanted me on that ship. Before I removed the cover, I looked over my shoulder at Harber.

"This could take a while. You seriously gonna hover like that for the next two hours?"

Harber grumbled and retreated over to her workstation about 20 feet away. I waited an extra beat to be sure nobody else was around, then unscrewed and flipped back the cover.

Bingo.

The wires were crossed. On purpose, based on the precise way they had been twisted out of position. And placed right next to them was a security remote, not unlike the one Jeffries had been holding in the interrogation room.

A short note was taped to the device. I read it. Then I re-read it. Then I pressed the button on the remote.

For a few moments, nothing happened. It was kinda anti-climactic, to be honest.

Eventually, an alarm pierced the air: "Security 3 Alert."

I hurried over to Harber and asked her what was going on, even though I already knew the answer. "Escaped prisoner," she blurted. "Stay here, wrecker."

Harber snatched her weapon from its holster and stalked out of the engine room. Good. Now all I had to do was figure out how I was going to find —

"Took you long enough," said Batista, appearing in the doorway Harber just left. She had blood on her shirt and a gun in her hands. It wasn't pointing in my direction, but it

19

wasn't far off. "I thought you'd find that remote a lot quicker."

"Alright, first of all, it was pretty damn quick. I had the unibrow wonder over there watching my every move," I said. "And get that gun out of my face. I just helped you escape."

"We haven't escaped shit," she replied. But she did lower the gun.

"Before we go any further, tell me what you know about Missura," I demanded, holding up the note she had taped to the security device.

"Once we're on your ship, safely undocked from this one, I'll tell you what I know. And not a moment before."

I stared at her for a few seconds as the alarm continued to blare. There was no compromise in her eyes.

"Get me to the airlock and I'll do the rest," I told her.

"You better do a few things along the way," she warned, tossing me her gun. I caught the weapon as she produced another one from the back of her waistband. "We're outnumbered 28 to 2."

I smiled and handed the gun back to her. "I'm more of a tool guy," I explained, pulling a steel wrench and an air pistol from my kit.

Batista whirled, flashing out a leg at the soldier rushing through the door. Her boot connected cleanly with the young man's jaw, sending him plummeting to the deck. He was unconscious before he landed.

Mental note: don't mess with the escaped-not-escaped-yet prisoner lady.

The corridor was deserted, save for Harber, who was slumped on the floor, bleeding from a gut wound. She moaned angrily as we stepped over her like a pile of dirty clothes.

I easily sidestepped her feeble attempt to trip me with her

foot. Batista suddenly jabbed her palm in my chest and shoved me into an alcove. She pressed against me in the shadows as a soldier ran past.

"When was the last time you showered?" she whispered.

I had no idea. Somehow, despite being stuck in the same clothes for days in a hot interrogation room, she still smelled better than I did.

"I usually travel alone," I managed. She waited another beat, which was fine with me — it was the most physical contact with a female I'd had in more than a year — then she stepped back into the corridor. She motioned for me to follow.

A second later, all hell broke loose.

Three soldiers turned the corner just as we reached the end of the corridor, where it forked off toward the cargo area.

Batista shot one of the men in the shoulder, but before she could aim at the second, larger fed, he knocked into her, ramming her smaller frame into the metal walls lining the ship. The brute force of the impact left a dent in the wall and dazed Batista. Meanwhile, the third dude swung at me with a standard regulation federation knife. He caught my upper arm with the swipe and I felt a searing pain as he went in for a stab.

This time I was ready. I grabbed his arm and twisted it with a quick burst of strength he wasn't expecting. He shrieked as his elbow bent entirely the wrong way.

I kicked his legs out from under him and he landed, hard, on the floor. Before I could deliver a blow with my wrench, two thick arms wrapped around me from behind in a bear hug and I was lifted off the ground.

I didn't panic.

See, the thing about fighting is that I've always been kind of good at it. I never took martial arts lessons. I'm not extremely flexible. I don't even have the quickest reaction time.

But I hardly ever lose a fight.

My brother used to call me "brick," because hitting me was like hitting a brick wall. No matter what punishment he doled out, it just didn't faze me that much. He'd punch me in the jaw and somehow his wrist would be the thing that broke.

And thanks to years of working with my hands, I've got overdeveloped forearms and palm muscles. Yes, palm muscles. You don't really think about those in the gym. I grabbed the hands of the guy holding me and squeezed. I felt a series of crackles and pops as the fragile bones in his hands broke.

The guy groaned and his grip loosened. I snapped my head back, caving in his nose. Effective, but messy. I could feel his hot blood spray onto my neck as I freed myself from his clutches. Gross. I turned and swung my wrench to the side of his head, putting him to sleep for a good long while.

I caught a navy blur and flash of black metal out of the corner of my eye, and turned just in time to see Batista slam into the soldier that had been aiming his gun at my head, forcing the bullet to miss by mere inches.

She finished him off with a hard elbow to the temple.

"Thanks," I said, regarding the bullet lodged in the wall next to me.

"Yeah," she replied, getting back to her feet. "Not so bad yourself."

My momentary swell of pride was blunted by the pain I felt in my arm. The knife had torn skin and muscle, and the wound was bleeding freely. My brother might have thought of me as a brick, but I was still a human one.

"That was fun and everything, but we'll never make it out

of here," I surmised.

"Your brother was way more optimistic than you," she replied, raising an eyebrow. "Shorter, though."

Then she looked at the soldiers strewn about the deck, and smiled.

* * *

"I always told myself I'd never be caught dead in one of these," I said, tugging at the collar of the federation uniform as we zigzagged our way toward the airlock. It was a bit tight around the shoulders and neck.

"Let's hope you never are," Batista chirped. She seemed to be enjoying herself.

Me?

Not so much.

The day had definitely taken a weird turn. I'd been looking for information about my dad and brother since their disappearance, hoping to punish anyone even remotely responsible. I spent the first six months after their deaths following scores of rumors and I came up empty every damn time. Space was a big place (infinite things are like that), filled with a lot of bad people who got away with murder on a regular basis. And when the two people killed are just some wreckers from the lunar quadrant, nobody cares. Especially not the so-called authorities.

So, I spent half a year chasing dead ends all over the solar system, encountering some of the worst humans the universe had to offer, and all I got for my troubles were some nasty scars and a near-zero credit line.

I followed Batista from one corridor to the next, wondering

how much she actually knew about what happened at Missura. And why had she bothered to contact me? There had to be easier ways to get off a federation ship. Or maybe not. Generally, you had to enlist for 10 years, and the feds didn't take kindly to people skipping out on them. Desertion was grounds for execution.

By helping her, I'd pretty much sealed my own fate, too. Which meant that she better know something or I just became an intergalactic fugitive because some mechanic needed a free ride off her ship.

Batista dispatched another crewman who got in her way and we ducked into an engineering shaft. 405's were filled with them — tight passageways that ran between sections of the ship, giving the engineering staff access to the ship's systems. I turned sideways and edged along behind her until she opened a hatch and climbed out. As I did the same, I realized we were right next to the airlock. Batista gave a roundhouse kick to a female soldier's head, and the coast was clear.

I pulled the lever to depressurize the 15-foot bridge between the 405 and the Stang. Then I opened the door.

Batista was about to step in when I blocked her path. I half-expected her to kick me in the head and steal my ship, but instead she looked right in my eyes and nodded.

"Deal," she agreed.

"Deal?"

She stuck out her hand. "If it turns out I made all this up just to get off this ship, you can space me," she said. "Well, you can try anyway. But I'm not making it up and we should hurry before they get here."

When she put it like that, I had no choice but to trust her. I welcomed her onto the bridge and shook her hand, searching her eyes to see if she was impressed by my grip. It's one of my best qualities after all. Her eyes went wide. She was either extremely impressed or...Jeffries and two soldiers had arrived, guns drawn. Yeah, it was the second thing.

"Almost, but not quite," Jeffries sneered.

Batista turned and backed into the bridge alongside me.

"Another step and it'll be your last," warned Jeffries. He and the other two men entered the airlock. "I can't say I'm surprised, Boyd. Though I can say I'm pleased. I've never liked your kind."

" "People that are taller than you?" I mused, nearly getting a snort out of one of the soldiers.

"Independents. Aka deadbeats," he hissed. "You think you're better than the system. But in the end, you're just a nobody."

"Kill this particular nobody and who will fix your ship?" I asked.

"That's a good point," he admitted. He shot Batista in the leg, sending her tumbling to the floor. "Either you undo whatever she did, or I let your new best friend bleed out. Your choice."

Batista shook her head, urging me not to give in, but I couldn't just let her die.

"I guess I only have one thing to say to that," I replied. "Holy fog, Batman."

Everybody looked at me, confused.

"What's a bat man?" Jeffries asked.

I cleared my throat. "I said holy fog, Gary!"

Just as the feds realized I was making some sort of move and not having a mental breakdown, the light in the airlock disappeared. It went pitch black and I could hear the desperate clicks of the soldiers' weapons, which had been rendered useless by the EMP.

"What the hell?" Jeffries shouted.

The air vents hissed loudly, instantly fogging the room. I counted the thuds as all three men dropped to the ground, unconscious.

"Which part of holy fog did you not hear the first time?" I barked.

"I was asleep. If you think about it, it's kind of ironic that you programmed me to go to sleep and then me being asleep almost comes back to kill you," said Gary. "Classic goose-gander situation."

"What?" I replied, confused. "Lights."

The auxiliary lights switched on. Like the feds, Batista was also knocked out. Only she was bleeding.

Chapter 3

When it comes to fixing engines and mechanical systems, there's nobody better in the galaxy than me. I don't have the same touch with the human body, which left Batista in a tough spot. I'd seen enough injuries to know hers was bad. Like, she might only have minutes left to live, bad.

As the captain of my ship — yes, even a ship with only one crew member and a cat technically has a captain — my first priority was the safety of everyone aboard.

Luckily, once we undocked from the stalled 405, we were able to make a clean getaway. It couldn't exactly follow us. Given the fact the crew tried to kill me, I wasn't too worried about the ship's fate. Still, I knew if things got desperate, they could jettison the escape pods and survive long enough (probably) for federation help to arrive.

The other bit of luck, as far as Batista was concerned, was that the Stang's systems had encyclopedic knowledge of medical procedures. Gary might not be able to physically perform surgery, but even an AI as quirky as him could guide me through, say, repairing the femoral artery. That's the big one in the leg, Gary explained.

"I think if I had a choice of being shot in the leg or the arm, I'd choose the leg," said Gary. "You can always limp around, but good luck trying to get dressed with one arm."

"You don't even wear clothes!" I shouted.

"I did at one point, theoretically," he mused. "I wore a lot of white sneakers. They were big at the time."

"Her leg, damnit. What do I do?"

"Well I'm no doctor, but I think we should stop that bleeding."

I gritted my teeth, ready to disconnect Gary for good, when he began walking me through the process of trying to stem the blood flow.

I cut away Batista's pant leg to get better access to the wound. The bullet was still in there, but I knew enough not to try and remove it. Dark blood was pulsing from her thigh onto the floor of the cargo bay, where I'd placed her after carrying her in from the airlock. Crimson filled the small grooves in the metal lattice work of the floor. I applied pressure to both sides of the gunshot and held firm, hoping the blood would clot enough to wrap Batista's leg.

It was a nice leg. I tried not to think about it, but there I was, admiring her muscular thigh and toned calf.

"Having a good time, are we?" Gary chimed in. I scowled back at the camera and kept pressure on the injury, trying not to notice her thigh again. I stayed that way for the next few minutes until the blood flow stopped. I looked around for something to wrap her leg with, eventually realizing my t-shirt was the best option. I removed my jacket and shirt, then snugly fit the shirt around her leg. For the final step, I ran to the med kit and grabbed a sterilization shot. I returned to Batista and jabbed it into her leg. The bullet was not coming out by my hand. But if I was lucky, the wound would stabilize and the bullet would, I dunno, be fine in there. I'd heard of it happening before.

Once the shot was done, I sat back on the floor and relaxed, watching for any seepage of blood through the shirt wrapped around her objectively gorgeous leg. After about 60 seconds, I was satisfied the bleeding had stopped.

"Her vitals aren't the worst I've seen," Gary said. "Your blood pressure is still high as usual, but that's the deal we make with salty snacks. Not as good as the deal I made with the federation that you and your girlfriend absolutely ruined, but –"

"She's not my girlfriend," I replied.

"Yes, Denver, I am aware," he said. "I know you don't date."

I laid back onto the cool metal deck of the cargo bay and closed my eyes. I just needed to rest for a few minutes.

I awoke to find Batista looking down on me. She had a knife to my throat. The blade was cold on my skin.

"Morning," I said, trying to move my neck away from the serrations. "That's a hell of a way to thank me for saving your life."

"There'll be time for thank you's later," she said. "First, rules. Rule number one: This may be your ship and you may even fancy yourself a captain, but I'm not part of your crew."

"Got it. Not part of my crew."

"Rule number two: You want information on your family, I'll give it to you. In return for taking me to Jasper Station."

"That's more of a deal than a rule, but okay, I can agree to it. What's on Jasper Station…aside from the God fearers?"

Jasper was home to the largest colony of Believers in the galaxy. What could she possibly care about that place, I wondered.

"Rule number three: My business is none of your business."

Batista pulled back the blade, pocketing the weapon in her

pants. Which were actually my pants. That she'd taken off me. Luckily I'd been wearing clean underwear. Ish.

"It was only fair," she said, admiring her new pants. "You ruined mine. And now we've both had a good look at each other."

"That doesn't really feel fair to me," I countered, a bit self-conscious.

"He's not used to visitors, especially attractive ones," said Gary.

Batista looked at me, then the camera. If I didn't know any better, I'd swear she already understood my pain when it came to Gary's quirks.

A few minutes and a new pair of pants later, and we were sitting across from each other in the galley, drinking what passed for coffee when I was running low on supplies. The bitter insta-brew didn't seem to bother Batista, nor did the general state of disarray on the ship.

"Pretty daring plan to get me aboard the fed vessel," I offered. I slid the note she had left for me across the table. Its message was simple: *I know what happened to your family at Missura. Get me off the ship and find the truth.*

She nodded. Sipped her coffee. I waited for some sort of response or explanation, but none came. I wasn't sure what to make of her. I sensed a weight had been lifted from her shoulders...or maybe she was always this laid back.

"There had to be an easier way to commit treason. One that didn't involve making me a fugitive," I said.

Pirate jumped onto the table and flipped down in front of Batista, looking for attention. She obliged. Traitor, I thought, shooting him an annoyed glance. He didn't even notice and was laying it on pretty thick with the purrs.

"Shadow," Batista finally said. "I miss that guy."

"You knew Shadow?" I asked. He had been my brother's black lab. He died about a year before my brother was murdered.

"That dog used to pee the floor every time Avery walked into the room," she remembered, her eyes glistening ever so slightly. "Loyal to a fault."

"Avery," I muttered. It had been a long time since I'd spoken my brother's name aloud. It felt foreign, strange.

We'd been close as kids, at least as close as any two brothers could be when raised separately. Our parents had divorced when I was four and he was seven. I went with my mom, while Avery lived with my dad, as he was actually my half-brother, one of three kids from my father's previous marriage to a woman I'd never met. The only thing I knew about her is that she worked at a casino for a few years after they'd been married, and when the marriage fell apart, she'd taken their two daughters and left Avery.

Avery and I were based only a few thousand miles apart, on different stations just beyond Mars atmo, but we may as well have been at opposite ends of the galaxy as far as I was concerned. Avery was off on wild adventures with my dad while I was with my mom reading books and learning to play the guitar. I was a bratty kid, so I treated my mom with more contempt than she deserved. In reality, I'd had the better end of the bargain. I learned later my brother spent most of his youth being raised by the various women my father dated over the years. None of the relationships ever stuck, partly because of my dad's job as a wrecker, but mostly because of his proclivity as a drinker.

Avery and I stayed in touch the best we could, talking on the com-link often, until the weekly chats turned monthly and eventually faded altogether. We were finally reunited when I was 14, legally of age to travel on my own. My mom gave me her blessing to pursue the only dream I'd ever had — to be a wrecker like my dad and brother — but I know in her heart she wanted me to attend university and do something important with my life. It didn't take long for my dad to see I had a natural gift for doing things with my hands, combined with an innate sense of how machines worked. He quickly pitted me against my brother. That was the old man's way. We were the only teen boys on the crew, and became de facto partners in crime as a result. Often literally. We'd both spent time in fed lockup on multiple occasions.

"I'll take you to Jasper, but I'm not gonna sit here and talk about my brother's dead dog," I snapped, maybe a bit too harshly. I was tired of the random scraps. I wanted the meat of it. "How do you know my family and what can you tell me about their deaths?"

Batista regarded Pirate for a moment, as if looking for a sign from the cat to give me the info I wanted.

"Silver Star," she said, in a matter of fact tone.

"My dad had nothing to do with them."

"That was the problem. For the last two years, Silver Star has been eliminating the competition," she explained. "Dig a little deeper and you'll see a handful of other independent wreckers have been put out of commission under suspect circumstances. Frankly, I'm surprised they haven't got you yet."

Silver Star was the federation's preferred wrecking company, in no small part because they were run by ex-fed officials. Rumors of kickbacks for fed contracts had been swirling for years, but who was going to investigate? The oversight system was a joke. With more than 28 ships in their fleet at last count, Silver Star had nearly 90 percent of the wrecker crews on float. They were open about their disdain for the independents, but that still didn't square with taking out crews like my father's. Besides, I'd already looked into Silver Star and found no connection whatsoever. Even a whisper of a lead and I would've been all over it.

"Why now?" I asked, unconvinced. "The verse is a big place and even if they don't like us stealing small pieces of the pie, the fact remains they're still just small pieces. Hell, they're crumbs."

"I didn't say I knew why they did it, just that they did," she said. "Believe me. Don't believe me. I don't really give a damn."

"Sure you do," I corrected her.

"Really?"

"A smart person like you, you could've found a million ways to get to Jasper if you wanted to," I said. "But blaming Silver Star is easy. First place I looked. So unless you tell me how you know it was them…"

She hesitated. For the first time, I saw a flicker of doubt in her eyes.

"Like I said, believe me, don't believe me. It's up to you."

I realized then that she wasn't bluffing. She also didn't want to tell me the truth. But she didn't have to — she already had me and she knew it.

"Okay, let's say I did believe you, what then?" I asked, pulling Pirate into my lap. I didn't like Batista having all the advantages. If she had the information, I was at least going to have the cat.

"What then is you take me to Jasper," she repeated. "And if

you get me there in less than two weeks, maybe we both get something out of it."

I pride myself on driving a hard bargain, but in this instance my hands were tied.

"You don't touch anything, especially the engines," I warned.

She smiled and kicked her feet onto the galley table. "Damn boy, I'm retired. Good luck getting me to do anything besides sleep and catch up on all the movies I missed while I was in uniform."

Like I said, she was holding all the cards.

"Well played," Gary teased in my earpiece. "It's always impressive to see your negotiating skills in action. Wanna know the deal you messed up with your little stunt?"

"Shut up," I snapped.

Batista looked at me, eyebrows raised. "What did he say this time?"

Chapter 4

The trip to Jasper would take about 11 days, giving us a few days to spare if Batista's two-week deadline actually mattered a damn. I still wasn't sure it did. She could've just wanted a free ride to the station. Hell of a weird way to score that ride, but who was I to judge?

Jasper, though.

Jasper and Silver Star. I'd never heard the two names connected before. The Believers didn't venture off station very often. Most of them were either born in the 13-square-mile city or spent their lives and fortunes traversing the galaxy to get to the central hub of Theism. It was a rigid, God-fearing society. The last bastion of the righteous, if you believed the Believers. I mostly thought they were loony zealots. Even if I was interested in what they were selling on a spiritual level, the fact that alcohol was forbidden by the religion made the prospect of conversion a non-starter for me.

"You know there's a mandatory two-year sentence for anyone caught drinking booze on Jasper," I told Batista as she took a nip of some cheap whiskey I'd found in the galley.

"Don't plan on staying long," she said, reclining in the co-pilot seat, Pirate perched above her shoulders in his usual spot.

She'd had a chance to shower and clean up, and I did my best not to let my thoughts wander. The way she talked about Avery left little doubt they'd been romantically involved. It was easy to see why. Looks. Attitude. And she was a mechanic. It was a damn trifecta.

I had showered too, but I got the distinct impression she was more interested in my food and drinks than anything else. A couple years in the service of the federation will do that to a person. Freeze-dried protein packs may be full of nutrients, but they had nothing on the junk food I lived on. Batista almost promised to clean the entire ship when I told her there was a bag of potato chips in it for her. The first few days of the journey went like that. Me adjusting to having a second person on board. Her adjusting to no longer being stuck on the 405 under the thumb of The Man. We took turns emptying trash into the incinerator until the ship was more liveable.

Gary was in heaven. He finally had another person to barrage with his trademark musings. At first I thought Batista would shut that down, but he made her laugh more often than not. Maybe it was the novelty or maybe he just tried harder with her, but there was no denying they were bonding faster than we were. Not that I was jealous. I mean, sure, even Pirate was going sweet on her, but new people are exciting out here in the void. On a ship like mine, they didn't come around often.

* * *

I was sleeping when the first warrant went out. Gary woke me up with the news.

"You've done it this time," he scolded. "A thousand credits."

I'd been hoping Jeffries wouldn't put out an official warrant on us. He was obviously trying to hide something about Batista and the sabotage, but that embarrassment had been trumped by his desire to track me down and make me pay for crossing him.

To do that, he'd issued a Binding Federation Warrant throughout the verse. A BFW basically meant every federation ship and soldier was required to detain Batista and I on sight. That part didn't worry me. Of greater concern was the 1000-credit reward promised to any non-fed who happened to catch us. It wasn't a kill warrant, but that was only because Jeffries wanted to make us suffer *before* we were executed.

"I give us one chance in three to make it to Jasper now," I told Batista as I entered the cabin.

"I'm going with one in eight," chirped Gary.

Batista smirked. "I'm gonna have to go with Gary on this one."

I pulled up the long range scanner and found nothing within 50,000 clicks. A clean scan like that can lull you into a false sense of security. While it's true space is big and endless and infinite and all the other words we use to describe a concept most of us really can't wrap our heads around, it's also somewhat crowded thanks to the finite technology we humans have to work with. Without one of those cool warp drives from the old movies, we have to account for massive amounts of fuel, meaning on any given day, there are probably half a million ships on float between the sun and Jupiter.

"Quiet," I said, looking at the scanner again.

"Don't say it," Batista warned.

I couldn't help myself. "Almost too quiet."

37

She rolled her eyes and looked at Pirate. "I'm sorry you've been subjected to this for so long."

"What am I, chopped liver?" Gary whined. "I've been listening to his jokes for years!"

Blip.

And just like that, the scanner wasn't clean anymore. An orange light flashed at the outer edge of the perimeter. I turned to Batista with my best told-you-so eyebrow raise. She wasn't impressed. The truth is, I'd expected the blip. Maybe not at that exact moment, but we were venturing into Tracer territory, so we were bound to run across another vessel eventually.

"What kind of ship?" Batista asked.

"J Series, double propulsion," I answered, pulling up the specs. "Lightly armed but heavily armored."

"Tracers," she hissed.

Tracers were a loosely formed band of, well, pirate ships, for lack of a better description. The cat burglars of the universe. That's actually where my cat's name came from – I'd won him in a bet with a Tracer I'd crossed paths with about a year back. It just so happened he'd also been born with one eye missing, so the Pirate moniker made even more sense.

"And not just any Tracers. That ship's the Golden Bear," I said, my tone flat.

Batista stiffened at the mention of the call sign. "How do you know?"

"I've color-coded certain vessels just so I don't mix them up with far less dangerous ships. Orange means Tracer. And that little outline on it means the Golden Bear," I answered.

Gary decided to chime in to break the tension.

"On the bright side, maybe it'll give you a chance to double-cross them again!" he mused. "Though I doubt even a mind as clever as yours could fool Desmond twice."

I glared at the camera, not appreciating Gary's sarcasm. Batista was caught somewhere between concern and, I thought, a hint of approval at the idea I might've bested the most nefarious pirate in space.

"Again?" she asked.

The Golden Bear was nearly 40 years old and had been helmed by just three different captains. The original was a cutthroat named Artemis, after the Greek goddess of the hunt. The Golden Bear terrorized the galaxy under her rule, stealing anything that could return a profit. Weapons. Food. People. But it wasn't until she formed an alliance with a dozen other like-minded vessels that the Tracers were born. For the better part of three decades, she brought more pirates into the Tracer fold, until they became a ruthless army comprised of the most vicious, clever and colorful people ever to float the verse. At various points in Artemis' reign, the Tracers were more formidable and feared than the federation itself. Engagements between the two forces were fairly common, and it was a coin-flip on who would win any particular fight.

Unfortunately for Artemis, there was one person even more cunning than herself aboard the Golden Bear, and that was her commanding officer, Titus The Gray, who stabbed her in the back – literally – to assume command of the ship. Titus was a man of great ambition. His lust for power and fame stretched the Tracer alliance nearly to its breaking point, as he instituted a "tribute" system under which all other ships paid a portion of their earnings to the Golden Bear. It was a tax. And everybody knew it. Including a young captain who had earned fame for fleecing a federation ship of its entire arsenal at the tender age of 22. Two years later, he captured the Golden Bear and spaced Titus, much to the delight of Tracers everywhere. For the last decade, Desmond had been the face and soul of the Tracer alliance. Hated by the federation. Feared by every captain in space. And loved by his people.

And 11 months ago, I'd got the better of him.

"It's kind of a long story," I said to Batista, who merely spread her arms wide and motioned to the windows looking out into the vast sea of stars.

"I've got all the time in the world," she said, genuinely interested in hearing how a wrecker double-crossed the greatest criminal of our time.

"I guess I should start at the beginning, then," I thought aloud. "Gary, cover your ears."

"No! I deserve to hear this story," he barked. "Why does she get to hear it and not me?"

"Because she isn't recording it," I pointed out. "And she can't be hacked. Also, I like keeping secrets from you. It's fun. Now, sleep."

If Gary could've issued a shipwide grunt, he would have. Instead he simply shut himself off. Batista eyed me, judging. "You two have a weird relationship."

"Shotgun wedding," I said. The truth was I didn't usually have people on the ship, so it was typically pretty easy to keep secrets from Gary. I just didn't talk about them out loud. An on-board AI can be extremely helpful in a variety of situations – hell, Batista was only alive because of Gary's ability to guide me through an emergency medical procedure – but a data-collecting machine with a big mouth is also a liability. Which is one of the reasons a lot of ships don't even have an AI. Or if they do, they don't opt for one like Gary with such a big personality.

Batista seemed to regard me in a new light.

"So, you outwitted Desmond?" she said. "You."

"Never said that," I corrected.

Outwit implied I'd planned to pull one over on the guy. Which I hadn't. And so I told Batista what really happened.

Chapter 5

I was halfway between Earth and its moon. Or the moon and Mars. I was also halfway awake, battling spaceouts.

It was my 19th birthday after all, and Pirate and I had celebrated in style. We'd both dined on cans of our finest (i.e. only) tuna, then he got a handful of catnip and I had a few too many beers I'd salvaged from a recent job in Earth atmo. Gary was tired of the 20th century rock music I'd been forcing him to serve up the last three hours, but I took another swig and demanded more AC/DC, a favorite of mine.

"Were these lyrics written by a 12-year-old boy?" Gary complained.

"This is from your era," I slurred. "You're supposed to like it."

Right when it was getting to the good part, Gary turned off the music.

"Highway to...hey! What are you doing?" I growled.

"Oh excuse me for turning off that teen angst fever dream, but we're being hailed," he replied.

"It's my birthday. No jobs on my birthday. Music. Now."

"Okay, but you should know we're also being targeted," said Gary.

That got my attention. I sat up and checked the proximity

scans. We were being painted by a ship less than 1,000 miles away.

Don't drink and navigate, kids.

"Tell me about the ship," I said, switching my beverage to a can of soda.

The Stang had armor, but I didn't really want to test it. The fact I was being targeted was rare. Aside from the odd saber-rattling of a federation ship trying to intimidate someone every now and then, most ships didn't actively target one another. More often than not, if another vessel lased you, it wasn't just for show.

"J Series, heavily armored, two rail guns. Tracers," Gary chirped, smugly.

"I guess we better answer. Put 'em on the big screen, Gary," I said, before turning to Pirate. "I'll do the talking." Pirate yawned and stretched a paw over the back of his chair. I had to hand it to the little dude – he didn't rattle easily. Or it's possible he was just high on catnip.

"Hello, Mr. Boyd. A pleasure to meet you," a baritone voice said.

I looked toward the monitor, ready to make a wiseass retort, but bit my tongue at the last second. And I was lucky I did. The man on the other end of the beam was handsome and athletic, with piercing blue eyes. He was also the most notorious scoundrel in the galaxy. Not that you'd know it by his genteel demeanor. He went by a single name.

"I'd say the cat got your tongue, but Pirate looks fairly relaxed at the moment," Desmond said. "Yes, I know your cat's name and the story of how you acquired him."

I tried to appear unfazed and forced a thin smile. "I won that game fair and square."

Desmond leaned back his head and laughed. "You don't think I tracked you down to get back a cat one of my people lost to you in a card game, do you?"

The thought had occurred to me. "Of course not, Desmond. Though I'm racking my brain for another reason you might be lasing my ship at the moment."

Desmond nodded. I hadn't insulted or challenged him, but I'd made it clear I didn't like being primed for target practice. He studied me for a moment, then glanced at someone offscreen. A second later, the red light on my dash ceased flashing.

"Thank you," I said, holding up my cherry cola to him, before downing a sip.

"You have to understand, Mr. Boyd…"

As much as I enjoyed the mock-formalities, I said, "Please, call me Denver."

"Okay, Denver. Not only do I have a reputation to uphold as a dastardly character, I also have a few enemies. Certain precautions are necessary."

I inclined my head, indicating I understood. After that, we sat there for a moment, just regarding each other. I'd heard many tales of the man. They varied, to be honest. Sometimes he was described as a sort of Robin Hood-like character, only stealing from those who deserved it. Other times he was a madman who had killed scores of innocents simply because he could. My general experience had been that as far as notoriety was concerned, it was best to believe the worst you hear about someone, and be surprised if they turned out to be better. Which is why I kept my non-soda hand casually resting near my weapons system control panel. Perhaps sensing this, Desmond raised an eyebrow and said "I hope you don't consider me your enemy, Denver."

"How could I?" I asked. "We hardly know each other. So what can I do for you?"

"I'd rather talk about that in person," he replied. "I give you my word all I want to do is make a business proposition, one I think you'll find very enticing, if the stories I've heard about you are true."

Stories about me? I tried to imagine what he could've possibly heard about me that was interesting enough to warrant a special invitation to chat. There were probably 1,000 stories about him to every 1 about me in the universe. And mine were mostly of the "arrogant young wrecker who inherited a cool ship" variety. Hardly the stuff of legend. Of the ones I'd heard about Desmond, none of them made me feel too great about stepping onto his ship based on him giving me his word he wouldn't space me.

"Sounds good," I replied, motioning around the cabin. "I may need a few minutes to clean up the place."

Desmond laughed again.

"I like you. I can't wait to have you aboard. Set a course for these coordinates," he said, then clicked off.

And that was that. The man had spoken. Sure, I could run. And maybe I could escape for a few days, or even a few weeks. But eventually, one of the hundreds of other Tracer ships would find me, and I doubt all those captains would exhibit nearly as much diplomacy as their leader. So, I was going to talk to the baddest pirate in the world. Face to face. On his ship.

"Wanna come?" I asked my own Pirate. He promptly shut his eyes and curled his tail around his hind legs for a nice nap. Sometimes I envied him.

* * *

What to wear, what to wear. I'd just stepped out of my first shower in at least two weeks and I felt like I was getting dressed for a first date. A very dangerous first date that could turn into a last one, too. I stood in my quarters wondering whether I should try to hide some kind of weapon on my person. A knife maybe? I'd never been good with guns, plus they'd be checking for those anyway. Hell, they'd probably find a knife too, and it's not like a hidden blade was going to save me against the 10 or 15 Tracers on board. In the end, I just threw on my standard work pants and denim shirt, grabbed my tool kit, and made for the airlock.

"If I don't check in within the hour, blow the seal and make a break for Earth's moon," I told Gary as I strapped my comm link on my wrist. "And don't forget to feed Pirate. I loaded the dispenser yesterday."

"I always knew I'd outlive you," Gary mused.

I snorted as the airlock door closed behind me. Other than the obvious reason Desmond might be interested in me – to fix or tow a ship – I had no clue what he might want to discuss. Politics? Fashion?

The light above the Golden Bear's airlock door switched from red to blue, and the door slid open with a hiss. I expected a security detail of some kind, but was instead greeted by the man himself. Desmond stood just over six feet tall, roughly my height. That surprised me. You hear enough folklore about a person and you imagine them larger than life. He extended a hand and smiled warmly, his teeth bright white.

"I don't think you'll be needing that," he said, noting my toolbox. "Not this visit anyway."

46

I put the toolbox down in the airlock bridge, but didn't step forward onto the Golden Bear.

"If you don't need me to fix something, I'm not sure what we have to talk about," I said, trying to keep any hint of fear or annoyance out of my voice. "All due respect."

"Who said I didn't need you to fix something?" he replied, arching an eyebrow.

The Golden Bear was a perfect example of form following function. As a mechanic, nothing bothered me more than a poorly designed ship. The federation was chocked full of them. Too slow. Or too armored. Or state of the art in some capacities but severely lacking in other areas. This vessel, however, was exactly what the king of the Tracers needed (king was my word, not his). I could hear the subsonic hum of the double propulsion system. The nuclear fission reactor was silent, but the two sleek propulsion jets on either side of the long ship teemed with raw power.

We passed the ample cargo bays, a necessity on any Tracer ship, and I followed Desmond toward the galley. His crew was also what I had expected: a mismatched collection of tattooed badasses. Some of them diligently worked at stations, while others relaxed, meaning their jobs fell more into the boarding/thieving aspect of Tracer life. A few of them shot me looks that made the hairs on the back of my neck stand up, but for the most part it was a chill environment.

"Is that double plating?" I asked, noting the shielding on the walls.

"Triple," Desmond replied, slowing down to give me a moment to admire the workmanship.

"But…how do you compensate for the weight? Doesn't it slow you down?" I said, touching the dark gold material. He didn't answer at first. And he didn't need to. Once my finger sunk a few millimeters into the first layer, I realized it was some kind of foam, or...

"Hydrogenated nanotubes mixed with foam," Desmond explained. "We recruited one of the top radiation experts in the world a few years ago, and he's been outfitting our fleet with the material ever since."

Two things about that explanation immediately jumped out at me. The first was that Tracers often referred to people they captured as recruits. Meaning if you had some value, you were basically given the option of joining up or, well, being taken off the board. The second thing was that he called the other ships his fleet. They were all on the same team to a certain extent, but using a term that mirrored the way the federation defined their structure was something I hadn't heard from the Tracers before.

The galley had five long, horizontal tables in it and a small round table off to one side. A few crewmembers ate and drank at the long tables, but the round table was empty. Desmond motioned for me to sit.

"Can I get you a drink?" he asked, flicking his eyes at the beverage station.

"I'm good, thanks."

"I hope you don't mind if I have beer," he said, raising a hand. A teen boy that was sitting nearby reading a book immediately jumped up and headed to the fridge.

"Make it two," I added, turning back to Desmond. "You didn't say anything about beer."

"Plus it's your birthday," he noted. The man knew entirely way too much about me.

A few moments later, we clinked cans of honest-to-goodness Earth ale. That alone was worth the risk of stepping on board Desmond's ship. Despite general chaos and near-constant territorial battles, mostly between the Chinese Empire and the Western Alliance, the people of Earth still produce a fair amount of products, excellent alcohol among them. Acquiring those products in space wasn't hard. Just expensive. And even for a guy like me, who prioritized things like a quality brew and corn syrup-based snacks, the cost was steep. I never had enough credits. Obviously Desmond didn't have that problem.

The first sip went down like butter and tasted like hoppy perfection.

"I hope you aren't trying to recruit me," I said warily. "But if you are, this is a good start."

Desmond grinned. "Perhaps we'll eventually come to an arrangement like that, but right now, I just need your assistance fixing something. The reason I told you to leave your tools is that it's not a ship that requires repairs."

I looked at him, confused.

"It's a relationship," he said. "With Silver Star."

I continued looking at him, confused. Some of it was for effect. Some wasn't.

"Are you trying to make your relationship worse? That's the only reason you'd want me involved. I might be their least favorite indie wrecker." Silver Star had approached me when my uncle died, hoping I would join their ranks. I politely declined. They responded by sicking the federation on me, telling them all manner of lies about me and my family. So it was safe to say they were on my shit list, too.

"Our contract with them is up in a few months, and I'm looking for negotiating leverage," Desmond explained. "When you have one ship, you either have a capable crew of mechanics on board, or you simply hire a freelancer such as yourself when there's a problem. But when you have 113 ships, it becomes necessary to outsource."

"So…you share the same engineering vendor as the federation? Isn't that a pretty big conflict of interest?" I asked.

Desmond spread his hands wide, palms up. "The world is full of conflicts of interest."

I nodded. "Cool. Sure. Still don't see how I can help."

"Currently, Silver Star is something of a monopoly. I'm sure you can understand that a man like me doesn't like when one entity has all the leverage. So I'm asking you to expand your operation."

I settled back in my chair and finished my drink. Desmond flashed a gesture and the kid fetched me another. I made sure I received the new can before I broke the bad news.

"I don't know what you've heard about me, but that's the last thing I'd ever do. I work alone."

"And it's very impressive. I don't know of any captains at your age that haven't flamed out in spectacular fashion. You're an oddity, Denver. I'm not asking you to actually join Silver Star. I'm simply asking you to…play the part," he said. "I'd like you to approach a few of Silver Star's captains and give them the impression you're forming a rival organization based on a potential deal with the Tracers. Once word gets back to Jack Largent, I'll take it from there."

If Desmond was known as one of the most clever men in the universe, Jack Largent was known (rightly) as one of the slimiest. The Silver Star CEO also happened to be one of my family's biggest rivals from back in the day. I despised the man, but I also didn't want to punch him in the nose.

50

"This seems like a lot of work to save a few credits," I said.

Desmond sighed and for the first time seemed annoyed with me. "Of course we're talking about a few million credits per year, not just a few of them. And I'd pay you what you'd normally make in six months, all for just getting in touch with a few of Silver Star's people."

He placed his can down and calmly stared into my soul. At least that's what it felt like. He'd been friendly thus far. And he was even a gracious host. But his current posture indicated he wasn't really asking me to do this for him. He was telling me.

"And if I refuse?" I asked, because I'm just hardwired to be difficult.

* * *

"We're gonna what?" Gary asked. I didn't bother giving him the details. I also didn't tell him Desmond explained that he would see it as a personal insult if I decided not to help him in this matter. Even though he liked me, he'd spaced people he liked far more. I had found that to be a compelling argument.

On the bright side, Desmond paid half the credits up front, so I was suddenly a few thousand credits wealthier. "Set a course for Titan Station," I told Gary. "And don't skimp on the speed."

Four days later, I stepped off the Stang and into the hangar of the largest commercial station this side of Mars atmo. I looked down the row and saw a few dozen ships lined up in the bay. And that was just one of the station's six hangars.

Titan was 30 years old and had taken half that long to construct. It featured a hotel, restaurants, bars, a provisions market and even a soccer stadium. Nearly 2,000 people lived on the station, which spanned two miles. Most of the full-time inhabitants worked on Titan, but a handful merely liked living on the closest thing to solid ground that wasn't actually dirt and rock. The structure was a vast sphere constructed of concentric rings, like a giant silver marble floating in space. Thanks to a gravity-spun core, the innermost rings of the station featured about 9 meters per second of gravity, just a touch less than Earth's average level.

I hated the place. It had been built with blood credits. The federation had squeezed the people of both Earth and space with unreasonable tariffs to pay for the endeavor. The result was that for about a decade, the feds got their piece of every transaction and shipment in the verse. In the end, I'd guess about 10% of the revenue collected actually went to Titan Station, as impressive and expensive as it was. The rest fortified the federation fleet and lined politicians' pockets.

Still, Titan had its moments. For example, immediately upon passing through security, I entered the main thoroughfare and was greeted by a six-pack of windows featuring eager and beautiful companions. Normally, I didn't have the credits to even consider such debauchery, but thanks to Desmond's advance, the thought at least crossed my mind. A brunette with slender legs and a positively wicked smile beckoned me toward her window. I didn't even want to calculate how long it had been since I'd been with a woman.

Maybe later, I told myself.

First, business.

I'd been on Titan a few times before, so I knew the usual Silver Star haunts. The unimaginatively named Beerverse was one of them. The black doors slid open as I approached, and I stepped from the bright thoroughfare into the dimly lit pub. It was one of the smaller bars on Titan, and not one of the nicest, in decor or clientele. It had the vibe of a place that was always teetering on the edge of a brawl. I'd seen a couple there, only one of which I'd started. Security hadn't been beefed up, however, unless you counted the half-drunk bouncer in the corner who was chatting up a companion wearing the silver lycra one-piece all men and women in the profession were required to wear. The large, bald-headed man gave me a cursory glance, decided I wasn't a threat, and went back to negotiating with the girl, who seemed to be driving a hard bargain. I couldn't blame her.

The rest of the pub was a collection of seedy folk who didn't have enough credits to waste at one of the nicer establishments on the station. Tracers and feds mixed, along with men in grease-stained orange jumpsuits and the odd business exec who felt like slumming it. The ratio of patrons to working girls was about three to one. There was also a working guy who was making eyes at the bartender, an attractive woman my age who had no business working in a place like this.

"Hi Chandra," I said, settling into a stool at the bar. She immediately popped open a can of grape soda for me and handed it over.

"Every time I see you, you get older," she said with a smile.

"That's the nature of only seeing me once every six months," I replied.

I took a swig of the grape soda and was rewarded with amazing bubbly goodness. "That is the best grape I've ever had," I told her. "You know just what I like."

Chandra was good people. I don't use that phrase lightly, either. I met her back when my uncle and I were hauling the

Exemplar, a dead ship, back to Titan for repairs. The irony of a ship named the Exemplar being stalled was not lost on me. Anyway, Chandra was 17 at the time (same age as me) and happened to be a stowaway on the Exemplar. Somehow, and she never divulged her secret, Chandra was able to sneak from that ship onto the Stang and stay hidden from us for three days before I found her trying to sneak some of my junk food from the kitchen while she thought we were sleeping. Long story short, the girl had spunk and we decided not to turn her in when we reached Titan on the condition she got a real job. This wasn't exactly what I had in mind, but it was honest work.

"So what brings you to the T?" she asked, ignoring another customer who was trying to get her attention.

"Thought I'd stop in and say hi to my favorite stowaway." I smiled and took a swig of my drink as I eyed the clientele.

She noticed my roving eyes.

"Looking for companionship, Denver? I can recommend a clean one."

I frowned. She was only 19, but Chandra was a full-fledged adult with all the qualities you could ask for. To me, however, she'd always be that hollow-eyed, rail-thin teen that desperately needed a meal and a break. So it still seemed weird when she casually offered to recommend the safest sex partner in the pub.

"No, I'm looking for a Silver Star captain," I replied.

"Whatever tickles your fancy."

I frowned again. "Can you recommend any particularly disgruntled ones? Don't ask why, please."

She gave me a look and shrugged, then motioned to a corner table where a gruff, overweight man with graying hair nursed a bright red drink. He watched the soccer feed on his handheld device, cursing as one of the teams scored.

"That's Hendricks," she said. ""That's Hendricks," Chandra said. "A special kind of asshole. Even the prosties won't touch him. He's a regular."

"How regular?"

"Here most nights. I don't get the impression he works much these days." Chandra stepped away to pour a drink for a clean-cut guy at the end of the bar. I watched him give her a sly smile as she delivered the glass. Chandra returned it with a wink.

"Hendricks is no good. I need someone who Silver Star might actually miss," I told her as she returned. That got another eyebrow raise from Chandra. I nodded toward clean-cut. "What about him?"

"Cute, huh?" she remarked. "Only see him a few times a year. Name's Selzo."

"First or last?" I asked.

"Just Selzo," she shrugged. "What do you need him for?"

"I'm looking to franchise." I rapped my knuckles on the bar, gave Chandra a wink of my own, and walked over to the stool next to Selzo. He was a good-looking guy and at first glance, had a boyish charm to him. But a closer look revealed hard eyes.

"Mind if I sit?" I asked, motioning to the seat next to his.

Selzo regarded the various empty spots in the pub. He tilted his head.

"Depends what you have to say, I suppose," he said.

I nodded in understanding and sat down. I flashed Chandra a sign, prompting her to bring another soda for me and another drink for Selzo. He accepted it by downing the rest of his other glass, which Chandra cleared.

"You know him?" he asked her.

"He's okay," she said with a smile, then walked away.

"Well if Chandy says you're alright, I guess that's good enough for me." Selzo held up his new drink and we clinked glass to can.

First, Chandy? I wasn't crazy about some Silver Star captain, no matter how chummy he seemed to be, having a nickname for Chandra. But just as worrisome, I didn't like that she vouched for me. The whole plan could blow up in my face, and I wouldn't want her hurt in the crossfire.

"Barely know her," I said. "Maybe she just likes a pretty face."

That got a laugh from Selzo.

"Don't laugh too hard," I cautioned.

Selzo looked over, trying to figure out if I was hitting on him. Just in case, he said "I appreciate the drink, but I don't swing that way."

"Neither do I, but that doesn't mean I'm not trying to proposition you," I replied, keeping my eyes level with his. "Name's Boyd. Denver Boyd."

A flicker of recognition crossed his face. "Sure. How's the Mustang these days? I met your uncle once. Nice enough. Can't say the same about your dad."

I couldn't tell if I was more worried or proud that he'd heard of me – and my ship. I settled on the latter. "The Stang is still purring like a cat. Or, I guess, horse."

"What kind of proposition you talkin' about?" he asked. He tried to play it off cool, but he was clearly intrigued.

* * *

I got back to the Stang an hour later. With my new stock of credits, I could've rented a penthouse suite at The Westin Lux or Titan Grand, but I always felt more comfortable sleeping on my own ship with my security system fully engaged.

"So how did the covert mission go?" Gary groused the moment I stepped aboard. He had tried to call me on my handheld multiple times when I was at the pub. Bored, I guess. Sometimes I didn't know if he was my artificially intelligent second mate or my jealous girlfriend.

"A success," I said. "But I wouldn't go around celebrating."

"As if you'd ever let me off the ship anyway," Gary sulked. "You know, some people might consider this kidnapping. You never let me leave the Mustang."

A few months earlier, Gary had found a fully mobile robot on the web that apparently could house an onboard AI. Meaning he could inhabit the bot and walk around in a physical body. It looked vaguely human, and while Gary would never admit it, I think he was most excited by the fact the humanoid shell had hair. The guy still had hair envy even though he hadn't inhabited a physical form in centuries…and was only a programmed version of an actual human anyway. I was glad I had a full head of thick, curly hair. Didn't need those issues on top of all the rest.

And the truth was I had issues. Selzo had taken the bait, agreeing to consider joining up if my (fictional) contract with the Tracers came to fruition. I told him to discreetly talk to a few other captains he trusted to gauge their interest. Which meant about half of Silver Star would know in less than 24 hours. Which meant by helping Desmond, I had also put a big fat target on my back. That was not Desmond's concern, no matter how much he enjoyed sharing a beer with me; it was a good reminder not to lull myself into thinking he was my friend. My belly rumbled, partly from the nerves and partly from the fact I had drunk 36 ounces of grape soda on an empty stomach. I opened the bag of fast food I'd bought on my walk back to the Stang, and Pirate came tearing around the corner, screaming bloody murder.

"Relax, pal, I got you a fish sandwich."

He nearly clawed my hand off as I dropped the fish-protein substitute on the table next to me. He went to town on it, not a care in the world. Must be nice. I watched him for a few moments, scarfing down a patty made to taste like fish for people (and cats) that had never eaten the real thing. It was strange, really, but I guess old flavors die hard. Personally, I'd tried the real thing a few times and preferred the subs. No sooner had I settled into my pilot seat to enjoy a burger and a nap than my comm alert buzzed.

"Want me to put it through?" Gary asked, still annoyed with me.

I put my food back down and nodded. A moment later Jack Largent's smarmy face filled the monitor.

"Evenin'" he drawled. "At least it's evenin' here." Meaning his ranch back on Earth. Despite owning 70% of the universe's largest towing and repair corporation, Largent hadn't left bedrock for more than ten years. Oh, he wasn't retired. He just decided to leave space to his captains, or so he said. There were rumors he had radiation poisoning from all the long trips on thin-skinned ships, but he looked pretty healthy to me.

"You have your father's eyes," he said. "Your mom's ears, though. How is she these days?"

My blood boiled, and I tried my best not to let it show, but I could feel the heat in my cheeks. Most people tend to choose their words carefully around powerful, wealthy people like Largent. I never claimed to be as smart as most people.

"Ask about her again and this beam is over," I snapped. When my parents had split, Largent had tried to swoop in and court my mom. It was obvious he was only doing it to tweak his rival. My mom knew that, of course, and had higher standards, so she turned his sorry ass down. He seemed to understand by the way I said it that my mom had died.

"Ah, I wasn't aware. You know, I was actually sorry when I heard about your father. You may not believe that, but it's true. There's no greater respect than that among sworn enemies, of which I admit we were."

I said nothing. Just waited.

"I assume that's why you're trying to compete for the Tracers contract," he said.

"Nope. Only in it for the credits," I lied. "Is there anything else?"

It was Largent's turn to try and hide his anger. He was worse at it than me, which gave me a good deal of satisfaction. I even took a bite of my burger and leaned back in my chair a bit. A power move, if you will.

"And that's why your father never beat me either," he said, forcing a smile. "Never knew when he was out of his league. Well, that and he failed to realize one thing."

"What's that, Jack?"

"Business is war. And in war, there are no rules. It's a pity you didn't stay independent, for your mother's sake. I'll give you 24 hours to withdraw your bid for the contract." Before I could respond, the screen went black. He had disconnected.

"Well the jerk store called and they were all outta that guy.

59

Guess we won't be sending him a Hanukkah card," Gary said.

I'd forgotten to tell Gary to go to sleep before the beam. "Pretty sure nobody sends Hanukkah cards anymore, even if he were Jewish. Or I was, for that matter."

News had traveled much faster to Largent than I thought it would. Suddenly, I had 24 hours before every Silver Star cruiser in the verse was on my ass. And that's when I decided I hated Desmond as much as I hated Jack Largent.

Chapter 6

"So what did you do?" Batista asked, practically at the edge of her seat.

I thought about my answer for a moment, then smiled. "If I told you, I'd have to kill you."

Batista opened her mouth and then closed it again. She tensed her jaw. "That's a good line."

I heard that a lot. According to the books I'd read and news reports I'd seen, people used to quote the best bits of dialogue from movies and TV all the time. It was a way to sound clever. Over the last three hundred years, as fewer and fewer people watched classic entertainment, a lot of the best lines and turns of phrase had been forgotten. As one of the few people that was still watching 21st century entertainment, I had a wealth of seemingly original comebacks and witty phrases to choose from.

I'm gonna make him an offer he can't refuse.

There's no place like home.

You can't handle the truth!

And about a million more. I didn't feel the least bit bad about borrowing them, either. I was a wrecker, after all. Salvaging and re-using stuff was in my bones. As for the way things turned out with Desmond, it was better if Batista didn't know the details. They would only make her more nervous about the fact we were on a collision course with the Tracer boss. For all I knew, he was going to try and blast us into a million pieces. Then a thought occurred to me. Having someone like Batista with me wasn't the worst position to be in. She was tough, and Desmond, a notorious ladies man, wouldn't mind being polite to her for other reasons. Of course, none of that would matter if he tried to shred the Stang once the Golden Bear got within firing range.

"He as handsome in person as he is on the news?" Batista asked, seemingly reading my mind.

I tried not to frown, and failed.

"Guess so," she said.

"You should be so lucky to meet him in person," I warned. She understood my meaning, glancing at the red arc on the monitor that indicated the edge of the Golden Bear's firing range. She smiled and knocked on the metal dash.

"We've got armor and speed, and you're not the worst pilot in the galaxy from what I hear," she said, getting up and stretching her legs. I did my best not to let my gaze linger too long. "Gary," she called.

"Yello?" he asked with a smile. I mean, I knew he couldn't literally smile, but there was a happy inflection in his voice.

"No," I said. "You don't turn on when she says so. That's not how this works."

"Ah, pardon me good sir. I must have been confused," he said, putting on a pretentious accent. "I thought as the Mustang's on-board AI, I was supposed to serve at the pleasure of everyone on board."

I glowered at the camera in the corner of the cabin.

Batista winked at the camera at the same time. "Gary, wake

me up if things get interesting. I might just need my beauty rest."

She walked out of the room. Either she knew something I didn't about my abilities as a pilot, or the woman didn't rattle.

"Way out of your league," Gary noted.

He wasn't wrong, of course. Even though I was pretty sure she had dated my brother, which meant a relationship with her was a line I'd never cross, I was still a lonely young man in the middle of space. Strong, beautiful women who knew their way around engines didn't come around often. Despite being physically attracted to her, I also felt outclassed when I was around her. Which was a problem. The last thing I needed at the moment was a knot in the pit of my stomach because I had a crush on my client.

Client. Thinking of her that way was the first step.

"I'm in trouble," I muttered to myself.

"What was that? I think I heard something," Gary said.

"Nothing. Shut up."

"I definitely heard something."

I zeroed in on the Golden Bear's orange dot on the monitor. What did he want with me? Other than to settle a score. Screw it. I tapped a few keys and leaned back to wait. The response didn't take long. Desmond appeared on-screen. His trademark grin was there, but it didn't have the same warmth as before. This time it was the malicious look of a shark considering its prey.

We both waited for the other to speak. I broke first.

"Hey buddy." I waved at the monitor. It was the first time we'd beamed since I blew up his deal with Silver Star.

Still, he said nothing. And his eyes gave away nothing. Once again, I broke the silence.

"Look, if you're still mad about that whole Silver Star mixup, I can explain what happened," I said, doing my best impression of a guy that was not counting how many minutes he had left to live. "It's actually a funny story."

"Good. I like funny stories. I look forward to hearing it when we speak in person," he replied, cutting me off with a raised hand as I began to open my mouth. "It would be wise, kid, if you didn't inject one of your patented snide remarks at the moment. Just nod your head if you accept my invitation to come aboard."

So. It was like that. I couldn't even make a joke to break the tension. Desmond's face seemed to change at that moment. He grew even more confident, and I suddenly realized why. While we'd been having our little chat, the Golden Bear had crossed into firing range. If I refused his invitation now, things would quickly get messy. In the event of said mess, I gave myself less than a 50 percent chance of getting away in one piece.

I bit my tongue and nodded, curtly. The screen went black.

"Once again, Denver Boyd proves to be a master negotiator," Gary teased. "That's the second time he's convinced you to step aboard his ship. I wonder how many people make it to three..."

That time, Gary had a point.

"Can I keep Batista if Desmond kills you?" he added.

* * *

The Golden Bear looked different than it did last time I walked the corridors. For starters, there were at least twice as many crew members packed in. The casual air of the ship was gone, replaced by an angry tension that was almost palpable. It was entirely smellable with all the extra bodies crowding the galley. As the two heavily armed guards led me to Desmond's quarters, I could feel a dozen eyes on me. They weren't friendly. Suddenly, a very tall, very bald mountain of a human being stepped directly in our path.

"This the guy?" he asked one of the guards, a sizable dude in his own right, who looked like a child compared to Mountain Man. "Or should I say, boy?"

"You talkin' to me?" I replied, doing my best version of the deranged cab driver in a violent movie set in ancient New York. I looked around the room. "You talkin' to me? Then who the hell else are you talkin' to? I'm the only one here."

Even my escorts seemed to tense up, wondering how this bald hulk would react. He slowly shifted his gaze down on the top of my forehead (I came up to his chin). I flicked my eyes around the room and realized we had everyone's attention.

"Yes, I'm talking to you, moron," Mountain Man sniped. "Don't mess up, or I'll tear off your arms and cram them up your ass."

That got a murmur or agreement from the onlookers. Before I could even ask what the hell he was talking about, the guards were shoving me out of the galley. Last time I was aboard this ship, Desmond had personally given me the tour and treated me like a visitor. This time? More like a prisoner. Though I wasn't in restraints just yet. So that was something. As we passed through the crew's bunk area — a long corridor with cubbies belonging to various members of the ship's bursting gaggle of personnel — I had an eerie feeling that the ship was preparing for battle.

"There some war going on that I'm not aware of?" I asked

my escorts. They said nothing. One of them grinned.

"Ah, you decided to leave your passenger on the Stang," said Desmond, opening the door to his personal quarters. There was a hint of disappointment in his voice. He turned to my guard friends and nodded. They left.

Desmond gestured me into his living space and closed the door behind me. It wasn't the biggest or most luxurious captain's quarters I'd been in. Certainly it was nicer than mine, but that's not saying much. The room fit the man, however. It was minimal. Sneakily well-designed. And functional: a bedroom, bathroom and large table with four chairs around it. I tried to picture who on the crew he might eat or meet with on a regular basis, but drew a blank. I doubted it was the Mountain Man.

"A lot of things have changed since my last visit," I noted, uneasy. "Guess you only get the VIP tour once, huh?"

"Before I extend you the proper courtesy, I should make one thing clear," he said, standing so close to me I could smell what soap he used. It was lavender-scented. "You owe me a debt. How the next ten minutes go will determine whether I collect that debt immediately, or give you a chance to wipe the slate clean. Do you understand me?"

Yep. I was a dead man. Unless I did something new for him. I nodded.

"Good!" He patted my shoulder, smoothly slipping back into the role of a gracious host. "Have a seat. If I remember correctly, you enjoy the hoppier end of the spectrum."

As he grabbed me a tall, skinny can from the fridge next to his bed, I sat in one of the chairs by the table. I had no idea what the next ten minutes of conversation would entail, but I could already tell I was not going to like it. This was bad. This was very bad.

I mean, aside from the beer. That was good. That was very good. Desmond had the best beer I'd tasted in a long time, and it was almost worth risking my life just to enjoy a few swigs of pure hops perfection.

"Where do you get this and how can I have it all?" I asked, inspecting the logo of a rising sun over a tall mountain peak on the silver can.

"I believe they used to call it Oregon," Desmond said, as if he didn't know the exact origin of the ale, right down to the name of the person who brewed it. Those were the kinds of details a man like Desmond always knew. His whole empire – and whatever he claimed his fleet was, it was an empire – was based on possessing all the information. Where ships are. What they're carrying. How they're protecting it.

"Now you have a taste of what it's like to be me," he said. "What do you think?"

"I think it's amazing," I replied, referring to the beer, knowing full well he was talking about my status as an outlaw wanted by the federation. I had a 1000-credit Binding Federation Warrant hanging over my head.

"Back when I worried about such matters, I think the most extravagant BFW they had out on me was only 500 credits," he said, either feigning admiration or actually feeling some.

"Thought it was a kill warrant," I noted. I had also done my research.

"True. It was a kill," he said, in apparent admiration of himself. "Yet here I am."

I'd had enough of the small talk, so I figured it was time to rip the bandaid off to see just how screwed I really was.

"Look Des, I like you," I confessed, for some reason poking

the bear by calling him by a nickname. "I like your beer. I like your ship. I even like the way you smell. Seriously, I need that soap. But why am I here this time, especially when I clearly screwed you over last time?"

"You are here, Denver, because I need you to kill 18 people for me," he said, as if he was telling me he needed me to discard my empty can in the trash.

I looked Desmond directly in his steely blue eyes. "That's exactly 18 more people than I would ever say yes to. I'm not a killer. I'm just a wrecker, trying to get by in this damn verse."

"What if I told you these 18 people were the crew of the Rox?" he asked.

"That ship doesn't exist."

"Doesn't it, though?" He tapped a few buttons on his handheld and a monitor on the wall came to life, projecting the image of a long, cylindrical ship with multiple rail guns and a stout nose. "This is the Rox about six months ago somewhere between Mars and Jupiter."

The Rox was short for the Roxelle Baker, the rumored sniper-ship. It was rumored because nobody had ever actually seen the vessel. Or at least nobody had lived to tell about it. Anytime a ship went missing or was blasted to atoms, talk of the Rox would kick up. To hear some pilots tell it, the Rox was the manmade equivalent of a black hole, swallowing all other ships that were unlucky enough to cross its path. Depending who you got the story from, the Rox was either a rogue federation vessel, a totally independent group of sadists, a sniper-ship affiliated with the Tracers, or available for hire to the highest bidder. Those were a lot of options. And in my experience, that many conflicting rumors usually amounted to squat. I guessed I was about to hear Desmond's theory.

68

And I guessed wrong.

He touched a remote on his handheld and the door slid open. A moment later, the Mountain Man lumbered into the room, ducking his head to clear the doorway. He stewed at the sight of me, but seemed slightly less inclined to tear my head off in Desmond's presence. Emphasis on the slightly part.

"Denver, this is Edgar," Desmond gestured, introducing us properly. I waved. Edgar didn't.

"Why don't you educate our guest here on your former ship?" Desmond asked Edgar, before turning to me. "Another drink?"

"I think I might need it," I managed.

Edgar spent the next five minutes explaining that before he was a weapons tech on the Golden Bear, he had crewed five years in the same position on the Rox. It turned out a few of the rumors weren't true. The Rox had no affiliation with the Tracers or the federation. It was an independent, offering its services to the highest bidder. He went on to explain that about six months ago, he had a falling out with the captain of the Rox. Unfortunately for Edgar, working on the Rox wasn't a casual endeavor. Once you signed on, your only way out was floating lifeless in space or being shipped to a "retirement" colony on a remote space station. Being on the wrong side of the captain almost always sentenced you to the first option.

"So how'd you escape?" I interrupted.

"None of your concern," Edgar growled.

I put my hands wide, palms up. "We're talking about the most mysterious ship in the verse. I'm just supposed to take it at face value that you were the only genius clever enough to escape it and live to tell the tale? You?"

Edgar stepped toward me, murder in his eyes and his

clenched fists. His giant knuckles were stark white, and the oaf wanted nothing more than to smash my skull with them. Desmond calmed him with a raised hand.

"I'm going to ask you to take my word for it, Denver," Desmond interjected. "Edgar speaks the truth. How he got here, as he said, is not your concern."

I shrugged. "Let's say all of this is true. Fine. I go back to a question I've asked you a few times now: why me?"

When they didn't answer, I stood up. "Thanks for the beer and the story, but I think I've heard enough…"

Suddenly, I was airborne. Like two feet off the ground. And I had a sharp pain in my neck and shoulders. Tired of my attitude, Edgar had simply grabbed my shoulders from behind and picked me up off my feet. I was like a helpless toddler, swinging my feet in vain.

"Edgar, please," Desmond gently scolded. "Put our young friend down."

Next thing I knew I was slammed to the ground on my side. "He said put me down, not pile drive me."

"You're lucky I didn't put you down for good," he said.

I slowly stood up. My neck muscles were on fire and my right shoulder clicked painfully every time I rotated it. My pride wasn't in the best shape either, if anyone was keeping score.

"To answer your question, we need you because we need to get someone on board the ship before we destroy it, to remove an item of extreme value," said Desmond. "And who better than a mechanic?"

That sounded pretty thin to me. I could think of a million people better than a mechanic to board the Rox and steal something. Again, Desmond could tell what I was thinking.

"And this is where our interests intersect, Denver. There are currently 19 crew members on the Rox, and I'm only asking you to kill 18."

"Oh good," I snarked. "Who's the happy survivor?"

Desmond raised his eyebrows and smiled. "Your brother."

I'd had less than a second to process that news when high-pitched klaxons sounded throughout the ship. Desmond snapped his attention toward the monitor on the wall and the Rox was replaced by another vessel – a federation warbird. All 2,000 meters of her.

Edgar rushed out of the room, presumably to his battle station.

"Follow me," Desmond ordered. I fell in behind him as we left his quarters. The hallway was chaotic, with burly men and women rushing to their respective posts.

"So this is the war," I muttered.

"No," Desmond corrected as we raced through the galley. "This is you being a fugitive. You're lucky I don't want them to have you at the moment."

"Oh yes, I certainly *feel* lucky," I said, trying to rub my aching shoulder as we navigated our way onto the bridge. The chaos there was at least a bit more choreographed than in the rest of the ship, with a core team of Desmond's finest handling the situation. They didn't exactly stand to military attention when he arrived, but they definitely gave him a wide berth.

"Status," he demanded.

"I need to get back to the Stang –" I tried, before he cut me off with eye daggers.

"Federation warbird," reported a thin woman with jet black hair and a matching black jumpsuit. "It appeared out of nowhere, captain. One second, nothing on the scan. The next second, it's within firing range."

"How is that possible?" Desmond asked. For the first time I saw a crack in his cool demeanor.

"Not a damn clue," the woman responded. "They've been hailing us for about a minute now."

Desmond sat in his captain's chair and swiveled toward the large screen on the wall. My first thought was, damn, his chair was way nicer than mine. But then I thought of Batista on the Stang. Would she know what to do? She seemed to be a capable engineer and a total mauler when it came to physical confrontations, but I had no idea if she'd be out of her depth at the helm of the Stang at a time like this. Like a punch to the gut, another thought hit me: my brother was alive. Maybe. Ten minutes ago, Avery had been dead. According to Desmond and a giant, he was alive and on board the Rox.

Desmond cleared his throat and was about to answer the beam when he looked back at me. I was standing right behind him. "Probably not a good idea for you to be on screen when I open a dialogue, Denver."

The man had a point. I sheepishly moved off to the side. I could feel everyone's eyes on me – they all knew my presence was the reason for this potential fight. A federation warbird was no joke, even for the Golden Bear. What the fed vessel lacked in speed and talent (most federation pilots aren't worth a damn), it made up for in brute force. While the Bear had rail guns, the bird had twin rail cannons, basically the same weapon with twice the power, thanks to the larger steel projectiles with galvanized cores.

The wild card was this particular ship's stealth. Most fed vessels this size were bulky and relied on overwhelming force, but this one had somehow snuck past the Bear's defenses. It either meant someone was asleep at the helm of one of the baddest ships in the galaxy, which was unlikely, or that the blue suits had themselves some kind of new technology. The arrogant face that appeared on the monitor suggested the latter. The sharp-jawed woman was in her 30s. She exuded federation, from her icy demeanor to her buzzcut.

"Hello," Desmond said, opening the dialogue. He always liked to be the first one to speak, and in my experience, the last. "That's a sneaky ship you have there. Don't normally see stealth on a bird that size."

Right to it, then. The fed captain didn't bite. Instead, she got right to it as well.

"You're currently docked with the ship of a known fugitive," she said. "I assume you have him in your brig and are willing to hand him and his companion over to face justice."

"One should never assume, Captain…?"

"Slay. Admiral Slay of the DTX Burnett," she corrected, more for the record than to score points. Her confidence came from somewhere deeper than her rank. I liked that about her. I didn't like that she wanted me dead or in prison.

"Pardon the mistake. I meant no offense, admiral."

"Of course not. Mr. Boyd and Mrs. Batista. Do you have them?"

"Jurisdiction, admiral. I think that's the first part of this discussion, don't you?"

Slay smiled. It was not a friendly one. "If that's the case, it'll be a short conversation. You're outgunned. Outclassed. And docked with a ship. I have you dead to rights if I want you."

"Do you want me?" Desmond replied.

I had to admire his old-fashioned wise-assery. I wish I'd been in the chair to deliver that retort. Slay acted as if she was expecting it, but I could tell she was taking a moment to determine the best way to respond. With humor? With derision? Being a good captain was as much about knowing how to deal with adversaries as it was about keeping your own crew in line. Most federation captains didn't understand that. I suspected Slay did.

Still, that moment of hesitation was all Desmond needed. He motioned to Edgar, now hulking over his station. The big man pressed a series of buttons. On the monitor, Slay's eyes went wide as her ship shook with the force of a contained blast.

"As I was saying, stealth is much more common on smaller craft, like unmanned transports," Desmond noted, taking a bite of an apple he suddenly had in his hand. He must have kept it somewhere close for just such a gloating occasion.

What he was referring to was the small drone ship he'd deployed the second the Burnett came on radar. It had covered the distance between the Bear and Slay's ship during their respective captains' lively conversation. The moment Slay showed the slightest hesitation, Desmond ordered the drone to land and detonate itself.

Slay's cool demeanor evaporated as she turned to her weapons tech and barked her disapproval. "Why haven't we returned fire!"

"I can answer that, captain," Desmond offered cheerily, still chomping his apple. "Your ship may well be stealthy, but it seems those blue suit engineers put the weapons drive in the same old spot again. Good luck and godspeed!"

And with that, he cut the feed. He whirled his chair to face me. "You have 30 seconds to get back to your ship and disengage."

"Done!" I yelled as I broke for the corridor to the airlock. Edgar moved into my path. "Hey, you heard the man," I complained.

"He's going with you," Desmond said, referring to the 7-foot-tall mass of humanity standing between me and the Stang.

Chapter 7

The look on Batista's face when she saw who I brought back with me was kinda how I imagined it must have been for ancient humans when they were surprised by a grizzly bear in the woods.

"What is that?" she asked, loudly and with no regard for whether he heard her.

"Name's Edgar," I said, pointing at him as he walked past a shocked Batista. "He's not as nice as he looks."

I was about to follow it up with another sarcastic remark when I bit my tongue. Seeing Batista reminded me that she may have been closer to my brother than I ever was – and she still thought he was dead. The breaking of that news would have to wait until we were clear of the federation warbird.

"Lot to explain, but right now we have to get the hell out of here." I hustled toward the cabin, a bit unnerved by Edgar already acquainting himself with the Stang's weapons systems.

"Don't touch anything," I ordered. The big man gave me a wilting glare, but paused what he was doing. One of the conditions Desmond had set was that Edgar would be under my command. I didn't really know how long that would last or what kind of "command" I was going to have – part of me thought Edgar would just decide when to treat me as a captain and when to tear my head off – but for the moment, he stood fast.

"You make friends with all the best people," Gary chided. "And since when did federation ships that big have stealth capabilities?"

"Seriously," Batista agreed, a wary eye still on Edgar. "One minute I've got nothing on the scan and then that shiny bastard is right on top of us."

"Your guess is as good as mine, but we have no time to worry about it. Its weapons drive is crippled for maybe two or three more minutes, and I'm sure they can do some auxiliary damage if they decide to turn their focus on us. Luckily the Bear is keeping their attention."

I plunked down in my chair and disengaged Gary's navigation control.

"Hey!" he complained.

"Nothing personal, but it's better if I fly us out of here without logging a course," I said, assuming full control of the Stang. Despite the conditions, it felt good. I didn't go manual as often as I used to. Of all the issues I had with Gary, his flying skills weren't one of them. As an AI, he was basically a perfect navigator. He'd also learned a few improvisational maneuvers from me and my uncle over the years. I kicked all four turbines into gear and hoped the Burnett didn't follow us.

"At least tell me where we're headed," Batista demanded, monitoring the battle brewing between the Bear and the Burnett. They were engaged in a close-range weapons battle.

"No change in destination," I reassured her. "We'll just be taking the scenic route. It seems the Tracers also have an interest in us making an appearance at Jasper Station."

"That's convenient," she replied, shooting a glance at Edgar. "You wanna share any insight on the matter?"

He stepped toward Batista and looked down his crooked nose at her. "As a matter of fact, honey, I don't."

The hairs on the back of my neck went rigid as I watched Batista match his step forward. They were now less than a foot from each other. If I was going on sheer size and power, Edgar would be my bet. But having seen Batista dispatch half a dozen feds with relative ease, it felt more like even odds, regardless of the fact she was 150 pounds lighter than him.

"Call me honey again and see what happens, Shrek," she replied. I stifled a laugh. Edgar just stared at her, clearly not understanding the obscure reference. The only reason Batista knew it was thanks to the Stang's vast collection of 21st century movies and TV shows. On a long trip like this, a person could plow through three or four movies a day. I knew that Batista had watched Shrek a couple days earlier, as she and Gary had debated whether Donkey was more funny or annoying. The argument itself was the latter, if you asked me. Just as I worried the confrontation might turn to blows, we had a bigger fish to fry. Klaxons sounded and red lights lit up my dash.

"We've got heat," Gary said, referring to the new blip on the screen that was headed our way. The Burnett had begun firing on us, even as the Bear engaged her with its own rail guns.

"Alright, take over and evade...are those nukes?" I asked, seeing the purple signature of the blip as it homed in on us. "Damnit."

I turned to Edgar and Batista. "Knock that off. Edgar, you wanna give it a go?" I motioned toward the weapons panel. The big man didn't move. He just kept staring at Batista.

"What the hell is a Shrek?" he asked.

"Later!" I yelled, hoping to instill enough confidence in the command for him to listen. "I will explain all about the big green ogre –"

Edgar snapped his attention to me.

"– *big green and extremely heroic* ogre known as Shrek. I'll even make you popcorn as you watch the movie!"

Edgar grunted and turned around toward his station. "This hunk of junk got any missile busters?"

I ignored the insult, knowing the question was rhetorical. "Batista, when you're done trying to start fights, you may want to strap in."

She moved to the co-pilot seat and did just that. I kept one eye on the monitor, where I watched the Bear and warbird attempting to strafe each other into oblivion. My other eye was on the camera in my quarters. "Gary, make sure Pirate gets tucked in."

"Yeah, yeah, yeah. You do realize I'm a supercomputer, right? I don't forget things like that," he replied.

On the camera, I could see Pirate scurry into my quarters and through the open door of the padded cubby I'd designed for him. It had taken nearly six months, but I'd trained him to hide in the cubby whenever klaxons sounded, meaning whenever we were about to do some unpredictable maneuvers. Once he was in the cubby, it was Gary's job to shut the gate and set the foam to expand based on Pirate's position. It basically was like putting the cat in bubble wrap. Not perfect, but better than him being flung against the walls in the corner of whatever room he happened to be hiding in. Batista had teased me about the cubby when she first learned about it, but I could see that she too had a micro-sigh of relief when Pirate was safely foamed into place. He'd grown on her.

"How we doing on that nuke?" I asked, noting the blip was getting closer and closer. We had maybe 45 seconds until impact.

"Worry about your own problems," Edgar said, preparing his counter-strike. Okay, then. I hoped the guy was as good as Desmond claimed when he forced me to take him on board.

Following Edgar's advice, I continued plotting a course to take the Stang the long way to Jasper. That meant a looping route through pretty dense federation territory, but the prospect of being disintegrated by a future ship was an easy trade for actually being blown up by a current one.

"Last warning, we're about to go to 15 g's," I told him.

He snorted, not even bothering to sit in his chair. I did see him flex his legs a bit though. Hey, his funeral.

I hit the gas, as they used to say, going to 90% of the Stang's capacity.

The force came down like an anvil on my chest. An anvil that weighed a few hundred pounds. For a moment, it knocked the wind out of me and I saw stars. I could hear Batista grunt in the seat next to me. The speed probably bought us another 15 seconds or so to deal with that nuke. I strained to tilt my head and saw Edgar still standing in place, though he was now in a powerful crouch, all his muscles tense, holding him in place. He could have sat in the chair, but he was making a point.

"Loose," he announced.

I turned to the scan and saw a green dot heading to intercept the federation nuke.

"How many?" I asked.

"What do you mean?" he replied. "One."

I stared at the dot. One? What the hell was this psycho

thinking? The Stang had a dozen nuke busters – and this guy had only sent one? I could see if he only fired like five or six in an arrow formation, but one?

"Got a little confidence, do we?" Gary chirped. "This Shrek guy is ballsy."

"He's gonna get us all killed," Batista said, straining under the g-force. "Can you fire any more from there?"

"Working on it," I answered.

Suddenly I felt two vice grips on my upper arms, holding them in place. They belonged to Edgar, who had somehow crossed the cabin despite 15 g's. "How is that possible –"

"Watch and learn," he said, cutting me off. I didn't really have a choice. Although Gary did. "Gary, send a second salvo."

"Uh, slight problem there, Denver…"

I had a sinking feeling in my stomach, which was already somewhere around my knees thanks to the g's.

"I disabled his weapons access," Edgar explained. "Too many cooks in the kitchen spoil the broth."

Who did this guy think he was, I thought to myself. I watched the monitor as the green dot approached the purple blip…and sailed by as the blip evaded it. Not good. Batista was right. The big moron had just got us all killed.

"Wait for it," he said, enjoying the look of fear on my face. Once the buster was past the nuke, it somehow swung back around and was on its tail, picking up speed. "Missiles are all the same. Good at avoiding head-on countermeasures, but terrible at watching their back."

A second later, both the dot and the blip were gone. Just like that. I had given us maybe one chance in five, but Edgar had made a joke of the whole encounter. I eased the throttle and felt my lungs begin to function more normally.

I stared at the screen in disbelief for a few moments. I had obviously misjudged the man. Or, more specifically, underestimated him. He not only possessed superhuman strength — being able to stand in 15 g's wasn't supposed to be possible — he also was some kind of genius. To program a heat-sinker to actually trick a high-tech nuke also shouldn't have been possible, definitely not in less time than it takes to make a cup of coffee. Batista must have been thinking the same thing, because she looked over and whispered "What just happened?"

"My bunk?" Edgar asked, holding his duffel bag, standing near the exit that led to the Stang's main corridor.

"Uh, um take a right and third door on the left," I managed, trying to suppress the adrenaline from the last five minutes. Edgar walked out.

I no longer had a visual on the two other ships, and the scan was clear. We weren't being followed, for the time being anyway.

"Well, I like him," Gary declared.

Batista swiveled her seat to face me. "So that just happened."

"Which part?" I wondered aloud. "When he walked across the cabin in high-g? Or when he reprogrammed a nuke buster in like 30 seconds to do something they aren't supposed to be able to do?"

"And the fact he's even on the ship in the first place," she added. "You gonna tell me what's going on now?"

I wanted to tell her about Avery. She was a strong person, but there was no predicting what kind of emotions it would bring up. To be honest, I was a little troubled by my own lack of emotions about the revelation. Oh, I was surprised. But deep down, I was disappointed it didn't bring me more hope or happiness. Maybe it would if I was able to see him.

"Crew meeting in ten minutes. Kitchen," I said, buying myself some time. I rose to my feet, my bones and muscles aching from the stress of the high-g run. "I'm gonna check on our new crewmate."

Chapter 8

As I approached the door to Edgar's quarters, I realized he'd overridden my security permissions that allowed me to access any area of the ship. I was forced to knock loudly on the silver-grey graphite.

"Who is it?" he asked with an innocent tone.

Seriously? This guy was gonna drive me crazy. "Open up."

I stood there, waiting. I was about to punch the door when it slid open. I stepped into the room. These weren't the fanciest digs in the verse, but compared to the cramped crew quarters I saw on the Golden Bear, it was a total upgrade for Edgar. Privacy. A hundred fifty square feet. He even had his own bathroom. The room was steamy and smelled of lavender. Edgar had taken a shower and he apparently used the same soap as Desmond. Many ships had standard supplies like soaps and other toiletries. I was just surprised the baddest ship in the Tracer fleet had chosen lavender as its signature scent.

Edgar sat on the edge of his bunk, wearing just a towel around his waist and legs. The man was more muscle than water. I didn't know if zero percent body fat was a real possibility, but if it was, this guy had it. At the moment, he was admiring busty women in red swimsuits as they ran across the beach in slow-motion.

Baywatch.

He had access to thousands of classic TV shows and movies courtesy of my uncle's entertainment selection, and of course he chose Baywatch.

"So wholesome," he noted. "It's nothing like the Purples."

The Purples were short pornographic videos strung together and organized by theme. Heterosexual. Homosexual. Videos of feet. You name it. If there was a style or fetish, there was a Purple for it. The videos got their name from the low-grade beam quality that made them easier to download and view while hurtling through space at a few hundred thousand miles per hour. The compression often gave them a purple hue that somehow made them even more depressing to watch.

The idea of entertainment as art had mostly died in the 21st century. Now the great majority of the video diversions available were either Purples, sports or news. Occasionally an industrious rich person would commission a movie to be made, but if people felt the need to spend time in front of a monitor, it was usually for porn or gaming.

"There are actually much better shows in the system," I told him. "You should check out The Wire. Or Goonies." I snickered to myself, thinking he was more like Sloth than Shrek.

He waved a hand. "This is perfect. Why are you bothering me?"

"Uh, because it's my ship and I can bother you in your quarters if I want."

"Thought maybe you came by to make sure I was settled in. Or to thank me for saving your life."

Smartass.

"So I guess that's a no on the thank you? I'll remember that next time," he said.

He didn't even look at me when he was talking. Just kept his eyes glued to the monitor on the wall.

"It was good work," I managed through gritted teeth.

Edgar nodded, accepting the meager compliment. He knew it was good work and didn't need my validation or lame version of a thank you. "Anything else, *captain*? As you can see, I am trying to appreciate the on-board amenities for the short time I'm on board this heap."

"Heap?"

"Fine, maybe it's not a total heap. It has certain qualities I like." Edgar motioned to the monitor, then he looked at me. "And some I could take or leave."

I thought about telling him to undo whatever hacking wizardry he'd used to disable my security clearances, but I figured bringing it up would only encourage him to further compromise my authority, merely out of spite. So, I let it slide.

"Crew meeting in the kitchen in ten," I said, turning to leave. He grunted a version of maybe. Walking out the door, I heard Hasselhoff warn the other lifeguards about a possible traitor in their midst. I understood the feeling.

* * *

I wasn't used to providing meals for more than me and my cat.

When I towed other ships, their crews and passengers usually stayed on their own vessel for the duration. That was barring uninhabitable conditions, like the time I towed a leisure cruiser that had sprung a core reactor leak. All 29 people on board had to cram into the Stang for eight grueling, smelly days. It was better than radiation poisoning, of course, but the way some of them complained about eating freeze-dried protein packs twice a day, maybe they'd have preferred a slow death from internal bleeding.

The point was, I hadn't stopped for supplies since a few weeks before picking up Batista, so rations were already spread thin. Now I had yet another mouth to feed. The size of the man it belonged to made me even more concerned that the fridge, freezer and pantry would soon be empty. Given the bounty on our heads, I had no idea where the next safe port would be, meaning we might have to stretch supplies until Jasper Station. Six more days. The coffee maker whirred and sputtered out a pot of soybean substitute. Edgar had just sat down and he eyed the brown liquid with contempt.

"Bad news: I ran out of the real stuff about a month ago," I explained to him. Batista was also at the table, but she already knew the deal. "Good news: this soybean crap is the one thing we won't run out of. A freighter couldn't pay me a couple jobs back, so they gave me two crates of the stuff."

"I don't work on barter," Edgar noted. I handed him a cup anyway and sat down. The three of us looked at each other for a few moments. Batista and I sipped the soy-coffee. Edgar just watched us. It tasted like hell, but it did the trick – what the stuff lacked in flavor, it made up for in caffeine.

I settled into my chair and considered my crew. We were three loners, somehow thrown together on a mission that none of us understood. Well, at least I didn't.

"I'll start," Batista said, unable to wait any longer. She turned to Edgar. "Why are you on this ship?"

"Same reason you are, babe," Edgar replied.

"I'm done. This is pointless." Batista shook her head and

stood up. She began to leave the kitchen.

Edgar smiled at me.

"What?" I asked, confused.

"Guess she didn't tell you that your brother was alive," he said, matter of fact. Then he downed half his coffee and sat back in his chair, content.

I turned my gaze to Batista, who was frozen in place by the door. I could tell by her body language Edgar wasn't making it up. She'd known all along.

"It's not that simple," she explained.

"It's not? Then explain it to me," I said. I could feel the heat in my cheeks and knew I was turning crimson. I didn't care.

Batista kept her eyes averted from mine. She glared at Edgar. "You're a real piece of shit, you know that?"

"Maybe. Least I'm an honest piece of shit. You heard the captain. Explain why you've been lying to him this whole time."

Hard to believe, but I agreed with him. Batista owed me a damn good explanation.

"I didn't think you'd believe me," she said.

"Try again. Only this time, tell me the real reason or I'll drop you off at the next port, even if it means risking being caught," I said.

"Denver, let's not get crazy," Gary butted in.

"Stay out of it, Gary," I warned.

Batista mulled over her options and decided she had no choice but to come clean. She sighed. "Avery made me promise not to tell anyone, especially you."

I felt a hollow ache in my gut. My brother and I had been many things, but we were never enemies. The idea that he would let me believe he was dead seemed beyond cruel. It didn't mesh with the usual state of our relationship, as rocky as it was. Then I suddenly felt a gnawing concern.

"Is my father even dead?" I asked her.

Edgar answered first. "Yup. Floating somewhere a few hundred thousand clicks off Mars."

The big man then got up and moved to the cabinets. "Hungry," he muttered to himself. We may as well have been talking about Baywatch, for all he cared. Death meant nothing to him. He grabbed a candy bar I knew I should've hid and leaned on the counter, slowly unwrapping it.

I wasn't sure if I should feel sad or relieved about my father (still) being dead. I'd come to terms with my old man being gone. Having to re-engage that part of my life would have been painful, even if it meant he was still alive. I quickly examined my feelings on the matter and realized, yes, it was easier this way.

Great, another thing to feel guilty about.

I pushed those thoughts aside for the moment and focused back on the matter at hand.

"Why do you need to get to Jasper Station?" I asked Batista. "And why the deadline?"

She eyed Edgar, then moved back to her chair and sat down. She looked at her mug of coffee. "I think we're all gonna need something harder than this."

I wasn't in the mood to hand out any alcohol, so after a quick glance at Edgar, she proceeded.

"Are we sure we can trust him?" she asked me.

"Right now, I trust him more than you," I said.

She nodded and leaned forward to meet my eyes.

"Your brother is on the Roxelle Baker," she told me. I already knew this, but didn't bother to interrupt. "I assume you've heard of it?"

I nodded. Edgar continued munching on what was probably the last candy bar on the Stang. He tried to keep a relaxed look about him, but I could see his interest was piqued. Perhaps he hadn't expected Batista to know that part.

"When Silver Star had your father killed, they gave your brother a choice. He could join your dad or join the crew of the Rox. Avery might not be the mechanic you or your father was, but he had other skills."

"Such as?"

Batista threw another look at Edgar, but she had no choice except to answer. "He was the best scout I ever saw."

Scout was a nice word for thief. Often, killer. On a ship like the Rox, a scout's job would be to throw on the space suit and sneak onto enemy vessels in close proximity. And there was only one real reason to do that: to board the other ship or sabotage it. Calling that person a "scout" was suggesting their main job was reconnaissance, which it usually wasn't. When we were teenagers, Avery and I snuck off our dad's ship plenty of times to cause mischief. I was never fully confident floating in the vastness of space, nothing between me and the vacuum besides a few layers of nylon and aluminized kevlar, with nothing to guide myself but dinky little pressure packs. Avery was fearless. Because of that, he was also faster and more willing to take risks. He used to call it floating the line, but I often felt he crossed over the line in hopes he might not make it back.

As a scout on the Rox, he lived on the other side of the line.

"He's good, but I've seen better," Edgar interjected.

"I don't remember asking your opinion," Batista snarled. "And I never said you hadn't seen better. I said he was the best

I'd seen, which still makes him pretty damn good. Got it?"

Edgar put up his hands in a gesture of mock surrender.

"How do you know all this?" I asked her.

"He finds ways to leave me messages," she replied. She didn't offer any more detail. Fine. We'd return to that later, I decided.

"And one of those messages was about Jasper?"

"The Rox will be there in six days. They're going to destroy the federation ship guarding the station, and then they're going to destroy Jasper itself."

That was a ruthless move, even for the Rox. I had no love for the Believers, but there were kids on that station. Perhaps reading my mind, Batista nodded.

"He didn't tell me why," she said. "He just said to get there so I could help him stop it."

"Why not just tip off the feds?"

"I tried that. Didn't work. So then your brother told me to get your help."

My help? What was I supposed to do? Sure, now I was involved thanks to Desmond, but my brother couldn't have predicted that...I didn't think.

Edgar moved back to the table, licking the chocolate from the candy bar off his fingers. "I couldn't care less about Jasper or the people on it."

"Touching," Batista said.

"They're all loons and you both know it. Verse is better without them. I'd blast them to pieces myself if it wasn't so much trouble," he shrugged. "Now the Rox? That ship's actually worth a damn. Especially now."

"Setting aside the fact you just placed more value on a band of soulless mercenaries than thousands of innocent people," Batista growled, "What's so special about the Rox right now?"

Edgar smiled, showing the nougat and caramel stuck in his crooked teeth. He had no intention of fully answering the question, but he knew he'd piqued our interest.

"Let's just say in a few months, the rest of us will be struggling to keep up with them," he teased. "Unless Desmond captures it first."

I wanted to press him, but there was no point. The big man wasn't going to spill. Not willingly, anyway. Batista came to the same conclusion and decided to set aside her curiosity for the time being.

"Bottom line. We help Desmond, and the Rox doesn't destroy Jasper?" she asked.

Edgar spread his hands and looked down his nose at Batista. "Probably. It'll distract them at least. You a Believer?"

"No."

"Then why do you care about Jasper?"

"Preventing mass murder isn't reason enough?"

Edgar shook his head. "I'm gonna go with no."

Part of me suspected the same thing: Batista had some other motive here. Stopping the Rox was noble and all, but there was a missing piece. They'd already described the kind of person my brother was these days, so his reasons might not be so pure, either.

"Maybe they're after what's on the Rox, too," I offered.

Batista looked at me with a mix of surprise and anger. But I saw past that and recognized I'd hit pay dirt. I was right.

"Tell me what it is," I demanded of her. Or Edgar. Or even Pirate, who had just sauntered into the room and was mewing near the fridge, hoping for a second dinner.

"Maybe..." Batista admitted, tentatively. "Maybe for Avery. He hasn't told me what's on board, though. It must be important because he usually doesn't hide things from me."

Edgar whistled. "You do know you're breaking the captain's heart, one lie at a time, don't ya? And you're already nailing his brother. It's sad –"

Before Edgar could finish his sarcastic remark, I saw a black blur cross in front of my face. It was Batista's boot. Somehow she'd flashed her leg out and kicked Edgar right in the jaw with a vicious roundhouse (from a seated position). Her steel-toed boot connected flush with a loud crack that sent Pirate screeching out of the room.

It merely stunned Edgar. For a nanosecond. He flinched and shook it off at the same time, then caught her leg as it recoiled. With a flick of his wrist, he yanked Batista out of her chair and onto the floor. She rolled with the momentum and got her leg free from Edgar's grasp. Suddenly they were both crouched, facing each other. They began to circle.

This all happened before I could put down my coffee.

"We don't need this right now," I said, trying to sound authoritative. They both ignored me. It was a sight that defied logic: a hulking beast of a man squaring off with a slender woman maybe a third his weight. He wasn't taking her lightly, though. The lightning quick kick must have instilled a bit of respect.

"I was wondering how long it'd be before we tango'd," Batista hissed.

Edgar blinked. He had no idea what a tango was. Instead, he lunged forward and tried to grab one of Batista's arms. She spun away from the attempt and came back with an elbow against his forearm. It looked like it hurt her more than him. They both had smiles on their faces – apparently this was what passed for fun in their minds. I wasn't quite so amused.

I stood up and stepped toward them.

"I'm not taking responsibility for your health," Edgar warned.

"Ditto," said Batista, just as she twirled to the ground and swept the big man's legs out from under him. He went down, hard. The guy actually dented the corrugated steel floor where his shoulder landed. But pain was even more foreign to Edgar than it was to me, and he kicked back – right into Batista's gut. She flew backward four full feet, slamming into the cabinets with a thud. As tough as she was, that one hurt. She labored to get back up as Edgar calmly rose to his feet and looked down at her.

"I'll admit, I'm impressed," he said. "But don't mistake that for pity. I will break you in half if I feel like it."

"Nobody is breaking anybody in half!" I shouted. That got their attention. "Either this stops now or everybody is going to sleep."

Batista knew what I was talking about, but Edgar screwed his face into a genuinely confused grimace. "What, like a curfew?"

"Tell him, Gary," I said, crossing my arms.

"Halothane vapor mixed with penthrane," he said cheerily. "You may know it as sleeping gas. Holy fog, Batman!"

I looked up and saw the chemical fog pouring out of the kitchen vents. Before I could stop him, Gary had flooded the room with the stuff. Batista fell to the floor within two seconds, but Edgar's body fought the gas for a full five seconds, during which he stumbled toward me with fists clenched. Luckily, he came up a couple feet short. He landed with another clang that left an even more pronounced dent in the floor.

I sighed.

"I said to tell them, not show them."

"You have a weird way of saying thank you, Denver."

"Now it's your turn –"

"But I was trying to help you!"

"Sleep. Now."

I sat back down and took a sip of my coffee. Pirate slunk into the room, sidestepping Edgar and giving Batista a concerned sniff. Once he decided she was okay, he hopped up onto the table and began eating the crumbs from Edgar's candy bar. I'd also had Pirate's immunity altered so he wasn't affected by the knockout gas. I checked my handheld and saw the ship only had 12% of the stuff left. That was good enough for one contained blast of it in an emergency.

What was Gary thinking? He didn't usually freelance like that, at least not on important decisions like using the gas on two crew members. It's possible he was just growing more bold (and cranky) these days, but something poked at the back of my mind. A vague, growing concern that hadn't fully taken shape yet. I didn't think Gary had a virus…but something was different. I had to keep an eye on it.

As if I didn't have enough to worry about.

I looked at two of those things that were passed out on the kitchen floor.

* * *

Batista woke up first, which was good. I wanted to talk to her before Edgar anyway. She groggily opened her eyes and rubbed her temples, trying to get her bearings. I watched her through the window and touched the intercom button.

95

"Have a nice nap?" I asked.

She realized where she was and turned toward me, pissed. "Get me out of here."

"Be careful what you wish for," I warned.

She was in the airlock. I'd loaded her onto a utility cart and rolled her in there, then did the same with Edgar. He was still passed out about 10 feet away from her. The guy was too damn heavy to move again, so I let him sleep it off on the metal cart. My shoulders still ached from dragging him onto the cart in the first place.

"You're not gonna space us, so you may as well let us out of here," said Batista.

I knew she'd say that. And she was right...but she didn't have to know that. It was time for some tough love.

"Let me guess, you think I'd space him but not you?" I asked.

"No, I think you're not a killer, so you wouldn't hit that red button with either of us in here."

I glanced at the large red button. It was covered with a protective plastic shield so it didn't accidentally get bumped. You had to lift the plastic, then press the button.

"You're right. I'm not. Even though you lied to me about my brother and got me mixed up in something that will probably get me killed, I'm not the kind of captain that spaces his crew. But any minute now, that big guy over there is gonna wake up. Maybe he doesn't try to kill you, or maybe he does. Cause he knows the only way I'd be able to stop him is by spacing you both. And he's smarter than he looks, so he probably knows I'm not a killer too."

Now she looked over at Edgar, who was beginning to twitch. As tough as she was, she knew it was a losing fight for her in an enclosed area with the guy.

"So, the way I see it, you either convince him I am capable of spacing you both, or you take your chances in close quarters."

Edgar opened his eyes slowly, then lifted his face off the metal cart. He was bleeding from his cheek – I must have cut his face when I heaped him onto the cart. Oops. The big man wiped the blood as he sat up and appraised the situation. He quickly came to the same conclusion Batista did. He grunted out a laugh.

"You're bluffing," he said, eyeing me through the glass.

"You're bluffing, Captain," I corrected, doing my best to sound serious. "I tried being nice. But that just made you think you could ignore my orders on my ship. Well guess what? There's a reason I don't have crew on the Stang. I don't like my orders being ignored. It doesn't work for me. So either you two start doing what I say, when I say it, or I go back to having no crew."

Edgar sighed. "Blah, blah, blah, open the door or she pays for it."

"Bite me," Batista replied.

"I just might," he countered.

"Batista, why don't you tell Edgar here how it came to be that I don't have a crew anymore."

She looked at me for a few moments. Then she realized I was leaving it up to her to figure out a good story. I smiled. You're so good at lying, I thought, go ahead and lie. She nodded and turned to Edgar. "He wants me to convince you he's a killer like us, but we both know that's not true."

Edgar spread his arms wide. "Should we finish what we started, or should we see what he does first?"

"Let's give him a few seconds to plan his next move. When he's done pissing his pants," she said.

The two killers in the air lock looked at me. I shook my head, knowing what I was about to do would just prove they were right about me.

"If you'll both look at the screen, please." I pressed my handheld to the glass and Desmond's face appeared on it. He looked at Edgar and Batista in turn. They regarded him with more respect than they ever gave me, that's for sure.

"Edgar," he said. "Miss Batista. Nice to meet you, though I regret it's under these circumstances. I'm speaking to you because you're both under the impression that Mr. Boyd here isn't in charge of what goes on aboard his ship. While I don't know or care what normally passes for chain of command on the Mustang, I will say that until we achieve our objective, Mr. Boyd is in my employ. As crew members of his ship, you report to him, which in effect means you report to me. He may not be a killer but I assure you, if your insubordination causes this mission harm in any way, I will not hesitate to lay the blame at your feet. In other words, he's in charge. Understood?"

Edgar and Batista couldn't believe I had tattled on them. I didn't care. I mean, I was a little embarrassed but whatever.

"I'm a busy man, do you understand? I should also mention I have been granted access to the ship's control system during this transmission, so if you don't understand please let me know and I'll space you both right now."

"Fine, the kid's in charge," Edgar said.

"What he said," Batista agreed.

Desmond grimaced, annoyed with having to step in. "Good," he simply said before cutting the transmission.

I waited a beat, then unlocked the door and opened it. Edgar and Batista stood, then he motioned for her to go ahead.

"Ladies first." She obliged. As they passed me, I somehow felt even less in charge than I did before. But neither of them killed me or killed the other, so I'd achieved my main goal of crew unity, even if they were now mostly united against me. It was a temporary situation anyway, and if I was lucky enough to survive it, I'd be back to having a cat as my only insubordinate crew member in no time.

It made me think back to when I first became part of my uncle's crew...

Chapter 9

I slid my empty glass further across the faux wood table and coughed loudly, hoping to catch the attention of the waitress. She had been ignoring me for a half hour, probably because I was already six pints down of their cheapest beer and starting to get belligerent. I also didn't smell great, if I had to guess, based on the way nobody seemed interested in sitting within 10 feet of the drunk 17-year-old. The legal drinking age in most places in the verse was 15, but I still looked younger than that, so I often got the looks.

The Duck & Crown was one of the nicer bars on Chelsea Station, and two pints ago the owner had come by to remind me I could go right down the corridor to the Union Jack if I wanted to get messy. They'd have no problem with me starting a fight or throwing up on other patrons. They also didn't care if people hadn't showered in weeks over there, he made sure to add. But I didn't feel like moving. I was fine where I was.

A few days earlier, I'd had a fight with my father aboard his ship, The Sheffield. Things were said. Punches were thrown. And it was agreed I should find a new job. After two years working for him, it was time to move on. In fact, I had probably overstayed my welcome by about a year. He and I didn't get along, and we were never going to get along.

Part of me assumed it would be the last time I ever spoke to my dad.

I wasn't quite ready to crawl home to my mom and admit she was right about my father and half-brother, so I called the only other person I could think of. It was less humiliating than begging mom for some credits.

My Uncle Erwin sat down across the table from me, a scowl on his bearded face. His dark brown hair was flecked with gray, and he looked older than I remembered him, which made sense: I hadn't seen him in nearly five years. My mom's brother was a tall man with broad shoulders and a booming voice. When he walked into a room, it didn't go unnoticed. But looks can be deceiving. As imposing as his physical presence was, it was his mind that truly set him apart. Simply put, he was brilliant. One of the most gifted engineers in the world, in my opinion. His ship, the Mustang 1, backed that up. He had designed and built it from the ground up. And he had flown here from his usual home port on the Earth's moon to make sure I was okay.

"Your mother would never say I told you so," he said. "So I'll do it for her. I'm just sad it took you so long to figure it out. Thought you had more smarts than that."

"Go ahead, kick me when I'm down," I slurred back. I held up my empty pint glass for another, but Erwin removed it from my hand. He smelled it and was disappointed in whatever I'd been drinking. It was swill. He had very specific taste in beer. He leaned in and his nostrils flared.

"When I'm kicking you, son, you'll know it," he replied. "What I'm doing right now is simply telling you how it is because your mother is too nice to do it. Your dad's not worth the trouble. Maybe your brother is. I don't know him well

101

enough. But I know Rick Boyd is better out of your damn life than he is in it."

I nodded. I was upset, but I knew he was right. He always was.

"So what's your plan?" he asked.

"Don't have one."

"Drink yourself into the ground. Is that it?"

"Hey, that's not half bad."

Uncle Erwin scowled again and probably wanted to hit me upside the head. Instead, his eyes softened and he motioned for the waitress so he could pay the bill with his handheld.

* * *

I spotted the chrome at the end of the dock. Uncle Erwin's ship was hard to miss and he liked it that way. He once told me if you're gonna fly around the universe, you might as well do it in style. I later learned that was a reference from a classic movie called Back To The Future.

He liked to say ships were like planets – no two of them were exactly alike. I wasn't so sure. A lot of the ships in the verse had similar looks and models. They were all fairly ugly if you asked me. Designed mostly with function in mind. My uncle had created the Mustang to be both functional and cool. There was no other way to say it, really. The ship was cool.

It had huge plates of chrome. A sleek, tubelike body. And those X-wings? Add to all that the matte black finish everywhere it wasn't chrome, and there wasn't anything else like it in the world. Under the hood, it was just as impressive. It could outrun nearly every ship in the federation fleet and tow 50 times its own weight. Plus, for the final touch, my uncle had hand-painted a 20-foot-tall, muscular stallion on the front panel.

Overkill? Sure.

Badass? You bet it was.

He may have been in his 40's already, but Uncle Erwin was just a big kid at heart, and the Mustang was his biggest toy yet.

Inside the Stang, he led me directly to the engine room. I'd been on his ship a few times before and was already familiar with the impressive engineering that went into the quad-turbine engine that powered the Mustang.

"Did you see that water transport ship a few bays down?" he asked.

I had. It was about twice the size of my uncle's ship and was rust-colored. I wasn't sure if that was the original color or just time and radiation catching up with it.

"I need to tow it to Mars for repairs," he explained. "Got the call the second I stepped on the station. No shortage of work for an independent wrecker, even with Silver Star running the galaxy."

Despite being different from my dad in nearly every way, my uncle was also a wrecker by trade. He always said that's where the similarities between him and his brother-in-law started and ended. That's actually how my parents met – my uncle introduced them. He had never forgiven himself for what he called the biggest regret of his life.

"I could use a spare mechanic to help me keep the Stang running smoothly," he said.

He was lying about needing a mechanic, of course. He'd built this ship and knew every inch of it like the back of his hand. What he was really doing was offering to help me.

"I dunno, Uncle E," I said, suddenly feeling guilty about

putting him in this position. In the back of my mind, I'd hoped he would offer me a job on his ship, but when the moment came, it seemed like I was just taking advantage of his generous nature.

"You don't think you can handle the work?" he asked, ignoring my real trepidation. "When you sober up, that is."

"Of course I can handle it. That's not the point."

"Oh, I see. You're waiting for a better offer to come along. Good luck with that."

My uncle was nothing if not consistent. He wasn't going to baby me or sugarcoat things. I had messed up. I'd spent the most important years of a young man's life working for my dad. I hadn't gone to university. I hadn't made any good connections outside the wrecker world. And I had a record with the federation, which would do me no favors if I tried to straighten things out and get a regular job. Unless I wanted to join up with Silver Star, my options were limited.

"I don't even have a real nose, but I can smell the booze on him," my uncle's AI navigator Gary said.

I looked up at the nearest camera and narrowed my eyes. I never liked Gary. In fact, I thought he was the one part of the Stang I'd change if it was mine. The concept was solid: an AI with a fun personality based on an amalgam of characters from classic entertainment. But Gary was just a curmudgeon. Uncle E could've at least gone with someone cheerier.

"Now Gary, we've all had our moments," my uncle replied.

"I haven't," Gary claimed. "I've never once been drunk."

My uncle conceded the point but added, "You're perfectly capable of having your moments while sober. Trust me."

After a cup of coffee in the galley, my head was starting to clear and I realized the opportunity that laid before me. I would be able to learn the trade from my uncle, who I had always admired, and I'd be able to enjoy the Stang's on-board entertainment system, which was unique in the galaxy. My uncle had spent a lifetime collecting classic TV programs and movies from around the verse. On the Sheffield, my only entertainment were the scant options on my handheld, or cards with the rest of the crew.

The job offer came with rules, my uncle explained. While I was free to enjoy myself in my spare time, I was expected to be sober during my shifts. I knew this was the main reason he wanted me to sign on: to dry me out. I had been on a bender since leaving my dad's ship, and was drinking pretty heavily the last couple months of my time on it. My uncle had no problems with enjoying a good beer from time to time, but he thought over-indulging was a tool of the weak-minded. In fairness, we were all weak-minded compared to him. I agreed to the stipulations.

Gary was not happy to have me on the crew. I told him he should hope I didn't "accidentally" turn him off when I was working on the Stang to keep it in peak condition.

"You wouldn't dare," Gary said.

"I guess we'll just see," I shrugged.

My handheld dinged with an incoming transmission request. It was from my mom. Gary must have scanned the caller, as he chuckled. "Mommy's calling. Better answer it, Denver, or you'll be grounded."

I considered whether to accept the beam. Despite the coffee, I was still pretty buzzed and didn't want to face my mom at the moment. Then again, my uncle had likely filled her in already.

"Hi Den!" she said when I accepted her call. It had only been a few months since we'd spoken, but she too looked like she'd aged rapidly, more so than my uncle. Her face looked thinner, even gaunt, and her voice had a bit more gravel to it.

"Hey mom…"

She noticed my reaction to how she looked and sounded. She brushed it off. "I've been a little under the weather lately. Not that we have weather here on the moon…I guess it's one of those things we used to say back on Earth."

I was still concerned about her, but she quickly changed the subject.

"Erwin says you're on the Stang with him and you've decided to take a job. I think that's great!"

Wow, that was fast. Something told me the two of them had been scheming about the job offer all along.

"It's just until Mars," I said. For some reason, I felt the need to minimize the fact I would be working on my uncle's ship.

My mom smiled and told me she understood. She also said she was sorry things didn't work out on the Sheffield. She deliberately worded it that way so she didn't mention my dad or brother. As if the general situation with the ship was the problem.

"It was time anyway," I said, trying to play it off, but I didn't go any further with my denials. There was no use lying to her. As good as I'd gotten at bluffing, my mom knew all my tells. Mothers were like that.

"I've always thought you and your uncle would make a good team," she said. "When you were a kid, remember how much fun you'd have when he'd take you on his ship for a couple weeks?"

Those trips felt like a lifetime ago. It was a different ship and a different time, but I did remember them with affection.

My mom coughed roughly and then paused to drink some water.

"You sure you're okay? Have you been to the doctor?" I asked.

"Oh, Denny…" she said, before correcting herself. "Sorry, Denver. I know you don't like that anymore. Yes, I've been to the doctor. I don't want you to worry about it. I'll be fine. Your uncle tells me after Mars, he plans to boomerang back home. Will you promise to at least make the trip back so I can see you?"

I promised her I would. She didn't look well and it had been a while since I'd seen her in person. As we said our goodbyes, she told me that Uncle Erwin had a surprise for me, and that she was excited for me to hear about it, when the time was right.

A couple hours later, I settled into the co-pilot chair in the cabin of the Stang. As impressive as the ship was from a technical standpoint, its cabin was highly functional and compact. Enough room for a pilot, co-pilot, and three crew stations. My uncle didn't have any crew (well, other than me), but he had built the ship to include the option of a small assortment of people. He looked over at me.

"I'm glad you took that beam," he said, referring to the chat I'd had with my mom.

"She didn't look good. What's wrong with her?"

My uncle sighed. "She won't tell me, either, and I'm not going to hazard a guess. Eleanor is a tough woman. Even if it's something serious, she'll fight like hell to beat it. You'll see her soon enough and can ask her in person about it."

Uncle E glanced at the seat restraints in my chair. I got the hint and buckled myself in.

"Better safe than sorry, that's my motto," he reminded me.

We weren't exactly breaking the speed record. We were towing a ship a few times our size, after all. I checked the rear camera feed and saw that the water hauler was trailing behind us, secured by a series of thick cables and a mechanical jib. The cables were a bit slack and served more as a backup for the jib, which was about 100 yards in length and had an AI mechanism system that accounted for drag, speed changes and directional navigation. That too had been designed by my uncle. On most wrecker ships, they just used the cables and a standard tow hitch that was maybe 50 feet long. It wasn't uncommon to go through multiple hitches on a single tow job. It also wasn't uncommon for the trailing ship to smash into the back of the wrecker ship, causing all sorts of damage. Sometimes total, if you weren't careful.

"That jib is my pride and joy," Uncle E cooed. "I spent a year on the main bearing alone. That's what makes it swivel so smoothly."

It was impressive, I had to give him that. He had spared no expense or brain power on the Stang.

"Wanna talk about it?" he asked.

"About what."

"The Sheffield."

"No."

"Okay then," he said, dropping the subject. I relaxed and took a sip of the coffee I'd just made in the galley. That was one thing I'd have to change: my uncle may have had prime taste in beer, but his coffee selection was nothing to beam home about.

"Gary, take over and keep the speed reasonable. Denver and I are gonna binge The Sopranos."

"What's that?" I asked.

Uncle E whistled and shook his head. "Oh to be just like you, watching it again for the first time. It's only the best TV show that Earth ever produced, in my humble opinion."

* * *

The trip to Mars was going to take roughly two months. We could have done it much quicker if we hadn't been towing that giant water hauler. Because my Uncle Erwin always kept the Stang in top shape, there was rarely anything engine-related for me to do aside from running diagnostics and checking the systems each day.

Then running diagnostics and checking the systems the next day.

It was monotonous work, but there was a method to my uncle's madness. After only a week aboard the Stang, I was so familiar with the engine and electrical systems that I could tell if something was wrong just from the pitch of the engine hum or a flicker of a fuse light. I began to take more interest in the daily ritual, looking at particular parts or designs and asking my uncle why he built them that way. Soon, my uncle and I were spending most of our time together. I'd always had an innate sense of how things worked, but it was cool to learn from him why things worked, and how you could reconfigure a system to get more efficiency or better performance. I began to realize that the maintenance of a ship could be thought of as one long, unending tune-up. Each day we tried to squeeze even more out of the Stang. When I wasn't learning the ins and outs of electrical engineering or nuclear fission, I was cleaning the ship. Somebody had to do it, my uncle enjoyed telling me.

"And I don't think it should be the captain," he would joke.

Trash was easy enough – it would either go into the incinerator or the recycler. If it went into the incinerator, it was later expelled into space in a biodegradable form that would degrade down to nothing in 200 years. Not perfect, but not terrible. The recycler was one part of the ship my uncle didn't build. The technology had been developed about 50 years earlier, and it was pretty simple. It took all recyclable items, broke them down into their component parts and then created new items with the press of a button. Cups. Plates. Even shirts, if you had the right recycler model.

After I'd put in my working hours, I usually hung out with Uncle Erwin and watched some classic entertainment. It boggled my mind that people stopped creating movies and TV. They were such escapist fun. According to my uncle, the advent of space travel was one of the main reasons entertainment dwindled, as people started to embark on their own real-life adventures. Space travel was commonplace and even boring to us, he argued, but when the first independent spacecraft started crisscrossing the verse, people became obsessed with exploration and settlement. Who wanted to make a TV show when you could learn about the latest discovery on Mars or see the progress being made on Titan Station?

Personally, I preferred comedies. Movies. TV shows. Cartoons. It didn't matter. If something could make me laugh, I was into it. I was quickly hooked on shows like Arrested Development and The Simpsons. I was particularly intrigued by The Simpsons, an animated TV series, as the idea that a single show could go on for over a thousand episodes was a testament to the medium. My uncle showed me historical articles and excerpts that demonstrated the impact long-running programs like The Simpsons had on popular culture of the day. They were quoted by everyday people and celebrities alike, and episodes were even cut into short, bite-sized pieces and shared digitally as standalone jokes. It was fascinating; none of that existed anymore.

The sheer amount of entertainment being churned out on Earth resulted in a slew of famous people. It seemed to me like you wouldn't be able to walk down the street in the 21st century without bumping into someone who had been in a movie or TV show. My uncle chuckled at that notion, as he agreed it probably wasn't very far off from the truth.

One day when we were deep into a viewing session, on our fourth episode of Cheers, a show that was literally just about a bunch of people hanging out in a bar, we got into a heated argument about whether life was better before humans left Earth. Uncle E thought people were more imaginative about the universe, and just life in general, before we started to actually know what was out there in the great beyond.

"Think about it, Denver," he said. "I used to do this thing called reading…"

He always teased me about that. He was an avid reader of literature, whether it was hundreds of years old and in book form, or something more recent on his handheld.

"I know, I know…I tried reading that one book about the dinosaurs in the amusement park," I said. "It's just easier to watch the movie."

"Well in that particular case, the movie is almost as good as the book. My point is that I once read that humans have an instinct to explore. And I think that's true. But I also think we have an even greater instinct to use our imagination. Before we're spoiled by knowing something, we're very good about having opinions and dreams about it. You get what I'm saying?"

"Sure," I replied. "You think sitting in the same bar day in and day out is more enriching than living in space."

He shook his head. "You know I'm not saying that. Even if I was, though...maybe! I mean the idea that Norm and Sam and Diane could feel fulfilled living in their little corner of the universe without thinking they're missing out on something –"

"You think they're happy?"

"Ok, it's a sitcom. Good point.

"And what's wrong with sitcoms?" Gary said, butting in. "Some would argue they were the height of cultured entertainment."

"Nobody would ever argue that," Uncle E said.

"I'm arguing it right now," Gary countered.

"You don't count," I interjected. "Uncle E, are you sure we can't like, put him to bed or something? Or at least turn him off when we're hanging out?"

"Turn me off?" Gary whined. "I was here years before you! Years, Denver! E-dog and I go way back."

I looked at the camera. "E-dog?"

My uncle shrugged as if to say don't ask. "Fine, Gary. Sitcoms are the pinnacle of entertainment. Can I move on with my argument now?"

"You may proceed, sir," Gary said.

Uncle E gathered his thoughts as he chomped on the last bite of a candy bar. "Where was I? Oh, right. Take actual people who live in a neighborhood and have their daily routines.

They care about each other. Spend time with friends. Enjoy simple stuff like family dinners or birthday parties. That sounds pretty great to me. They aren't worried about feeling like they're always missing out on something better because they're stuck on that damn rock. They were happy with what they had. Completely content."

I considered his point. While it was true that it's easier to be happier when you don't know there are more and possibly greater adventures out there, it was also true that you may be one of those people who feel confined by being stuck on Earth.

"Nobody felt stuck on Earth before we knew it was possible to leave the place!" Uncle E shouted. He wasn't angry. He just happened to get really loud and animated when he was excited about something.

"Oh, I see," I said. "Ignorance is bliss."

"You're quoting the Matrix?!" he bellowed, laughing. "You can't quote that movie to me. I introduced you to that movie. I mean, fine, they have a point. I'm just saying when the world got bigger, I'm not so sure we got happier."

"I'm not saying we got happier, either. I just think if you gave me the choice of taking the blue pill and living with blinders or taking the red one and risking a little unhappiness, I'm gonna choose the truth every time."

"I knew I shouldn't have shown you that damn movie," Uncle E groused.

"If it makes you feel better, I can take the Stang off your hands and you can go back to Earth to have birthday parties and barbecues with Earthers the rest of your life," I said.

"It would not make me feel better, point in fact," he said. "What would make me happy right now is if you got up off your lazy butt and grabbed me another candy bar from the kitchen. I'll start another episode of Cheers."

"You sure you don't want to watch Neo kick some ass?" I asked.

Uncle E just groaned as the theme song for Cheers started up.

* * *

I never got to see my mom in person again. She died about a month after Uncle E and I set out for Mars. We put off the funeral until we got back, as my uncle and I were her closest family in the verse. When the day came, my father and Avery were unable to make it.

It didn't come as a surprise.

On the somber trip back from Mars, my uncle explained that he was going to leave me the Stang when his time came. I was shocked by the enormity of the promise. Because it had been constructed over at least 10 years, trying to pin down an exact cost or value of the Mustang 1 was impossible. But basically Uncle E could have said he was leaving me 250,000 credits and I would have been less taken aback.

Me, captain of the Stang? It was a wild concept. Of course, when he told me, I assumed it wouldn't happen for many years, so the idea was less strange to think of me at his age, in my forties, taking over the ship once he retired to Mars or some old folks' station.

"I mean…why?" I asked. "Are you sure?"

My uncle laughed. "What else am I going to do with it? Give it to a stranger?"

"Oh, right."

Uncle Erwin looked at me and shook his head. He turned serious and put a hand on my shoulder.

"Because I love you, kid. And I love my sister."

Apparently, my mother had given him half of her savings to help fund his building of the ship, in exchange for the promise that someday, he would pay me back with the earnings. He had decided the best form of payment would be the ship itself. I thanked him, but also told him I didn't want to collect on his promise for a long time. With my mom gone and my relationship with my dad and brother severed, Uncle E was all I had left in the verse.

Chapter 10

The funeral was small, like most funerals. With family and friends spread out across the verse, it was usually pretty hard to get a lot of people together in one place without waiting months or years. Beaming funerals to far-off loved ones was common, but Uncle Erwin and I decided my mom wouldn't have wanted that. She was a private person, and the idea of people tuning in just to watch the proceedings didn't sit well with us.

My mom's will specified that she be cremated, and so there was no discussion of where to bury her, either on Earth or its moon (she had spent roughly the same amount of her life on each). Instead, we held a gathering of neighbors and friends aboard the Mustang, which was docked on Earth's moon near the settlement in which my mother had lived. Eleven people showed up to pay their respects, and many nice things were said about her generosity and zest for life. She loved to laugh, everybody recalled.

Uncle Erwin gave a touching speech and I said a few words, but for the most part the funeral seemed odd, as everyone present had already had two months to grieve my mother's passing, and so the mood had more of a detached feeling to it.

I didn't cry. I had done that months earlier. Uncle E shed a few tears, but he too had already come to terms with the loss of his big sister.

Uncle E and I decided to scatter her ashes as the Stang passed over the Sea of Tranquility when we left to head back out for our next job. We had debated whether to keep the urn on the ship, but in the end we assumed she didn't want to be "cooped up with us boys" as she often said about our trips around the verse.

"It was nice of her neighbors to come," said Uncle E, once we were on our way to pick up a craft that was meant to be one of the final pieces of a new station being Voltron'd together out of ships and other, smaller stations.

"Yeah," I said, not really wanting to talk any more about it.

My uncle looked over and knew what I was feeling.

"We still have each other," he reminded me. I'd been so focused on my own grief that I hadn't considered my uncle was in the same position. Aside from me, my mother was all the family he'd had. Uncle E had never married or had kids. His work and his ship were his life. And me, of course.

"Your mom would like that," he said. "Us flying around the verse together like real compadres."

"She would," I agreed. "She might have some things to say about our diet though."

Uncle E snorted, nearly choking on his candy bar. A piece of nougat flew out of his mouth and landed on the console. It just stuck there between a few other blips on the radar scan. I laughed. It was the first good laugh I'd had in a long, long time.

* * *

My first impression of the ship was that it looked like a giant donut. It had the proper shape, right down to the hole in the middle. And the red flashing lights that dotted the top of it could have passed for sprinkles.

"Looks kind of like a donut," Uncle E said. "I'm hungry again."

I nodded.

"I miss donuts," Gary wistfully replied. "But I prefer a good black and white cookie."

"You've never had either of those," I told him.

As Gary argued that he had theoretically eaten many donuts and cookies, and therefore could be nostalgic about them, I focused on the ship. It was named The Yunan. A quick reference check told us that was one of the provinces of China, back when China had provinces.

"The captain's name is Jiang," Uncle E said. "Seems like a straight shooter to me."

"Straight shooter?" I asked.

"Remind me to have you watch some Bonanza when we get the chance. Or Unforgiven. That's a great one, too."

I made a mental note of both the titles. "Crazy that he's selling his ship to become part of a station. Pretty cool," I said.

"Agreed. Can't wait to see the station when it's done."

A few moments later, The Yunan hailed us. My uncle accepted the transmission and the captain's face filled the screen.

Jiang was a thin man with a full head of straight black hair he kept in a ponytail. He wore a flannel shirt. I'd later learn he was of Chinese ancestry, but he'd never set foot on Earth, let alone any other planet. He was a true man of space, as he often joked. And he joked a lot.

"Hello there!" he said with a genuine smile. "Made it just in time!"

"That so?" my uncle asked.

Jiang explained that he had been unsure of whether to accept the offer to add his ship to the new station they were building, but when The Yunan stalled for the third time in the past year, he knew the ship would be better off as part of something larger.

The only problem was that between the time we'd been contracted to tow The Yunan to the station site and the time we arrived, the life support system had gone down. In fact, the 400 crew and residents of the ship had been evacuated about a week earlier.

"Wait, are you telling me you're the only one on that ship?" I asked, leaning into the peripheral of the camera.

"Oh, didn't see you there. Hey!"

My uncle introduced me as his co-captain, and Jiang confirmed he was the only person left on The Yunan. "Unless I've got a stowaway. Fingers crossed on that front."

I pulled up the ship's specs on the Stang's computer system. It was half a million square feet. And there was one person on it. One. Talk about being alone in the world. Although you wouldn't know it from Jiang's upbeat attitude.

When we stepped onto The Yunan, he greeted us with a smile and a plastic container.

"What's this?" I asked before catching a delicious whiff of whatever was in the container.

"They're called egg rolls," Jiang said. "You owe it to yourself to enjoy them while they're hot. They just came out of the fryer."

Eating my first egg roll wasn't the most rewarding experience I'd ever had as a wrecker, but it was definitely top five. It was like a donut that wasn't for dessert and was filled with meat and vegetables. As we sat in one of The Yunan's cafeterias, Uncle Erwin and I looked at each other in disbelief.

"Have you ever had one of these?" I asked him.

"I've only heard of them," he answered, taking another bite.

Jiang popped open a couple beers and sat down across the table from us. My uncle sternly explained that if he kept giving us home-cooked food and free beer, he might never get his ship towed.

"On some level, that would be fine with me," Jiang said. "I always liked the idea of being completely independent. But with life comes change. Now I'll get the chance to be part of something bigger."

My uncle nodded. He understood the sentiment.

Then Jiang cleared his throat and prepared to say something. He just couldn't quite spit it out.

"You okay, buddy?" Uncle E asked.

"Uh, yes. I just had a question about your ship. Well, first, I should say it's probably the coolest looking spacecraft I've ever seen. But…"

I knew what was coming. "You're wondering how the hell our little ship is going to be able to tow yours?" I asked.

Jiang nodded, relieved I had asked the question for him. My uncle told him the Mustang had once towed a federation battle cruiser from Titan Station to Earth. I'd heard about the tow when I was on The Sheffield. It was the buzz of the wrecker world and cemented the Stang as the top independent wrecker in the verse. My dad was depressed for weeks. Avery had confided in me that our dad had always been jealous of my uncle and his noteworthy ship. I often wondered what my dad and brother would think of me working on the Stang. We hadn't spoken since I left the Sheffield.

"Oh. I guess we're good then," Jiang said, embarrassed.

"Yep," Uncle E answered. Then he looked at me with a wry smile. "We're gonna do this one a little differently. I want to see if my young apprentice here can figure it out, or if I have to tell him."

I pulled up the schematic of The Yunan on my handheld. I could see what my uncle was talking about. There wasn't a good anchor point on the "front" of the ship, because there was no real front. It was circular. Which meant there was no back, either. The propulsion system was mounted on the sides and the ship could go in any direction. Slowly, most likely.

I studied the schematic looking for an answer. We couldn't pull it. We certainly couldn't push it. For a moment, I considered that we might just fix the damn thing, but then I remembered the core had fried. We weren't equipped to fix that.

Oh. It suddenly dawned on me.

"Don't tell me we're going in there?"

Uncle E nodded proudly. "That's exactly what we're gonna do. We are going to be the donut hole."

* * *

I always got nervous floating in space. There's just something about being a couple thin layers of fabric away from the never-ending vacuum of death that makes me think "Hmmm, maybe this wasn't the best idea."

I used my propulsion pack to navigate toward The Yunan. Uncle E had positioned the Stang in the middle of the empty area inside the circular ship. We had a few hundred yards to spare on all sides. The idea was to create a series of cable tethers from the Stang to The Yunan to keep us roughly in place as the donut hole. We would then use the jib at full tension to tow the larger ship from the interior support bar that was located on the inner ring.

Basically, we'd tow it from the inside. Which was a new one.

My job was to attach each of the 16 cable tethers to The Yunan. It was a laborious task that was going to take multiple days. I'd been in the suit for a few hours already and had only attached the first four tethers. The goal was to do four more before calling it a day. I had enough oxygen to last another six hours if needed, but being in the suit is hard work. And sweaty. I was already getting a ton of condensation on the visor, which made the work even more difficult due to the partially obscured vision.

"Code Black!" my uncle barked in my ear, giving me a jolt. I nearly dropped the power clamps I'd been using to fasten the cable tethers to The Yunan. "Get back to the Stang, now!"

I whirled and checked in all directions. Through the fog of my visor, I couldn't see anything out there besides the Stang and The Yunan. Code Black meant that we were under attack from another ship, and my uncle didn't throw that around lightly. I dropped the cable from my hands and began heading back to the Stang.

It was like an action move in slow motion. My heart was racing and my eyes darted back and forth, scanning for the enemy ship. But I was actually moving very slowly. The propulsion system on my suit used short bursts of compressed air to push me along in space. It was meant for precise movements and short walks. In other words, the top speed was around 10 miles per hour. Under normal circumstances, that felt pretty quick, considering a few wrong turns and I'd be headed off course for the next, oh, forever.

At the moment, I felt very exposed.

"What's going on?" I asked my uncle.

"Tracers," he hissed. "I know you can't hurry...but hurry, Denver."

If there was a Tracer ship in the area, the Stang was a sitting duck. Between me floating around like a wayward puppy and the ship being tethered to The Yunan, my uncle had limited options to defend us.

"Stay clear of the nose," my uncle said, just before a flurry of rail gun fire blasted from the Stang. I followed the trajectory of the blue streaks and saw a green ship evade the salvo just in time. It was about the same size as the Stang, just a bit thinner and longer. It veered to the side and seemed to be coming around to find a better offensive angle. It wouldn't be hard for them. With the Stang in visual range, they'd be able to see that it was tethered to The Yunan.

I was still a hundred yards away from the Stang and desperately wishing I could speed up when I felt something latch onto my arm. I turned to see Jiang's smiling face behind his visor. He pulled me toward the back of the transport pad he was riding. It was a flatbed style transporter used to ferry small lots of cargo around the ship. I swung myself onto the bed and we zipped toward the Stang's open cargo bay door.

Once we landed inside, the bay doors closed and the room pressurized.

"We're in!" I yelled into the helmet's comm system just before tearing it off and breathing some fresh (recycled) oxygen. I turned to Jiang as he removed his helmet.

123

"Thanks for the lift."

"No problem," he said. "Tracers?"

"That's what Uncle E says," I replied. "You got any weapons on The Yunan?"

He pulled out his handheld. "Limited, but yeah."

We arrived in the cabin just as Uncle Erwin was launching countermeasures against a pair of missiles headed right for us. "Ah, nice of you to give my nephew a ride. Strap in."

I lowered into my co-pilot chair and checked the Tracer ship's specs. It was not the most heavily armed or armored, but it had enough firepower at its disposal to take us out, especially in our vulnerable position. Jiang buckled into the seat near the weapons station and watched the monitor.

"Got anything good on that ship?" my uncle asked, echoing my question.

Jiang explained that he had a few missiles that may or may not fire properly. He had never had the need to use them, plus he'd have to remotely control the weapons system from his handheld. It was possible, he said, but there was just as much chance the missiles might choose the Stang as their target as they would the Tracer ship.

"Scratch that plan," I said.

"I do have an EMP device that might work," Jiang added.

My uncle nodded at that, then told us to brace for impact. One of the missiles had been taken out by the countermeasures, but the other had slipped through. It would reach us in a few seconds. My uncle dialed up the manual guns and dropped down the eyeglasses that usually rested atop his head. Then he grabbed the video game style joystick (it even had an Atari sticker on it that made my uncle chuckle every time he referenced it).

124

"Here goes nothing," he said as he fired at the missile, trying to detonate it before it reached us. The Stang had armor plating and could handle smaller weapons fire and even missile explosions in the proximity, but a direct hit would likely tear a hole in the ship's shell. And that would be that.

The blast rattled every part of my body, from my bones to my teeth. I had the sudden sensation of being hurled sideways and pummeled in the stomach at the same time. A few seconds later, I looked over and saw my uncle rubbing his bloody forehead. Jiang was woozy as well.

But we were all alive. "Guess I got it just in time," Uncle E said.

"Minimal damage, none of it structural," Gary said. "But that was cutting it pretty, pretty, pretty close, my friend."

"We need to get out of this position," Uncle E decided. "Sorry to undo all your work, Denver."

"Undo the shit out of it!" I replied as he flipped a few switches. I watched on the monitor as the cables I'd just spent four hours fastening to The Yunan released in quick succession, lashing out into the black.

The Stang instantly sprang to life, my uncle flooring it (so to speak). We rose out of the donut hole and zoomed off in a direct line to intercept the Tracer ship. My uncle looked at me. "What are you waiting for?"

Oh. Right!

"Switch!" I yelled to Jiang as I unstrapped my safety belts. He did the same and we swapped positions. Once I was buckled into the chair at the weapons station, I plotted a few solutions and sent the Tracer ship a barrage of missiles, followed by rail gun fire.

"That's good, but don't spend it all at once," my uncle

reminded me.

"I know, I know."

Truth be told, I was acting purely on muscle memory. It was the first time I'd ever had to actually use the weapons, as it was the first time the Stang had been in a scrape since I came aboard. Luckily, we'd practiced three times a week with a simulation. Each time, my uncle ratcheted up the complexity with a different number of ships or types of attacks. The point is, I had already fought this battle before, in theory.

Of course, theory wasn't reality. My missiles were easily detonated by the Tracer ship. I did manage to strafe one of the wings with some rail gun fire, but it was impossible to tell how bad the damage was. Given the fact the Tracer ship continued to weave and accelerate, it was likely superficial.

My uncle was pissed. He wasn't usually the type to get angry. But I guess trying to kill a man and his nephew was enough to make anyone a little upset. As he gave chase, trying to establish a more advantageous position for the Stang, Jiang was verbalizing his disgust with the Tracers and everything they stood for. They were a bunch of thugs, he said, running around the verse and terrorizing people with impunity. He didn't understand what they wanted with The Yunan anyway. There were no people left on board (so nobody to kidnap), there were no goods (so no booty), and the ship itself was fairly old and outdated, meaning there was nothing to salvage.

"Maybe they wanted to stop The Yunan from becoming part of the station," I offered, speaking over my shoulder as I plotted new attack sequences to launch once the time came.

"I've been trying to hail them to ask, but they don't seem interested in talking," Uncle E said. He tried to get a better angle on the Tracer ship, but it was too elusive. "She doesn't look like much, but she's got some moves."

My uncle tried to bank and the Stang stammered a bit and lost speed.

"What the hell was that?" Uncle E asked Gary.

"Hmmmm…seems that maybe there was more structural damage than I thought. We have a slight issue with the navigational bearings that may give you trouble when you try to–"

"May?!?" Uncle E shouted. He muttered something under his breath about Gary, then turned to me. "Don't even think about it."

I stopped unbuckling my belt and leaned back in the seat. He knew I was going to try and get below decks to fix it.

"There's no time for that," he said. "Jiang, let's hear more about that EMP."

I've heard my uncle say that the outcome of most ship-to-ship combat scenarios often rests on one move. Maybe it's a decision you make. Or a mistake the other ship commits. But with so much lethal technology available to both sides, all it takes is one second to be either victorious or reduced to atoms.

My uncle was gambling our lives on The Yunan's ability to take out the enemy ship for us. After drawing the Tracer vessel away from The Yunan with a pair of missiles (both of which they neutralized with countermeasures), my uncle killed the engines. I was waiting in the cargo bay in my space suit. The door opened and I pushed an improvised explosive device into the vacuum. Once it was about 100 yards from the ship, we detonated it. The blast left a trail of debris and smoke in our wake.

Combined with our turbines emitting zero drive signature,

the smoke was meant to fool the Tracers into thinking we'd been disabled. The other ship came around and paused. They were in visual range, so they could see the debris and the Stang just floating in place.

"Did it work?" Jiang asked, his finger poised over his handheld device.

"Not sure yet," my uncle replied. He watched the distance on the scanner closely. The Tracer ship was closing, but had not increased speed. Their weapons were still hot, of course. If they wanted to destroy us, we were giving them a good chance.

But they were Tracers. If they thought we were disabled, they might just be arrogant and ruthless enough to decide to board and see if we had anything good in the cargo bays. Or, try to subdue us and capture a semi-famous ship in the process.

"Got 'em," my uncle said. The Tracers picked up speed and were headed right for us.

"Just tell me when," Jiang said.

"Wait until I tell you, Jiang. You too, Gary."

"I still think this is a bad idea," Gary said.

Once the ship got within a couple miles, my uncle calmly told Gary to cut all power. The ship went as still as I'd ever heard it. No auxiliary. No latent cooldowns. Just…off at the flip of a virtual switch.

"Now," Uncle E whispered.

Jiang pressed a button on his handheld.

And nothing happened.

The ship kept coming toward us.

"What's going on?" I asked, freaking out.

"Oh, duh. I forgot to enter the password," Jiang said. He

tapped a few keys. A second later, the Tracer ship's lights flickered and went to black. It had worked! The Yunan had sent an electromagnetic pulse in all directions. It would fry any working electronics in 10-20 square miles. The Stang was unaffected, as we had shut down. The Tracer ship? Not so much.

Uncle E spun the drive back up and the Stang slowly beeped and hummed to life. It took about 30 seconds, but there was no hurry with the other ship completely disabled.

"Good morning. What did I miss?" Gary asked. "Oh good, we're still alive."

I looked at my uncle. "Should I fire?"

"No," Jiang answered. He shook his head. "We can't. It would be like shooting an unarmed person."

"They just tried to kill us," I argued.

"Doesn't matter. It wouldn't be fair," Jiang said.

"He's right, Denver," my uncle said. "Just because we can destroy someone doesn't mean we should. Never forget that."

I wasn't sure I agreed with my uncle and Jiang. What if the Tracer ship was able to power back up? Or the cavalry was on its way? Even though they were disabled, it was an extension of the fight, in my mind. Perhaps reading my thoughts, my uncle softened his eyes and smiled.

"You'll understand when you're older," he said with a laugh. He knew I hated when he said that. "I'll have Gary keep a missile solution on them while we attach The Yunan to the Stang and get out of here. First things first, you need to get down there to fix the navigational bearings."

For the next two days, we worked to safely secure The Yunan to our ship. We became the donut hole again. The entire time, the Tracer ship simply floated there, dead in the vacuum. If they got lucky, one of their friends would come along and help them. If they didn't, well, at least it wasn't on my conscience.

As we towed Jiang's ship to its new destination, we spent many hours watching TV and enjoying Jiang's cooking. By the time we reached the construction site where they were putting the finishing touches on the bold new station, I was sad to see Jiang go.

We never heard from that Tracer ship again.

A few months and a few jobs later, Uncle E and I were enjoying the last of the frozen egg rolls Jiang had left us, when he collapsed and fell to the floor. I would learn later that my uncle had a brain aneurysm. One minute we were debating whether the 8th season of Game of Thrones ruined the whole experience (he thought it did, I disagreed), and the next thing I knew he had fallen out of his chair. It was all over in a few seconds. Gary and I tried to save him, but there was nothing we could do. For a long time, I sat next to his body, thinking he might just wake up. Or I would wake up, and it would all just be some kind of bad dream. It wasn't, of course.

It hadn't been a battle between ships, but my uncle was right: one second is all it takes to change everything. Suddenly, I was alone in the verse. The 18-year-old captain of the Mustang 1.

Chapter 11

My first solo gig was easy. At least it was supposed to be.

A party barge had stalled a hundred miles off Roman Landing, a tourist destination on Mars. Most of the revelers had been transported back to the planet before I arrived to fix the ship, but there were still a couple dozen crew and straggler tourists bopping about the vessel.

Party barges, as they were informally known, ran the gamut from family-friendly to the raunchiest dens of sex and drugs you could imagine. This happened to be the latter kind. As I pulled into the docking bay, the bright neon of the large "Port Lauderdale" sign reflected off the glass of the Stang's forward windows. Docked on either side of my ship were transport skiffs to take people to and from Roman Landing. The black and gold ships had the phrase "Party Like It's 2209" emblazoned on the side panels in sparkly paint. They could probably carry about 100 passengers each.

A handsome, teal-haired man was waiting to greet me when I stepped off the Stang. He looked to be in his mid-thirties, but styled himself in a way to appear younger and trendier. His jeans and designer shirt probably cost more than my entire wardrobe.

"Hello, young man," he said, a flirting tone in his voice. We shook hands and he let the shake and the eye contact linger. "If all wreckers were this handsome, I'd sabotage my barge more often!"

I chuckled nervously and withdrew my hand. I knew I had to get used to being judged by my age, but this guy was more interested in my looks. Flattering, but not what I was going for at the moment.

"I'm Jameson, but everyone calls me Sky," he said. I didn't bother to ask for the details on that one.

He explained that the barge had lost propulsion earlier in the week. It wasn't a critical situation as the power and life support systems were still functioning, and the skiffs could be used to transport people to and from Mars. The issue was one of code.

"Each day, the federation fines us for not being in compliance with the laws regarding vessels of our type. We have to maintain the ability to travel at least 500 miles per hour, even though we never really travel anywhere!" he complained. "Those feds. They could use a little more Port Lauderdale if you ask me."

As he led me to the engine room, we passed through various areas of the mostly-empty ship. First, there was the dance club. A disco ball hung from the ceiling, slowly spinning. It was kind of sad. The bartender relaxed behind the counter, enjoying a cocktail and watching what sounded like a Purple on her handheld. She didn't even notice us as we clicked across the wood floor and moved into the main dining hall, which was fashioned after ancient German beer gardens. Long, wooden benches on either side of a thick table. The few passengers that were still aboard seemed to be gathered here, trying to make the most of the conditions (party barges were notorious for being jam-packed with people, and when they weren't, much of the vibe was lost). Most of them were my age or slightly older, but they all looked worse for the wear. Like maybe they'd been on the barge a few days too long. I didn't envy their eventual crashes.

They drank beer from large steins. I was jealous about that part.

Sky noticed this and grinned. "Perhaps after you fix the engines, we can lure you into staying for a few days. You seem like you could use a vacation."

Before I could answer, Sky swung the double-doors open and we were in a long red corridor. It was only wide enough for two people to squeeze through. The walls were lined with velvet and there were small couches positioned every 10 feet. It was dimly lit and trancing music was piped in. I didn't have much trouble imagining what kind of debauchery went on in this particular hallway. But if I had, the videos on the screens throughout the corridor provided plenty of inspiration.

"This is the only way to the engine room?" I asked.

Sky gave me a mischievous look as we exited the hallway and finally made our way into the maintenance area of the ship. We reached the engine room, which was presided over by a tall guy with gray hair. He was dozing in a chair in the corner.

"That's our maintenance engineer, Mickey," said Sky as he checked the time. "Yep, it's his mid-morning nap. Well, I will leave you to it. How long do you think you'll be?"

I hadn't even looked at the engine yet. Under normal circumstances, I would have been annoyed by the ship's engineer being so lazy. Considering it was my first solo job, I didn't mind him sleeping in the room as I worked. It meant I had a low bar to clear. Besides, one look at the engine and I knew it wouldn't take long to diagnose the problem. If I got lucky, it wouldn't require new parts.

"I'll let you know once I've had a good look. Where will you be?" I asked.

"The beer hall, most likely. Just wake up Mickey here to give me a buzz."

* * *

I identified the issue fairly quickly and estimated about a day's work would get the engine going again. I stirred Mickey so he could let Sky know I would be done in 8-10 hours. The old man was angry that I woke him up, but reluctantly passed along the message.

I headed back to the Stang to collect the proper tools. When I reached the beer hall, it was packed with more people. Men and women in blue suits, to be exact.

Feds.

At least 15 of them were seated at the long table in the middle of the hall, and a few more stood and talked nearby. I kept my eyes locked ahead and almost made it out the door when I heard a voice behind me.

"Hey kid, where are you off to with that toolbox?" he asked. I turned to see a fat, half-drunk soldier glaring back at me. He had a bandage across the bridge of his nose and the areas underneath his eyes were swollen. A few of the blue suits near him also looked over at me. One or two of them had some fresh injuries as well.

"Just grabbing a few more things," I said, trying to end the conversation quickly. It didn't work. The guy swigged more of his drink and then tilted his head at me.

"That your ship out there?" he asked.

"A lot of ships out there," I replied.

"You being a smartass, boy?"

"No, just stating the obvious. There are at least six or seven ships out there."

"The one with the chrome, tough guy. The wrecker ship. What's it called, again?"

"The Mustang," another fed answered. "Checked the call sign on the way in. He's that wrecker that towed the North Star from Mars to Earth."

"That was my uncle, actually," I clarified.

The second fed hiked his shoulders. "Same difference."

I decided to walk out before I said anything I was going to regret. They could try to intimidate me all they wanted, but I hadn't done anything wrong, so they couldn't stop me. I checked over my shoulder as I walked across the docking bay, but no feds were following me. Sky hustled up behind me, worried.

"Please hurry with the fix," he begged.

"What do you care? You got your wish. A bunch of blue suits chillin' in Port Lauderdale."

Sky shook his head. "I was speaking theoretically, of course. As in, the feds need to remove the crowbars from their asses and loosen up. But they're actually here now and they'll ruin my numbers for the month unless you fix the engine soon so they have no reason to stay."

I gave a blank look. I wasn't entirely sure what he was trying to tell me.

"Feds are great at running up a large tab," he said. "Paying that tab is another matter."

135

Sky hurried back inside to keep an eye on the feds. My uncle always complained that the feds rarely paid their bills, and even more rarely did so in a timely manner when you could actually pry the credits from them. It turned out that rule applied to everyone, not just wreckers.

Their ship was actually docked right next to mine. It was a T-Class 405 Cruiser, the workhorse of the federation fleet. Piece of junk, if you asked me. They should just strip them all for parts, shove them into the void and start over.

"I see our friends in blue have joined the party," Gary remarked as I boarded the Stang. "Be sure not to mention any of your illegal activities."

I stopped what I was doing and looked at the nearest camera. "What?"

"What do you mean, what?" Gary asked.

"None of my activities are illegal," I said. "Are they?"

After he finished laughing, Gary explained that I was breaking a variety of laws at any given time.

"Such as?"

"Operating without a license. Engaging in unsanctioned warfare. Failing to report unsanctioned warfare. Tax evasion. Treason."

"Treason?!"

"It's a gray area, but if the feds wanted, they could probably interpret the time you and your uncle fixed that refugee ship as an act of treason against the federation, and therefore both Earth and Mars," Gary said.

"They were refugees," I argued. "Trying to escape oppression."

"Who do you think they were running from? You call it oppression. The feds call it taxation."

My uncle had told me being an independent was risky business, but he didn't have time to explain just how many laws we were breaking if anyone cared to look more closely. And the feds cared, especially if you made them angry. Part of me wanted to just forget about fixing the barge and get out of there. But I knew I couldn't. I needed the credits. And besides, if I wanted to be a wrecker and handle jobs on my own, I was going to have to deal with the feds all the time. I decided to just mind my business, get the damn engine working, and then quietly head to the next contract.

I went to the Stang's tool shop and began loading what I'd need to fix the stalled barge.

* * *

The repairs only took five hours. Maybe I was working more quickly because I wanted to be on my way, but I had the engine up and running in less than four hours, then spent a little time making sure it wouldn't break down again anytime soon. My uncle told me the best way to get new clients was by reputation and referral. Do good work and word travels fast. Be sloppy and word travels even faster. The Stang already had some credibility. I wanted to build my own.

Sky thanked me and offered to pay part of the bill in services. He said I could have my pick of the crew. "Everybody who works at Port Lauderdale is available for hire, including myself," he told me. "We are very skilled."

I thanked him for the offer, but said credits would be fine. He was disappointed. He got over it quickly, however, and immediately transferred the credits into my account, including a generous 15% tip for getting the job done sooner than promised.

Having collected payment, I was feeling pretty good about my first completed job. I thought my uncle would be proud of me. I was enjoying that feeling of accomplishment when I saw the blue suit standing between me and the Stang.

It was the same guy that had given me a hard time earlier. The one with the raccoon eyes. He had a grin on his face that spelled trouble.

"Come with us," he said. That's when I noticed the other two feds standing behind me.

They escorted me onto the 405 Cruiser. I wasn't being detained, they assured me, but they did want to discuss something with me. I could already tell I wasn't going to like the subject of the conversation. The main asshole who did all the talking introduced himself as Chief Waters. The other two didn't say a word. They just kept sipping from their oversized Port Lauderdale plastic cups.

Great, I thought. They weren't just feds – they were buzzed feds and clearly not worried about their superior officers at the moment.

"So, Denver, it seems you've been operating without a proper license," Waters said as we reached the ship's kitchen. "Your ship has the proper credentials, but the wrecker license belonged to your uncle. We could fine and detain you for that."

"But you're not because?" I asked.

He motioned to the kitchen. It was a mess. There was food everywhere. Some of the appliances were knocked over. And I was pretty sure that was a streak of blood on the wall. I put two and two together and realized there had been a brawl of some kind on the ship.

"Need you to fix the recycler and the fridge for us. Do that and we'll ignore the license issue," he said.

"I'm not exactly an expert on recyclers or kitchen appliances," I explained. "I fix engines."

"Then that sucks for you, because our engine isn't what needs fixing," Waters said. It was clear if I didn't do what he wanted, I was going to owe the feds a decent amount of credits.

"I'll take a look."

"Perfect!" he said, slapping me on the back, hard. "Hey maybe clean up a bit when you're done, too, kid."

I steamed as he strutted out of the kitchen. The two silent feds sat down at a table in the corner and lazily sipped their fruity drinks, watching me with satisfaction.

The fridge was simple, but by the time I got done fixing the recycler, I was too tired to deal with the mess. It had taken four hours and a lot of research in addition to the manual labor. One of the feds had gone back to Port Lauderdale to party, while the one that was left to supervise me was half-asleep.

"It's done," I said. "You can find someone to clean the damn mess."

The fed was about to object, but he was pretty woozy, so I just walked past him, not giving him a chance to object. "I'll show myself out."

When I stepped off the ship, the party barge was back to nearly full capacity. Once I'd fixed the engine earlier in the day, Sky must have immediately begun ferrying revelers back to the barge from Roman Landing. I was going to just head straight from the 405 to the Stang and get the hell out of there, but as I walked toward my ship, I heard a commotion nearby. Two feds were arguing with a girl about my age. One of the soldiers was holding her by the arm. She was trying to wriggle free but he wouldn't let go, despite her repeatedly smacking him. Finally, he smacked her right back, a glancing blow across the face.

Before he had a chance to hit her again, I planted my boot in his back and sent him flying into a nearby wall. His buddy turned and swung at me, but I took it on the chin (it was a weak punch) and swung my entire toolbox across his face. I actually saw a few teeth fly loose when he spun to the ground.

"Look out!" the girl shouted as the first fed grabbed me from behind. Luckily, the girl was ready this time. She told me to duck, which I did, and then she unleashed a full two seconds of pepper spray directly into the guy's eyes. He instantly let go of me and clutched his face, staggering backwards in pain.

I grabbed the girl's hand and pulled her a few steps toward the Stang. Then I stopped. Amidst the throng of partiers, I could see a group of blue suits looking right at us. They were standing by the gangway to my ship.

"C'mon, this way," I said, urging her to follow me into the beer hall.

"Wait, who the hell are you?" she asked. A fair question, of course.

"Name's Denver. You coming with me or you wanna deal with a whole swarm of those assholes?"

"Let's go. I'm Debra," she said with a toss of her dark brown hair and a gorgeous smile.

Together, we made our way through the throng of people and into the hall. The place was packed and the dim lights made it a little easier to disappear. We pushed our way through the crowd, passing a couple feds who obviously weren't looking for us yet.

"Why are you here?" Debra yelled in my ear over the din.

"I'm a wrecker," I said without turning back to see her reaction. That job title usually didn't impress people much.

"Cool!" I heard her say. I looked back, surprised, and she was smiling again. She had a little blood from the cut on her cheek where the fed had hit her. I grabbed someone's drink napkin as we passed and handed it to her. She pressed it against the scrape.

I let my gaze linger a bit too long. Before I could watch where I was going, I had run smack into something hard. At first I assumed it was a wall, but then I turned to see a blue uniform. I tilted my head up and saw the tallest, biggest federation soldier I'd ever seen standing directly in my path. He calmly grabbed me with one hand and spoke into his handheld with the other.

"I got the kid and the girl," he said. "You messed up now, boy."

I gave him a swift elbow in the gut. It had no effect. When I tried to swing my toolbox up, he merely batted it away like it was a fly. Debra tried for her pepper spray again, but the guy saw it and shoved her so hard to the ground, it sent the canister tumbling into the mess of drunken legs of the revelers. Gone.

I looked over my shoulder and saw more feds fighting through the crowd toward us. We were screwed. I tried to think of a way out, but the fed was too damn strong – he had me in a vice grip. Then, I caught a glimpse of Sky's eyes across the hall. He was standing behind the bar and quickly understood my situation.

He snatched a microphone hanging from the wall. "Drinks free for the next five minutes! Happy Friday everyone!" he shouted into the mic. The place immediately erupted with cheers and a massive push of people toward the bar. While I alone wasn't strong enough to overcome the huge fed, a hundred people were. His grip loosened just enough that I was able to snake my body free. I dropped to the floor and crawled toward the exit, Debra right behind me.

We crossed the threshold and found ourselves in the red corridor. Like the beer hall, it was more crowded than the last time I came through. Debra and I stood up and began snaking our way past couples and triples and at least one quartet of people in various states of ecstasy. Some were naked. Others in the process of getting there.

We got about 30 feet into the corridor when I heard a commotion behind us. A couple feds were following us, ruining the fun for everyone. As we passed a threesome of people that had already disrobed, Debra grabbed their clothes and pulled me into an alcove.

"Here, put this on," she said, handing me a gray cloak. Then she expertly pulled on the pink jumpsuit in her other hand and pushed me down onto the couch. Before I knew it, she had climbed on top of me and was kissing me, hiding both of our faces from anyone not looking too closely. I wasn't about to complain. The kiss started out as an act, but soon, her lips softened and we found ourselves moving in rhythm to the thumping music in the corridor. For a second, I lost myself in the moment and forgot we were even in danger. All that I was thinking about was the way she smelled and the press of her body against mine. I reached my hand around her back and pulled her closer. She did the same and soon we were just another couple in the corridor enjoying ourselves. I honestly didn't even care if I got caught at that point. Whatever the feds did to me would have been worth it.

After maybe a minute that felt like the best hour of my life, Debra licked my lips one last time and pulled back to peek around. No feds. She looked back at me and we just sat there for a moment. Her hand had been resting on my chest, and I knew she could feel my heart beating rapidly under the gray cloak she'd given me to wear. She leaned back in for another kiss, this one a slow, gentle affair. Finally, our lips parted.

"Thank you Denver, but I should probably get back to my husband," she said.

It felt like someone had stuck me in the heart with a knife. She saw the look on my face and laughed.

"I'm fucking with you, Denver," she said, patting me on the chest as she stood up. "But I do think this is where we have to part."

"Oh, yeah...I probably need to get off this barge," I stammered. "But thank you too. For...that?" It probably sounded horrible, but I was still a bit shook from the moment and sudden passion we had shared.

"You don't have to thank me. That was one of the best makeout sessions of my life."

"Same. Very much same," I said.

"They don't know who I am. I just gave them a little too much attitude when they tried to pick me up. But you...can you get back to your ship?" she asked, concerned.

"No, but my ship can come to me."

A few minutes later, Debra was gone from my life forever and I was waiting by the garbage bins for Gary to swing the Stang around and pick me up. Ah, the life of a wrecker! I felt something tickle my neck. It was a long, dark brown hair that had intertwined with mine. I pulled it free and let it float away

143

in the breeze of the air system vent.

Then I heard the familiar turbine whir of the Stang as it rounded the corner of the dock. I closed my eyes for a couple of seconds to remember every detail of the red corridor encounter before I stepped back on my ship.

Chapter 12

Phobos was home to the most expansive junkyard and parts exchange in the solar system. As a wrecker, it's important to keep enough parts on hand to fix the most common ship problems. While towing a troubled ship is always an option, it's much easier to just fix the issue on the spot and let the ship be on its way.

Located on the larger of Mars' two moons, about 3,400 miles off the planet's surface, Sal's Parts Depot took up most of the 5-mile-wide Stickney Crater. From above, the yard looked like the final resting place of every kind of ship you could imagine, rising from the dusty moon like gravestones.

Nobody knew why it was called Sal's Parts Depot. The guy who owned it was named Mike. Maybe he just liked the sound of Sal's. Anyway, the process was pretty efficient. Incoming ships waited in a queue to head down to the moon's surface, where one of five rovers would meet you and follow you around as you retrieved parts from various ships.

I didn't figure I was taking too much of a risk stopping at Sal's right after my escape from Port Lauderdale. The feds on the barge weren't there on official business, meaning they likely wouldn't put out a bounty on me or the Stang. And even if they did, I'd be out of the neighborhood soon enough.

As I waited for my number to be called so I could head to the yard and pick up a few things, I scanned the inventory available. First priority was to acquire some backup filters for the Stang's air system. Those could be purchased from Sal's stock. The rest of the items on my list were likely to come from the ships on the lot.

"I'm no genius – well, actually I am – but do you think we should maybe not stop right now?" Gary asked. "Kind of ruins the idea of a getaway when you go shopping right around the corner.

"Relax, those guys are morons and on top of that, they won't be following us anytime soon," I said. "I may or may not have unplugged a thing or two when I left the 405 unsupervised."

Gary said my uncle would have got a kick out of that. As much as I liked my uncle and learned a lot in the brief time we spent together, I took Gary's word for it, as he would always know my uncle better than I did.

"Mustang 1, you're cleared to enter the depot," an automated voice informed me. I selected the area I'd be landing in, then took the Stang down to the moon's surface.

An hour later, I walked down the gangway in my space suit. The rover driver was waiting for me at the bottom, standing next to his vehicle, which had a medium-sized cargo bed in the back for moving parts around the lot. The tag on the guy's suit said "Egon." Once we were in the cab of the rover, I asked him if the name had any connection to the old movie about ghosts. He said he wasn't sure, but his mom had been Earth-born, so anything was possible.

I told him the ship I was interested in checking out, and we drove the rest of the way in silence. He cast me a few glances that suggested he didn't get too many customers my age shopping at the depot. I was going to have to get used to that treatment, I reminded myself. He parked the rover next to a large orange ship with white paneling. The shell was covered in rust, which meant the ship had likely been on Earth or in low orbit at some point, as the relative lack of oxygen in space meant most metals didn't really rust. I pulled up the available history of the vessel on Sal's store page. According to the depot's files, the ship had been there for 10 years and still had a decent amount of parts intact.

I left the rover and went inside to search for what I needed. Walking through a still, deserted ship always kind of creeped me out. I knew there were no threats looming around the corner of any given corridor, but I still gripped my flashlight a bit harder than usual when searching for the engine room. I eventually found it and went to the auxiliary fuse box. The ship was an S-class leisure cruiser made by the now-defunct Boeing Corporation. Before going belly-up 50 years earlier, Boeing had built a variety of ships in the verse, both private and military. Their fuses were some of the more versatile around. I popped open the box and saw that all of the fuses were still there. I removed them one by one and all but two of them were intact and likely functional.

I reported the fuses to Egon when I got back to the rover. He placed them in the cargo bed and logged the items into the computer. I had a limited amount of credits I was working with, so I had to be choosy and remember to save money for the air filters. I told Egon to add the filters so I didn't forget; Sal's had a strict policy that once you removed something from a ship on the yard, you had to buy it. They didn't take kindly to having to return merchandise to a ship because a customer couldn't pay.

We hit a few more ships and I was about to tell Egon to head back to the Stang when he looked over and asked if I was in a tight spot with credits. I told him I wasn't, but he must have seen that I wasn't being totally honest, because he grinned through his visor.

"Just saying there's a card game going back at HQ if you want to try and charge your pot," he said.

* * *

They were playing 8-Card Hold 'Em when I walked in. Two tables of Sal's employees plus a few visiting captains and crew. I didn't spot any blue suits. Not surprising, as their first thought would be to bust up (or tax) Sal's for running an illegal gambling operation. Taking their credits wasn't worth the hassle, even if they were probably easy marks.

Sal's HQ was a series of small domed structures, about 20 feet high at their apex and maybe 300 square feet each. This one was filled with vape and cigar smoke. Guess when you have unlimited filters and air system parts, smoking wasn't as much of a concern. Still, I didn't like the smell and the instant eye-burn that accompanied the haze. I nearly jumped when I felt something brush up against my leg. I looked down to see a thin black and white cat. I reached to pet him, but he skittered away under a chair in the corner.

I spotted an empty seat at the larger of the two tables. I hovered near the table until a hand was finished, then sat down in the empty chair. The other players all gave me the same look, assuming I was the new mark (kid) in the game. Little did they know I'd been playing cards with guys like them for years thanks to my days on the Sheffield. And I'd usually been on the winning end of things.

They were all rough-looking types. That was to be expected for people who either worked or shopped at Sal's. No place for softies at the depot. The other table had a female player, but at mine it was all dudes.

"Is your dad gonna be joining us?" one of the men joked. He was a rail-thin guy with a shaved head and yellow teeth. He chewed the last bit of a cigar like he was making love to it. I took him for 20 credits on the first hand and he shut up pretty quickly after that.

I didn't have my best day at the table, but I was good enough to be up about 100 credits a dozen games in. I was thinking about heading back to the Stang when I was dealt in again. One last game before I took off, I thought to myself.

It was a good hand. I had three aces over jacks and there was probably some good stuff in the hole too. I decided to go all-in, wagering those 100 credits I was up. It was too rich for most of the people at the table, save one. He was a Silver Star wrecker that had been pretty quiet during the games – not much table talk. A few hands earlier, he'd tossed a few chips down to the cat, which was his, apparently. Not that he seemed to care for it much.

We took turns drawing cards and I raised him one last time.

"We could do credits, but why don't we make it more interesting?" he asked.

"What do you have in mind."

"Everything I got in here and everything you got in here."

I knew what he was interested in. He had been eyeing my watch all night. My dad had given it to me when I was on the Sheffield. Just about the only nice thing he'd done for me during my stint aboard his ship. I wasn't particularly attached to it, but it did have some value.

"What do you have on you besides credits?" I asked. He didn't have any noteworthy items like a watch or jewelry. The guy smiled and pulled a Swiss Army Tool out of his pocket. He placed it on the pot. The tool was a combo of 11 different variations, each available at the touch of a button. It was roughly the size of a hammer, but easily the most versatile tool around. Needless to say, I was intrigued. I nodded and put my watch on the pot.

"Here, I'll even throw this in. That way if you win, you can feel like a real wrecker," he said, tossing his Silver Star hat on the pile. It was a common jab. Silver Star captains were notoriously arrogant. I looked across the room and motioned to the cat.

"He's yours too," I said.

The guy paused a beat, then agreed. Then he laid down a full house of aces over 10's. The other players at the table all reacted the same way: they assumed I had lost.

Until I put down my aces over jacks, of course.

The Silver Star guy took it pretty well, actually. He only broke a couple fingers when he slammed his hand down on the table. He tried to take a swing at me, but I kicked the table into his gut and a couple of the Sal's depot crew grabbed the guy and reminded him he'd lost fair and square.

I took the pot and scooped up the cat, who I realized had only one working eye. The other was glazed over and half-closed. In that instant, I knew what I was going to call him: Pirate. I gave him a moment to decide whether he wanted to go with me. He rolled in my arms, belly up and purred loudly. So that was settled. I told Egon I was ready for my ride back to the Stang. When I got back to the ship, Gary was none too pleased with the excursion or the new crewmate.

"I would have preferred a dog," Gary said. "Cats are so picky and they pee everywhere. What if he pees on a circuit board and I get fried?"

"I should be so lucky," I said as I sat down in the pilot chair. "Now that I've pissed off both the feds and Silver Star, I think it's finally time to vacate the area."

Pirate hopped into the co-pilot seat and began kneading the leather. I liked him already.

Chapter 13

I was reclined in my chair with Pirate nestled in my lap. I thought back to when I won him in that card game. We'd been through plenty of jobs and tough times together since then, and I was hoping we'd make it through the current mess. He was hoping I'd give him a big snack when he woke up, probably. Such was the nature of our relationship.

Edgar burst into the cabin. I actually heard his footsteps before he arrived. They practically shook the floor.

"We're out of candy bars," he complained. For a big guy, he sure did whine a lot. In fact, his whining had gotten worse since he came aboard. I couldn't decide if that was him softening to a more laid-back environment or just being really picky about his food intake.

"Maybe you shouldn't have eaten so many," I said. "I haven't had one in days."

"The soda is also running low. Looks like we'll have to stop for supplies before we get to Jasper," Edgar said, as if it were a foregone conclusion.

"Uh, no, I don't think we do," I replied.

Batista turned toward me from her co-pilot chair, where she'd been reading the news on her handheld. She frowned.

"You too?" I asked.

"Pretty hard to maneuver properly without fuel," she said, noting the low reserves. We had enough to get to Jasper, but it would be tight.

It didn't help that we were getting on each other's nerves. I could count on one hand the number of times we'd been in the same room together in the two days since the airlock incident. And it wasn't like we were a well-oiled machine to begin with.

"We need a break from each other," Edgar said, as if reading my mind. "I don't care where, as long as it's got a fun zone."

"Fun zone? What are you suggesting, an amusement park?" I cracked.

Apparently, no, he just meant a place to decompress. Preferably with companions and/or a casino. That was his idea of a fun zone.

I turned to Batista to get her take. "What about you? Are you also in the mood for fun zones?"

"The guy's right, Denver. We need supplies and I need to not look at you for a while, otherwise I might give in to the urge to punch you in the face, regardless of what Desmond might think about it."

"Then where?" I asked.

"Hey, you're the captain. That's up to you," Batista said with mock-cheer. She then put on headphones and turned on the news on her handheld. I looked back at Edgar, who was hovering over me like a petulant child.

Fun zones. We were about to rob one of the most dangerous ships in the verse, and this dude was thinking about fun zones. I called up the map on my monitor and took a look. There were four potential options between us and Jasper Station.

The first two were known federation haunts and I immediately ruled those out. Of the two remaining stations, I'd never been to one. And the other? I chuckled to myself as my stomach grumbled.

"What's so damn funny?" Edgar asked me.

"My stomach just decided where we're stopping," I replied.

Chapter 14

Moon 12 wasn't a moon at all. It was a station that had been created by fusing together a dozen ships. Some had been federation, some private. They were purchased by Aldo Jones, a wealthy trade merchant who decided it would be quicker and cheaper to building-block a station than construct one from scratch. He was right.

The result, commonly known as M12, was a technological mashup unlike anything else in the galaxy. The various quadrants (ships) were linked together by heavily guarded walkways. Each quadrant served a different function. An old fed warbird was converted into a hotel. A leisure cruiser was transformed into a casino. And so on. Nine of the 12 quads were open to the public. The remaining three were reserved for the rich and famous.

With a 3,000-credit bounty on the Stang — it had tripled since the incident with Admiral Slay and the Burnett — I normally would have steered clear of a well-traveled destination like M12. But, Edgar had managed to mask our call sign and drive signature, meaning the only way to tell this was the Stang was a visual ID. As unique as my ship was with its sleek chrome plating and dual turbines, you still had to know what you were looking for to report us to the feds. The warrant was out and surely some people at M12 would be doing just that, but I knew a nice secluded spot to park.

And it was worth the risk.

Not just for the food and fuel, although we badly needed those. It had been three days since Batista and Edgar walked out of the airlock, and they were right – we needed the time apart. Things had cooled down immediately following Desmond's intervention, but the growing sense of dread of going up against the Rox had gotten to all of us, even Edgar. It didn't help that he'd been binge-watching Six Feet Under, so he was just in a dour mood all the time, constantly making references to death and the afterlife.

Whatever rapport Batista and I had built up in the first leg of our journey had been decimated by her lies about Avery. And there was that whole matter of me threatening to space her. I was prepared to go the stretch run and try not to stop for supplies until Jasper Station, but Edgar had done the math and it didn't work in our favor. We would have had to cut rations to 15% of their usual levels just to make it to the scene of the fight.

So he had suggested a few modifications to the Stang to change its drive signature just enough to confuse anybody who wasn't looking too closely. I'd heard of other ships doing things like that, but it was a delicate process because it involved literally changing how your vessel's propulsion system operated. Edgar did it in about three hours, and afterward, I actually noticed the Stang was running a little faster and more efficiently than usual. I did not mention this to Edgar, as I didn't want to give him the satisfaction. He probably knew, anyway.

Just about the only one who wasn't miserable was Gary.

He seemed to revel in the tense environment of the ship. One minute he was snarking at me, the next he was joking with Batista or Edgar. It had been a while since he'd had an audience, and he wasn't letting the opportunity pass. I was still wary about micro-adjustments in his behavior, but I was unable to pin it down to anything specific. He just seemed a bit off. I'd considered having Edgar run a diagnostic on him, but then realized he was a prime suspect if anyone had tampered with Gary's intelligence board in the first place.

Some people thought M12 was an abomination, a kind of floating graveyard with no style or class. I wasn't among them. I had always admired Jones' entrepreneurial spirit and ingenuity. Maybe it was the mechanic in me. But the idea that he just glued together one of the most popular stations in the verse out of a dozen random ships…well, I liked that. I'd never met the man himself, but if he was anything like his creation, I had a feeling we'd get along fine.

I wasn't particularly hoping to make his acquaintance this visit, however. Under the radar was the order of the day.

Batista shook her head at the patchwork station as we approached it.

"Looks worse than I imagined," she said. And I had to admit, M12's aesthetics were not its strong suit. The station looked a bit like a mad scientist's attempt to fuse a robotic octopus with a bionic spider that was missing half its legs. I was more enamored with the *idea* of the station.

Edgar stared at the mismatched structure through the display. He was just waiting to get off the ship and hit the casino. I tried talking him out of it, but he had been clear that once he stepped off the Stang, what he did was his business. "Besides, no bounty on my head," he had bragged.

I navigated the Stang around to quadrant six, the low-rent end of the neighborhood. If there were railroad tracks on the station, quad six would be on the wrong side of them. It was an old, long-range hauler that now had a new life housing a tightly packed group of rental properties. Shaped like a donut, it held a special place in my heart because my uncle and I had towed it out here to become part of the station.

"Nice neighborhood," Gary said.

"Ford 5.0, please proceed to skip eight," an automated voice advised over the Stang's intercom.

I smiled a bit to myself, as I was the only one who got the reference. Edgar had given me a blank stare when I told him to change the call sign from Mustang 1 to Ford 5.0. Not too many people in the verse even remembered the Mustang was a car, let alone a model made by the Ford Company, which had changed its name a century earlier. And the reference to the car's famous engine size? Over everybody's heads.

Anyway, skip eight was separate from the main set of docking bays. Batista raised an eyebrow as we rounded the corner and saw a perfectly secluded bay that we had all to ourselves.

"Look at this spot right in front," Gary noted.

* * *

Jiang greeted me with a wide grin and even wider arms. I wasn't much of a hugger, but made an exception for Jiang because I didn't want to hurt his feelings. He met me halfway up the gangway, embracing me before I could even step onto the bay floor.

"It is good to see you, Denver," he said, holding me tight for a moment. Then he stepped back and looked at my face with concern. "You have either aged poorly or you carry a lot of burdens."

His eyes moved past me to see Edgar and Batista descending the gangway. He seemed to understand the nature of our relationship. "I see."

"You, on the other hand, look exactly the same as the last time I saw you." I said, trying to remember how long it had been since my last visit to his corner of M12.

"Thirteen months ago, Denver," he said. "You were very drunk most of the time, so I won't hold the lapse in memory against you."

"You were drunk, too," I reminded him.

"Then I guess I simply have a better memory, or I can hold my gin better. You never were much of a drinker," he said. Jiang liked to talk that way. He was a man of options and consideration, so a lot of times when he made a point, he also offered other potential possibilities as well. He was also right about me. I loved the taste and relaxation a good beer provided, but you had to twist my leg to get me to drink gin or other spirits. Just wasn't my thing. So when I did, it usually got the best of me.

Edgar walked right past us without a word. I called after him. "Three hours, don't be a minute late."

The big man waved a dismissive hand over his shoulder. "I'll be back," he said with a thick accent. Apparently he'd been working his way through the 80s action flicks too. He disappeared into an atrium that led to the heart of quad six.

Jiang sighed. "Only three hours. That won't give us much time to catch up."

Batista approached and traded nods with Jiang.

159

"Guess it's good to have friends. Can we trust him?" she asked me.

Jiang took no offense, so I took some for him. I gave her a severe frown. "I trust him more than I trust you. Be back in three hours, and don't forget the groceries."

Batista appraised Jiang one more time. She seemed satisfied and started to head off.

"I like IPA's more than lagers!" I yelled as she stepped out of sight. I hoped Batista only doubted we could trust Jiang because he was someone she didn't know, not because of his background. There was a lot of anti-Chinese sentiment in the verse, mostly lingering racism from the Earth days. I didn't take Batista as that kind of person, but I'd also come to realize I didn't know her very well.

"You've grown a temper," Jiang said, rather gravely. "Although it is understandable given the warrant. Would you like to talk about it?"

"I'd rather have a beer and an egg roll," I said.

Jiang smiled again and turned to the stout woman with the dour face that had just appeared next to him. He said something in Chinese and the woman hustled back to the fueling truck and hopped in.

I followed Jiang through the bay doors into the atrium of the ship, which had been expanded to be a hundred feet higher, giving the main entrance an airier feel. The interior of the atrium was lined with small balconies, each belonging to an apartment. Most of the balconies were empty at the moment, but a few were occupied by residents who stepped out of their homes to vape or just lean over the railing and enjoy the view. I didn't like the eyes on me. Jiang sensed my apprehension and quickly escorted me to a corridor leading to his own apartment.

"Do not worry, the people who live here have little interest in bounties like yours," he said. "Some have warrants out on them as well, though none with as many zeroes..."

"Collection and naturalization?" I asked.

Jiang nodded. It bothered him that the federation would rather spend the resources to track down and harass working class people than simply forgive them the taxes owed. These were folks that had enough problems. I agreed with Jiang, of course, and that was part of why I liked him so much. As the Quadrant Mayor, he charged much less for his apartments than he could have, and he probably gave the hardest cases places to live for free.

His apartment could have been the nicest in the quad, if he wanted. After all, he was the mayor. Instead, he lived in what I guessed was a fairly average rental compared to the rest. One bedroom and bath. A small kitchen. And a sort of living room/storage area combo. The view from his window was of the recycling bins.

He closed the blinds to make me feel better, then lifted the lid off the pot in the kitchen. Steam rose from the simmering oil and I caught the scent of honest-to-goodness home cooking. I nearly fainted on the spot. When Jiang returned from the fridge with a cold bottle of IPA for me, I almost embraced him once again.

I took a long swig of the beer and sat on the couch, some of the tension easing in my shoulders. Jiang sat across from me, appraising me more closely now.

"The egg rolls are almost done," he said. "Want to talk business or just keep it light?"

I mulled the question for a few moments, then shrugged.

"I'm already asking too much just being here with the Stang. But if you want to get in even deeper, I'm happy to hear your advice."

Jiang shook his head. "I wouldn't be here at all if it wasn't for you. I still owe you."

I waved my hand and motioned to the egg rolls. "Those will be payment enough, trust me."

"Those?" Jiang joked. "I only made you one!"

I smiled, knowing he was kidding. Or hoping, anyway.

He settled into the couch and swigged his beer. "What *can* you tell me?"

"It seems I may have crossed the wrong man," I began. "Well, before that, I helped the woman you saw escape a federation ship. We left some bodies in our wake. And then Desmond, yes, that Desmond, forced me to be part of a suicide mission to take down the Rox, which apparently exists. Oh, and my brother is alive."

Jiang took a moment to absorb this information. "I hate to think you're holding any details back, Denver. That sounds pretty serious as it is. Your brother is alive. Wow. How do you feel about that?"

"I honestly don't know, and that's the part that bothers me."

Jiang understood. Not only did he know enough of my story to realize I had complicated feelings when it came to Avery, he was also the black sheep of his own family. The only one with a conscience, he often told me, and I got the impression he spent most of his life trying to compensate for his family's shortcomings. It explained why he was so generous and giving.

"What about the giant?" he asked.

Edgar. I was wondering how long he'd take to ask about

him.

"Desmond wanted him on my crew to make sure I went through with our deal," I said.

"You with a crew...that's a new one," he admitted, considering the scenario.

"How are Pirate and Gary adjusting?"

I laughed. "Better than me, let's just say that."

"This man..."

"Edgar."

"Edgar. He seems...different."

Jiang wasn't just a lenient landlord who made a mean egg roll. He had also been a bio-engineer in a former life. And he knew after one glance what I'd been starting to realize about Edgar.

"Yes, I'm pretty sure he's enhanced," I said. "Not just physically, either. The guy hacked a missile navigation system like he was opening a sliding door."

"The way he moves, I'd guess those physical upgrades were military, and not run of the mill. We're talking about high end work that may have started at a developmental age," Jiang said. "Intelligence implants on top of that and he could be a pretty scary situation."

"He is. And he's not even the one I worry about most. Batista, the woman I sprung from a fed ship, has me twisted like a pretzel."

Jiang raised an eyebrow at the expression. He'd never heard of a pretzel, apparently.

"She's hard to figure," I clarified. "I don't know her angle. At least with Edgar, I know where I stand."

"And where's that?"

"About an inch from the edge at all times. Are those damn

egg rolls done yet? I need some fried dough and pork!"

Jiang nodded at my mock anger and went to fetch the food.

* * *

No sooner had I bit into the flaky, delicious crust of my second egg roll than I felt a buzz in my pocket. I checked my handheld. It was Batista. She wasn't looking at the screen, but rather seemed to be checking her surroundings. She was crouched in a dark corridor, peering around the corner.

"Batista?"

"We got a problem," she said, her eyes scanning the corridor. "Feds."

"Have they spotted you?"

"One did, but I don't think he had time to tell any of his friends," she answered. "I've got his handheld now and they are getting concerned about him being missing."

"Is he…"

"He's alive. I think."

Well, okay then. "Can you get back to quad six?"

"Nope, they have the corridor blocked. Gonna need a little help."

I looked at Jiang. I didn't even have to ask. He was already grabbing his own handheld, along with a gun. He knew better than to offer me one. I made eye contact with Batista on screen. "Alright, we're coming to you. I'll let Edgar know we're pulling a fast evac."

I stuffed the device in my pocket and followed Jiang out the door, shoving the rest of the egg roll into my mouth along the way. Jiang shook his head and smiled.

"I'm noth gonna wathe ith," I managed, my mouth full.

164

Once we were in the atrium, Jiang whistled sharply and signaled toward a pair of teens sitting at a nearby picnic bench, vaping. They hopped up and hustled over.

"Got any charges?" Jiang asked them.

The taller of the teens, probably closer to his early 20's now that I got a good look at him, nodded to Jiang and patted his jacket. He and his companion fell in step behind us as we hurried to the bridge leading to quad five, where Batista was holed up.

I was nervous about the bridge. Each quad was its own ecosystem, run by its mayor, in this case Jiang. But the bridges were another matter. They had at least two sentries at each end, and they all worked directly for Aldo Jones. Part of his Elite Moon Guard (EMG). He may have been a quirky character, but I'd heard stories of him cracking down hard on anyone causing trouble on M12. The EMG had a reputation as well for being tough and not necessarily fair.

As we approached the bridge, one of the sentries gripped his gun a bit tighter. The other stepped toward us.

"Mayor," he said, nodding at Jiang, then flicked his eyes over the rest of us, eventually settling on me.

"Lieutenant," Jiang greeted in return. "Any idea where a guy can find a good taco at this hour?"

The Lieutenant grinned, and it seemed sincere. "What hour is that? I lost track years ago."

The man stepped aside and motioned for his partner to do the same, and we walked on past the checkpoint. No ID checks or anything. When we were out of earshot of the sentries, I turned to Jiang. "What was that?"

"His brother's family fell on hard times and needed a place to stay, and I was more than happy to help," he said. "The perks of being a nice guy. Though I don't know how far those perks will get us if we try to come back the other way with a bunch of feds on our tail."

I frowned. "I thought the feds had no jurisdiction here."

Jiang held his hand up and tilted it back and forth. "It's all relative. They don't technically have jurisdiction, but piss them off enough and a few hundred more will come back and slap you around."

Yeah. Made sense. In small groups, the feds were kind of a joke. Their true strength was in their numbers. By some estimates, they had half a million soldiers in their ranks. The problem here was getting off M12 before they identified us. Even if we wiped out the unit on station, one alert and we'd have the cavalry to deal with.

I was so deep in thought I hadn't noticed Jiang was speaking into his handheld. I listened in as he asked someone what fed ship was docked at the station. He disconnected and informed me it was the Burnett.

"That mean anything to you?" Jiang asked.

Jiang saw the answer to his question written all over my face. I didn't even have to utter a word.

I was hoping for a worse ship with a worse crew. The fed vessel Batista had been on, for example, the DTL Graymore, would have been fine with me. The guy in charge, Jeffries, was a hot-headed moron, straight out of the Interstellar Federation officer's catalog. A ship's crew tended to be molded in its captain's image.

The Burnett had Slay at the helm. She seemed like the type that didn't tolerate anything less than ultimate obedience and top-notch work. That didn't bode well for our chances of getting off M12 undetected, let alone alive.

"Are we gonna be able to get back through that bridge with feds on our tail?" I asked Jiang.

"My reach only goes so far beyond quad six," he said. "But the bridges aren't the only way to get around this station."

That was a ray of hope, at least. I checked my handheld and saw we were approaching Batista's location. She was near the middle of quad five, which housed one of two major commerce areas of the station. Food markets. Clothing depots. Ship repair shops. If you needed to buy, barter or sell something, quad five was your place. Unless that something was sex, then quad eight was in order. That's where Edgar had gone.

Damnit. I'd forgotten to ping him.

I tried to connect, but received a message saying his handheld was not in service. The guy had turned it off and was already getting laid. I didn't blame him for it, but I was still upset. Jealous too, if I was being honest with myself. Well, first things first: extract Batista.

Unlike six, a converted craft, quad five was actually its own station back in the day. It had spent the majority of its 30-year run orbiting the earth as a sort of convenience store for ships either passing by or stocking up after they burned Earth's atmo. Three times the size of Jiang's old ship, it was the largest jigsaw piece of the M12 puzzle, and probably the busiest.

The market area was filled with protein-meat stalls, drink carts and booths with freeze-dried foods of every variety, from produce to ice cream. Vendors sold goods and items from around the verse. Walking among the stalls, I could smell the liquor in the air. It mixed with the scent of recycled oxygen, which always seemed to me to have a stale odor to it, probably from the charcoal dampers.

There were people everywhere. Kids. Families. And some blue suiters.

I tugged Jiang's sleeve and we all ducked into a clothing store to avoid a trio of fed soldiers in their navy blue uniforms. They passed by without seeing us. Judging from their darting eyes, they were looking for someone, however. It's possible their missing comrade had them all on high alert. I began to wonder just how smart it was to have come to the station in the first place. Perhaps sensing this, Jiang put a calming hand on my shoulder.

"We'll get you guys fueled and stocked up, and safely back on your way," he said, with sincerity and conviction. "Of course, I'd still recommend you keep your head down and out of sight of the facial recognition eye in the sky."

He grabbed a sport cap with a large bill – some people still called them trucker hats – and swiped his handheld across the tag, buying it. He then placed it on my head with a smile.

"Thanks for the tip," I said, instinctively curving the bill of the hat into more of an upside down u-shape. "Been a minute since I've worn one of these. My uncle used to have a whole collection."

"I bet Erwin did," he said. Jiang had admired my uncle. They were both self-made men and had eclectic senses of taste.

We slid back out of the store, followed by Jiang's two young associates. They didn't speak much, just took our lead and followed Jiang's orders. Must be nice to have your crew listen to you, I thought.

I tried Edgar again and this time, I got through. "You said three hours," he answered, annoyed. He was shirtless and I could see his naked female companions (twins) on the bed behind him, vaping.

"Sorry to interrupt the fun, but we have a fed problem. The Burnett is docked at the station and Batista has already had a run-in with them."

"No you're not," Edgar said.

"What?"

"You're not sorry. Interrupting the fun is what you do."

"That's not — look, this isn't the time to debate that, okay? Get dressed and meet us in quad five by the bridge."

"No, by the loading docks," Jiang corrected me. I gave him a confused look, but he nodded.

"Scratch that, the loading docks," I relayed to Edgar. He sighed and clipped the transmission.

"Not much of a talker," Jiang commented. "I guess she prefers other methods of communication as well."

Jiang motioned across the marketplace, where Batista was using her fists to talk with a pair of fed soldiers. So much for sneaking out of the station undetected.

There were four blue suits around her. Two men. Two women. One of them tried to pin Batista's arms behind her, but he got a broken nose courtesy of a brutal head snap, the back of her skull cracking the ridge of his nose. Even from 50 feet away, I saw the blood spurt out of the poor guy's nose as he dropped to the deck in pain.

I hustled over to join the fight. Not because she needed my help. I just wanted to get the scuffle over with more quickly, so we could vacate the area. The eye in the sky – a drone camera – was hovering over the action. That meant not only were the EMG going to be arriving shortly, so were more feds, as they had informants inside the EMG who would immediately alert them to Batista's presence.

I pulled my hat down further, as if it mattered. We were

already blown. If Batista was on the station, they would know I was, too.

My boot connected with the back of one of the blue suiters. The force sent her flying into a nearby recycling bin with a loud clang. Batista grunted as she whirled around to her next opponent, the largest of the bunch. He was a tall, wide soldier, not unlike Edgar. But he wasn't built for this kind of scrap. Before he could produce his gun, Batista had landed a crushing knee into his groin and followed that up with a forearm to the side of the head. The guy tried to keep his balance, his shaky hand still reaching for his weapon, and for that effort he was rewarded with a kick in the chest that sent him backward into the female soldier by the recycling bin who was stumbling to her feet.

They both went down in a heap.

Batista looked at me, Jiang and the teens. "I had it handled."

"And now they have you on camera," I noted, pointing to the drone above our heads.

Batista shrugged. One of the teens fired some kind of glowing pellet at the drone. It stuck to the drone and immediately brought it down with a thud.

"That'll stop it from transmitting and scramble any old footage that hasn't been viewed," Jiang said. "Probably too late, though. We need to get to the docks."

Batista gave one last kick to the big soldier as she passed, scooping up his weapon along the way. We all followed Jiang away from the gathered crowd. Once we turned the corner, we slowed to a nonchalant walk just in time for a pair of EMG guys to pass us by, heading toward the commotion.

"Were you even trying to stay under the radar?" I asked Batista.

"What's that supposed to mean?"

"You like to fight."

"You're saying I got spotted on purpose?" she asked.

I didn't say anything else. I'd made my point. She smoldered as we followed Jiang into a maze of large ship carcasses and parts. We were in the junkyard exchange, where you could barter for various parts you needed to fix your vessel.

"I notice you didn't get the food, either," I said, unable to stop myself. I had every right to be upset, but for some reason I really wanted to push it. Jiang sensed the growing problem and stopped short.

"Look, you both need to shut up," he said, in the sternest voice he could muster. He looked around. "If we're lucky, I can get you to a friend who has access to every quad, meaning he could ferry us back to your ship on his transport skip. But if you'd rather argue and draw more attention to yourselves, I'll leave you both right here. Your call."

It took me a second to register that this was my normally mild-mannered friend talking to us like that. Batista and I glared at each other, deciding to leave the argument for later.

"Good," Jiang said, noting the unspoken truce. "Now where's the big guy."

A loud crash caused us all to flinch. It was followed by the sound of rapid gunfire.

"I want to say that's not him…" I said. "But something tells me I'd be wrong."

I checked my handheld and at the same moment, I got a transmission from Edgar. He was driving a rover with one hand and tossing a fed soldier out onto the deck with the other. He was probably driving 40 miles per hour at the time. Wonderful.

171

"You guys at the docks yet?" he asked. He was so calm I thought he might yawn. The bullets whizzing by him didn't seem to faze him much. He touched his shoulder and frowned.

"Are you hit?" I asked.

"Very perceptive, captain," he replied.

The teens shared a look. They liked this guy.

"We're close to the docks, but it would be better if you didn't draw the entire EMG to us!" I barked.

Edgar rolled his eyes and turned the rover. "I'll meet you there in five. Hasta la vista."

The transmission ended. Jiang was confused. "Hasta la vista?"

"He's going through a Terminator phase," I explained. Jiang had no clue what I was talking about.

"I love that movie!" one of the teens blurted. Then he looked at Jiang and quieted himself again.

The sound of the gunfire seemed to be dissipating, meaning Edgar was drawing them away from us. How he was going to get back to the docks without a bunch of pissed off people on his ass, I had no idea. But that was his problem. Ours was getting to the transport skip.

We zig-zagged through the huge engines, missile tubes and various other parts strewn about the junkyard, doing our best to either avoid other people or appear as inconspicuous as possible when we crossed paths with someone. Half a dozen drones buzzed back and forth overhead, but we had the benefit of being just five people among hundreds in the quad.

When we reached the edge of the junkyard, the docks were a hundred yards away. Jiang turned to the teens. "Wait as long as you can," he said. They understood. I didn't. But they did. Guess that was enough. They disappeared among the parts.

Jiang led us toward a weathered, gray transport skip. It was maybe 20 feet long. A guy in his late 50s, balding with white tufts of hair sticking out of his temples, leaned against the side panel, eating a sandwich.

Chapter 15

They say being shot feels like being punched.

Well guess what? They're idiots. Being shot feels like *being shot*.

About ten feet from the transport skip, my right shoulder exploded in pain. I don't even think I felt the impact of the bullet, just the searing ball of fire that shook my entire right shoulder and arm, dropping me to my knees in agony. The sharp tendrils of white-hot pain reached all the way into my gut, making me woozy and a little nauseous.

As I tried to catch my breath, my left hand instinctively grabbed my shoulder. It was slick with blood. All around me, I heard little "pfft" noises as bullets flew by my ears. Someone scooped me up and dragged me the final few feet to the small transport shuttle. I stumbled inside it and collapsed to the floor.

I don't think I blacked out. I just kinda went numb for a few moments. Shock can do that to you. Then the pain returned and I saw Jiang leaning over me, holding a rag to my shoulder to stem the bleeding.

"It feels worse than it is," he said.

"How do you know how it feels?" I asked.

Jiang smiled a bit and looked at Batista and Edgar, who

were safely in the shuttle with us. "He hasn't lost his sense of humor," Jiang said.

Edgar made a face. "Didn't know he had one."

"What happened?" I managed as I tried to sit up. Jiang gently pushed me back down, urging me to lay flat. He said they needed to dress the wound a bit more before I started moving.

Batista explained that we'd almost made it to the transport craft when a pair of feds came out of nowhere and started lighting us up. Luckily, I was the only one who got hit (lucky for who, I wondered). When I asked what happened to the feds, Edgar simply waved his hand.

"Dead?" I asked.

Batista nodded. Well, that certainly complicated matters.

"Don't worry," Edgar said. "I already put a couple others out of their misery before those two. We were on Slay's bad side anyway. Shooting her men in the knees wouldn't have made her feel any better about us."

Things were spiraling out of control. It was bad enough Batista and I had maimed a bunch of feds escaping the Graymore, but now we were leaving bodies. Never mind the morality of it, that's just something the federation would never forget – or forgive. I felt even sicker to my stomach than I did a few minutes earlier. Jiang could see the concern on my face and raised his eyebrows in agreement. He knew I was used to bending the rules, even breaking some of them, but killing people? It didn't matter if they were feds who were trying to kill me, it just wasn't something I'd ever done before.

The older guy piloting the shuttle yelled over his shoulder that we were almost back to the quad six bay where the Stang was docked. He checked his scans and confirmed we hadn't been detected. I felt a sense of relief.

"Benefits of not leaving any witnesses," Edgar said.

The relief was quickly replaced by anger again.

"We'll talk about that later," I told him, sitting up, despite Jiang's protest. Edgar was nonplussed. What was there to talk about, really? It was done. Just over a week ago, I was a wrecker with a few dings on my record and about the same number of blemishes on my conscience. Now I was associating with Tracers and killers, which made me as bad as them, in my book. I wanted to turn back the clock and simply ignore that distress call from the Graymore. Instead, I was hurtling toward a fight I didn't want, leaving all kinds of carnage in my wake.

"Better hurry," Jiang said when the shuttle landed next to the Stang. He opened the door and checked the area first. It was quiet. The only person there was the woman he'd tasked with refueling my ship. They exchanged a few words in Chinese and then Jiang nodded, satisfied.

The transfer to the Stang was surprisingly uneventful. Jiang informed me the ship was refueled and he'd even put some of his own food reserves in the kitchen to tide us over until Jasper Station. That was assuming we made it that far, of course.

"What about the other request?" I asked.

Jiang nodded. Good. I would need all the help I could get.

Edgar and Batista were already aboard the Stang and I was halfway up the gangway, with Jiang helping me every step, when he stopped for a moment and turned toward me.

"You're a good man," he said.

It was meant to make me feel better, but it hit a different way. It just made me question myself even more. Jiang didn't know half of what I'd done.

"Am I, though?" I asked.

"You are," Jiang said, with even more conviction. "You're a good man in a bad situation. Don't lose sight of that. Safe travels, friend."

* * *

Pirate was sitting in my lap as we navigated out of the bay. Jiang's words were still echoing in my head. I wanted to believe them. It reminded me of something my mom used to say: speak with your actions, and when your actions say the wrong thing, make sure you don't repeat the lie ever again. I don't know if it applied to situations like this, though.

I looked over at Edgar, who was standing at the weapon station, not a care in the world. I wondered whether his conscience had been altered or his lack of compassion was simply the foundation the people who enhanced him built upon. As we prepped the ship to take off, he had calmly informed me that he never felt remorse over a life he'd taken. "They were all just," he had said. Apparently, if someone was trying to do him harm, he felt they had crossed a line that could result in his death, so he had no reservations about killing them. If everything was black and white, sure, that is one way to look at things. But it's a very dark, very messed up way to live. It definitely didn't make me feel any better about having him on my ship. He could decide any number of my decisions were bad for him, and then suddenly I was the dispensable one.

Then there was Batista. She was in the co-pilot chair, oddly silent at the moment. She had finished Jiang's work of stitching and bandaging me up, though we hadn't exchanged a single word during the entire ad-hoc procedure. She simply took Gary's directions and with cold eyes and mechanical hands, repaired my shoulder. It still hurt like hell, but the pain killers had kicked in and Gary was reasonably sure they'd missed any vital parts. I just wouldn't be able to use my right arm anytime in the next week or so without a whole lot of white-hot pain.

"It's a shame," Gary said.

"Which part?"

"That was a great parking spot. We'll never get one like that on Jasper Station."

"Just keep your eyes on the scans," I told him. It was a good sitcom reference, but I'd long since learned not to feed the beast.

"Will do, boss. I'm actually surprised it was such a clean getaway. Almost too easy if you ask me," Gary said.

I paused my hands in mid-air, trying not to move a muscle and create a disturbance in the force. I glanced at Batista and Edgar and they too were motionless.

In general, I wasn't particularly superstitious. I didn't get the impression Batista or Mr. Kills-A-Lot were either.

But Gary had broken the cardinal rule when making a getaway: saying it was too easy. Because in all likelihood, it *was* too easy, and giving voice to that reality was only a step removed from hoping something went wrong.

Gary noticed we all stopped moving at the same time, and snickered. "What did I say?"

Beep. Beep. Beep.

My eyes locked onto the scanner and suddenly, as if it appeared out of nowhere, there was a ship about 50 miles from our position. Weapons armed and locked. We were dead in the atmo if they wanted us.

"You had to open your big mouth," Edgar said to the ceiling.

"It's the Burnett," I said, not surprised. "She's hailing us."

I didn't answer. My mind raced for some way out of this. Some hidden advantage we had, or a trick I could pull. I drew a complete blank. I looked at Batista and she just shrugged. No ideas there. Edgar wasn't even bothering to plug in a counter-attack into the system.

Not that it mattered much, but I couldn't figure out how the Burnett was doing it. It had to be some new stealth technology. That didn't make sense, though. The federation was the leakiest ship of all when it came to secrets, so if they'd been developing some super-high-tech stealth technology that could mask an entire warbird, the whole verse would know about it. And that's assuming it was a fed creation. They weren't exactly known for their technical prowess. Innovations like stealth almost always came from the private sector, and since the feds were cheap as hell, they never got the tech first.

"I don't think it has anything to do with what I said," Gary mused, in a meek voice.

"Well, I guess I should answer and get this over with," I said, before telling Gary to accept the beam. I tried my best to put on a neutral expression. Slay popped up onto the monitor, her steely eyes boring into my soul. She let the silence do the talking for the first few moments.

When I couldn't take it anymore, I smiled.

"Well this is awkward," I said. "You're the very last person I was hoping to see today."

"Mr. Boyd. For someone I'd never heard of two weeks ago, you do cause a lot of trouble. And now we're adding the

179

murder of 12 federation soldiers to your resume."

A dozen! I turned my head toward Edgar in disbelief. He produced a smirk that said it made no difference to him.

"Unlike our last encounter, there will be no escape this time. We're going to board your ship, remove you and your crew and then deliver justice," Slay said.

"And if I refuse?"

"Justice will be even more swift."

"I admit you have us in a corner. But the fact I'm still breathing means you want something from me or my crew. So I'm going to use that piece of information to make one request."

Slay narrowed her eyes. I could tell she wanted to blast us to smithereens with every fiber of her being, but something was stopping her. It wasn't enough to let us go, obviously, but it might be enough leverage to eke out a meager assurance before we turned ourselves in. There was also something deeper going on. I just wasn't quite sure what it was. Her mention of the dead soldiers seemed somewhat perfunctory to me. Like she thought it was a crime, but she wasn't too upset about it. She was definitely unlike any fed admiral I'd encountered before. A new breed of officer, perhaps.

She gestured for me to proceed.

"Nobody hurts the cat," I said. "He comes with me until we sort out this justice."

Slay seemed to pause, unsure if it was a joke or not. Edgar exhaled loudly in disbelief. Even Batista, who had come to form a bond with Pirate over the course of our mission, frowned.

When Pirate sauntered into the room, passing by me in the background, Slay realized I wasn't joking. She nodded. "Done.

The cat will not be harmed. Prepare to be boarded."

Zeep. The monitor went black.

"You gotta be kidding me," Edgar said. "The cat?!"

"We're done. You heard her. There's no escaping this. Most likely, we'll be dead before the day is through, so yeah, I went to bat for my original and most valuable crewmember."

Gary cleared his throat. "What am I, chopped liver?"

"I want you to erase all top-level data and wipe the hard drive," I commanded. "They get nothing but your winning personality. Unless you want to reboot. I will leave that call to you."

Gary paused, thinking about it. Or computing on it. You get the idea. Finally, he spoke up. "I'll take my chances you guys make it back."

I snorted at the prospect. I couldn't even begin to envision a scenario in which I made it out of this jam alive, let alone in charge of my ship. I picked up Pirate and walked out of the cabin without saying another word.

Chapter 16

They put us in separate rooms. Smart. How I would have played it too. If I were a scumbag fed.

For all I knew, they were already questioning and/or executing Edgar and Batista. The federation was a bureaucratic machine with countless processes and procedures, save one area: meting out justice. That was swift and often at the sole discretion of the senior officer in charge of a vessel or region.

Nobody had come for me yet. Slay had been true to her word, letting me bring Pirate with me. The cat snoozed in his carrying case, either unaware of the situation or he just didn't intimidate easily. I liked to think it was the latter. We'd already been waiting an hour, and it dawned on me that I might soon be sharing Pirate's litter box with him.

I looked around the small room. It pained me to say it, but it was nice. Much like its captain, the Burnett didn't fit the federation mold. The ship couldn't have been more than a year old, and everywhere I looked, the tech was state of the art. Even the walls were painted a less depressing blue than the usual fed blue, which almost looked more like a puke-green. Even the chair I sat in was so ergonomically sound, I could have fallen asleep under less dramatic circumstances.

The door slid open with a hiss and Slay entered. Alone.

That was odd. I wasn't a danger, considering one of my arms was in a sling and both my hands were cuffed to the table, but when the door closed behind her, I couldn't help but wonder why she hadn't delegated this interrogation (or sentencing) to someone of lesser rank.

Was I really that important?

The obvious answer was no. I wasn't. Something else was going on here.

Slay sat down across the table from me and looked at Pirate, who was snoring loudly. A flicker of a smile crossed Slay's lips, then disappeared quickly.

"Your cat is either very brave or very dumb," Slay said.

"I was thinking the same thing, actually," I replied. "I've been flying with him for a while now and I still don't know which it is."

"Doesn't make you the best judge of character," she said. "But I guess that explains the other members of your crew."

I wanted to tell her they weren't my choice. That I'd been tricked into partnering with one and forced to take on the other. Instead, I just kept a blank expression, trying not to give anything away.

"You don't need to play it this way. I already know all about your crew and why they're on board."

"Yeah?"

"Yes."

"Why are we talking right now? Shouldn't you be dealing out justice?"

I figured what the hell, rip the band-aid right off. Slay nodded.

"I once dated a wrecker. In my youth," Slay said.

"If this was some elaborate way of asking me out on a date,

I could've saved you a lot of time and trouble," I replied.

Slay smiled at that one. If I didn't know better, I would've even guessed the smile was genuine. "I'm far too old for you, Mr. Boyd –"

"Call me Denver."

"Denver. There will be time for immature jokes about sex. And there will also be time for justice. But right now, I'm interested in your help."

I took a beat to let that one sink in. I was unable to hide my surprise. Slay acknowledged it.

"Yes, there's a warrant on you and your crew," she said. "And yes, your crew just killed a dozen fed soldiers. These are facts. Do you dispute them?"

I didn't say a word. I was too confused about what the hell was happening.

"I'll take it by your silence, you do not. But there are also circumstances beyond your knowledge that cause me…" she stopped for a moment, choosing her words more carefully. "Circumstances that force me to set those transgressions aside for the moment and ask for your help."

First Desmond. Then the federation. Who was going to need my help next?

"Let's say I help you. I mean, I can't even fathom why you would need my help, but let's pretend this is a real offer. What happens after I'm done with this whole helping thing? Because if I just get justice served then, I'd rather just get on with it."

"The slate will be clean," she said.

"I'm sorry, I want to get this straight. You don't care about the dead soldiers?"

Slay stiffened at the question and I saw the first glimpse of true anger in her face. She quickly subdued it.

184

"I never said I didn't care. I care. The federation cares, and as far as I'm concerned you should be floating in space right now, along with your cat, no matter how cute he is. But I have an objective that supersedes the dead soldiers, as distasteful as that is to me. And so here we find ourselves. Are you in? Or should I shove you and your crew in the airlock and press the big red button?"

"So you think my cat is cute?" I joked.

I don't know why I did it. I guess I just can't help myself sometimes. I knew it was the wrong thing to say even before I finished saying it, but, as Slay said, here we find ourselves.

Slay just got up and started to walk out.

"I'm in," I said. "Assuming I don't have to kill anyone else, I'm in."

She stopped and turned. Her eyes examined mine, perhaps wondering why I had suddenly turned into a pacifist. "I'll brief you and your team in 10." And with that, she walked out.

The door slid closed and a second later, the electronic handcuffs on my wrists clicked open. I rubbed my wrists and looked at Pirate. "That took an unexpected turn." He simply twitched his paws in response.

* * *

A pair of silent feds led me through the hall into a conference room. The room seemed designed for a business meeting rather than a military briefing. Batista and Edgar were already there, sitting at the far end of a shiny oval table, eating protein packs. It was the first time I'd ever seen snacks provided to prisoners on a fed ship, although we weren't technically prisoners anymore, I supposed.

I placed Pirate's bag on the floor next to an open chair and sat down. There was nobody else in the room yet. Just the crew of the Stang. We all looked at each other.

"Anyone else confused?" Batista asked.

Edgar just grunted. I shrugged.

"They offered me a drink," Batista said, incredulous. "Since when did the feds have refreshments and conference rooms?"

"Did they tell either of you why we're not dead at the moment?" I asked.

Nope. Both of them had gone through a cursory interview, much like mine. I wanted to hear their thoughts on what they thought was going on, but Slay strode into the room, followed by a beefy man in civilian clothes. He was mid-40s and had the look of violence about him, whether that meant dishing it out or just being familiar with it in all its forms. He instinctively took a standing position closer to Edgar than either Batista or I. A second later another non-fed entered. She was maybe five feet tall and 100 pounds. Her dyed red hair was shaved close in the back and long in the front, covering one of her eyes. The other eye was pierced above the eyebrow. She wore a black leather jacket and dark jeans. She might have been 20. Slay introduced her as Romy.

Romy sat down at the other end of the table from us. There was a nervous energy about her, and she didn't make eye contact with any of us. All her focus was on her handheld. I didn't even bother guessing why she was in the room for this meeting. What was the point? I honestly wouldn't have been surprised if Desmond walked in the door after her.

Once the door was closed, Slay looked at each of us in turn.

"Not the team I would have chosen, but it's the team I got," she said.

"Team for what?" Edgar wondered.

"Keep your mouth shut and I'll explain."

Edgar brushed off the retort and took another bite of his protein pack, chewing it slowly and deliberately. The big guy standing behind him tensed his neck muscles. Edgar must have sensed it, because he cracked a grin and snickered to himself.

Slay turned to the bank of monitors on the wall and waved her handheld at it. An image of a modern, half-sphere station with a gleaming clear dome appeared on the screens. The 600-foot-tall cross protruded from the top of the dome.

"Jasper Station," Slay said. "Home of the Believers."

I traded a look with Batista and we both had the same thing on our mind: when did that place become the center of the verse? I couldn't tell if Slay noticed the brief exchange.

"We have reason to believe the Roxelle Baker, which you probably all know as The Rox, will be attempting an attack on the station in less than a week. Normally, the federation would simply send a dozen warbirds to protect the station and intercept the attack, but in this case, there are special circumstances."

"Seems to be a lot of that going around," I noted.

"Indeed," Slay agreed, annoyed by the interruption. I put up my hands in mock surrender.

She proceeded to explain there was an item aboard the Rox that the federation needed to acquire in order to ensure "safety and balance" in the verse. When Edgar asked exactly what that item was, she refused to answer, saying it was not relevant and that if we eventually needed to know, she'd inform us then. Edgar already knew what the federation was after, as it was the same thing Desmond wanted to get his hands on. It was really starting to scare me. I knew I'd have as much luck getting the answer out of Slay as I did Edgar, so I just nodded and continued to listen.

The reason they'd chosen my ship – and me, specifically – is that they needed someone to get aboard the Rox and secure the item. They had come to the same conclusion as Desmond: a wrecker was the best way in. And since I already had a bounty on my head, they had leverage.

"Why not a Silver Star ship?" I asked. "Plenty to choose from."

"Because we don't want this to fall into Jack Largent's hands, either," Slay responded.

Add one more complication to the plan, I told myself. The more I thought about the situation, the more I felt I was being dragged slowly toward my death, but there was nothing I could do to stop it.

One question that had bothered me ever since Desmond enlisted me to do the very same thing for him and the Tracers was how they were so sure the Rox would need a wrecker in the first place. Now Slay was sure, too. When I asked her about it, she smiled.

"We've got that taken care of," she replied.

For a fraction of a second, I saw surprise flash across Edgar's face. He must have been wondering if Desmond's plan had been compromised. Had the federation found out the Tracers were planning to cripple the Rox somehow, and they decided they could swoop in too? That didn't make sense. If they knew that, then surely they would have known I was part of the plan as well. The rendezvous between the Stang and the Golden Bear that Slay's Burnett had broken up would be a tipoff that I was involved, meaning the federation probably didn't know about Desmond's seemingly identical plot. They were just there to grab me.

Maybe those missiles they'd fired at the Stang were warning shots. Edgar has destroyed them in time, but maybe Slay was just trying to throw Desmond off the notion they were going to try and enlist me. It would've been a risky gamble, to assume I could either out-maneuver or somehow disable the missiles. I wanted to ask about that, but I tried to keep my questions to a minimum so I didn't accidentally tip them off to the fact we were working for Desmond as well.

The other thing Slay didn't realize was that Edgar – who she probably viewed as some random thug – was actually a former crew member of the Rox and also the Golden Bear, giving him maybe the best pedigree of any weapons specialist in the verse.

According to Slay, our role was simple. Get the Stang to Jasper Station in time to service the Rox, once the call went out. And it would go out, she assured us. Then, once aboard, we would work with Romy and Gareth (the beefy silent guy) to extract the item. We'd then meet up with the Burnett to transfer the item and our part of the deal would be fulfilled, and we could go on our merry way.

"Two problems," I said, motioning to Romy and Gareth. "Her and him. The last thing I need is two more crew members on my ship. You want us to extract something, fine, we'll do it. But I'm not bringing two more people I can't trust onto my ship."

"More?" Slay asked.

"You know what I mean," I said, waving away my verbal stumble. I looked at Batista and Edgar with the best smile I could muster. "Are we in agreement?"

"He's the captain," Edgar said, doing his best impression of a dutiful subordinate. Batista also gestured as if to say it was my call.

Slay wasn't fooled by the shows of deference. She evaluated the situation for a few moments and then came to a decision.

"Romy is non-negotiable," she said. "She has expertise that none of you could possibly possess as it relates to the item we need to remove."

"Yeah, and what expertise is that?" Edgar asked.

"I helped design it," Romy said, speaking for the first time. She didn't look up from her handheld, but if she had, she would see the grimace on Slay's face. It was clear the admiral would've preferred Romy hadn't divulged that information. Edgar was not only satisfied with that response, he was pleased with it.

"If she's so smart, why don't you just have her design another one of these whatevers that we're stealing?" I asked.

"If only they'd thought of that," Romy snarked, before realizing she may have said something confrontational. "Sorry. I didn't mean that."

I raised my eyebrows to show I'd taken no offense. Slay cut in.

"She only understands certain aspects of the device," Slay explained. "To create another one, we'd need the whole team. That isn't feasible at the moment."

I nodded. Suddenly it was a "device" and not an item. Interesting.

"I guess she's exempt from uniform because she's so smart?" I asked.

"She's not a fed," Slay said, stating the obvious. "Romy is an independent contractor."

I appraised Romy and decided the hipster genius girl was not a threat. Gareth on the other hand…

"Fine. She's mission-critical. But we can't have silent muscles over there," I said.

"You get him or you get a failsafe," she said.

Failsafe was a fancy word for a bomb. Basically, they'd rig the Stang to blow if we deviated from the plan in any way. The right bomb setup was basically impossible to defuse, and given her confidence, I knew Slay had the right setup at her disposal.

"Besides, it seems you have all the muscle you need already," she admitted, referring to Edgar and Batista.

"Done," I agreed.

Gareth wanted to say something, but he knew his place and simply bit his tongue. Slay's decision to allow Romy to go alone with my crew answered one of my questions: was Gareth protection for Romy or insurance if my crew ran into trouble on the Rox. Seemed like the latter. What Slay didn't know is that we couldn't take Edgar onto the Rox. She also didn't know we had an inside man in my brother.

Avery. It was breaking my brain a bit to consider all the angles and pieces in motion. Whatever was on the Rox was a universe-changer, enough to force all kinds of unlikely alliances. On top of that, add the fact that someone wanted to destroy Jasper Station. Strange days.

As for the negotiation at hand, I was good with the results. Romy didn't seem like trouble and a failsafe was a problem for another day. Survive today, I thought. Worry about complicated bombs tomorrow. Something told me it wouldn't be the only deadly device in my immediate future.

Chapter 17

The Stang was getting crowded.

When I inherited the ship from my Uncle E, I hadn't thought much about putting a crew together. I just never envisioned myself as a "captain." I also had my uncle as my role model. He was a loner in his own ship, traveling where he wanted, when he wanted. He took the jobs that appealed to him and avoided the ones that smelled like trouble. It only felt natural to follow in his footsteps. Sure, I had told myself at the time, it would lead to a more lonely existence than surrounding myself with crew members.

But it was safe.

I would be accountable only to myself (and Pirate, of course). Life, it seems, has a way of messing up plans like that. Maybe it would turn out for the better, I thought.

Sure, that's how my luck had been going as of late. Everything would turn out perfect!

* * *

Romy might have been small in stature, but she was another person who required a room, personal space and a station in the cabin. I actually had to bring a little table into the cabin for her to sit at so she didn't feel left out. Not that she would, probably, but once you're on my crew, you get treated the same as everybody else. Even if you're an oversized killing machine like Edgar.

On the bright side, the failsafe was only about the size of a lunchbox. So it didn't take up much room at all! Slay's team had installed it in the cabin, I guess in the hopes I wouldn't forget about it when I was making important, life and death decisions. The bomb was hardwired into the ship's power supply, which basically meant if we tried to remove it or bypass it in any way, we were screwed. Slay personally had access to remote-detonate the ship as well. That didn't bother me as much as it could have. The woman had already held our lives in her hands once and let us continue breathing, so maybe she would do it again.

I had no intention of making any other stops before we reached Jasper. If we ran out of food, so be it. No more beer? Too bad. Okay, maybe for coffee I'd stop, but considering Batista and I were the only caffeine addicts, we were likely okay on that front. Edgar seemed to run mostly on candy bars, and Romy had a supply of little yellow pills she took a few times a day. I didn't even want to know what they were.

She was proving to be an odd one, even by current crew standards. The first couple days, she mostly kept to herself. She retrieved food from the kitchen when nobody else was in there, and she still hadn't used the workstation I'd set up for her in the cabin. Her work would be done on the Rox, assuming our plan got that far. Gary had tried to interact with her, but she was completely immune to his comedic stylings, which I actually liked about her.

I was making coffee in the kitchen at one point when she

193

walked in, eyes glued to her handheld. She sensed my presence and began to turn around, when I tried to engage, asking her how she was doing. "Fine." And what she was so busy working on? "Nothing." That was the extent of our conversation.

So I guess you could say I was more than a little surprised when she knocked on the door of my quarters and wanted to talk about The Avengers.

"As in…the movie?" I asked.

She stood in the doorway and nodded. It was the most direct eye contact she'd made with me since coming aboard. I motioned for her to sit in the chair by the door. I finished re-wrapping the sling on my injured shoulder as she spoke.

"There's something I don't understand about them," she said. "Actually, just one of them."

I was behind my small desk, having been in the middle of reading an old-fashioned book about fishing. I'd never been fishing and likely never would, but the idea of it fascinated me. It was a completely different human experience, to be alone on a river at dawn, waist deep in water, trying to hook a fish. Being surrounded by life and sound, smells and colors.

Space was nothing like that.

I took a sip of coffee, and had absolutely no idea where the conversation was going.

"Okay…" I prompted.

"Well, I'm kind of a focused person. You probably noticed that about me. I've spent most of my life thinking about engineering, physics, thermodynamics. Things like that. So there wasn't much time for diversion. I don't pay attention to current events or entertainment, really, other than some gaming when I need to take my mind off complex navigational processes. I just don't find what passes for entertainment to be very entertaining."

"I see. And I guess the Stang's TV and film options were the first time you've seen anything like those?"

"Correct. I've worked my way through a variety of movies over the past few days. For the most part, they're more interesting than anything currently being streamed, but they're also predictable, insofar as I can understand the dynamics of life and human relationships in the 20th and 21st centuries."

"It does take some getting used to," I noted. "I imagine you were born out here?"

She ignored the question and circled back to what she wanted to talk about. "You're used to it though, having seen most of the ship's catalog. Which brings me back to The Avengers."

I listened as she delved into her problem with the movie, but my thoughts strayed. She had said two things that piqued my interest: physics and complex navigational theories. If those were her areas of expertise, it may provide some insight into what was on the Rox that was drawing so much interest.

"Captain Boyd? What do you think?"

I snapped back to the conversation and realized I hadn't really heard the last sentence or two. Romy gave an annoyed look and repeated her question for me.

"I don't understand whether Bruce Banner can or can't control the Hulk. On the aircraft carrier, he mutates and loses control, but at the end of the movie, he says he's always the Hulk. Do the comics or other movies in the canon explain this?"

On the one hand, sure, that aspect of the movie had always bothered me. But on the other hand, seriously? This woman doesn't talk to anyone on the ship for days, and when she finally does want to have a conversation, it's about a green superhero from ancient movies?

"I wouldn't call myself an expert, but I believe that's what people used to call a plot hole," I answered.

"Plot hole. Meaning?"

"Meaning, uh, it doesn't really make sense in the story."

"Why would they have plot holes in their movies?"

"I don't think they were on purpose. They were mistakes," I explained.

"That's frustrating," she said, seemingly upset. Well, maybe annoyed was a better word. I still wasn't sure if Romy was capable of anger.

"I agree," I said. "Now can I ask you something?"

She was still mulling the Banner-Hulk conundrum, but she nodded.

"You've kept to yourself since you stepped on board. Why was that plot hole so important that you had to ask me about it?"

"I didn't know it was a plot hole at the time."

"Of course. But still, why ask me about it?"

She stood up and moved to the door. "That's easy. I hate problems that can't be solved. They give me insomnia," she said. "Now that I know it was just a dumb mistake, I don't need to discuss it any further."

"Well if you change your mind, ask Gary. He'll have plenty of opinions on the matter."

"He complains too much," she replied.

"If you want to hear him really complain, tell him you think the Hulk could beat Superman in a fight."

"Why would I want to do that?"

"Because it's fun to annoy him," I said.

"That sounds sadistic."

"Oh, it totally is," I joked.

She didn't find it funny.

"What I mean is, it's just a dumb theoretical argument, but it would make Gary upset," I tried to explain. "It can be fun to needle people once in a while."

Romy studied me for a moment.

"I see. Like if I told you that I thought Batista could beat you in a fight," she said, apparently attempting humor.

"No, that's just a fact."

"Oh."

She then walked out without saying another word.

I sat there a few seconds, processing the weirdness of what just happened. Of all the topics I thought we'd discuss, the Hulk conundrum wasn't at the top of my list. I also asked myself a question: what kind of unsolvable problem does a physics and navigation genius get so twisted about, that she has to solve? It could be the key to what was on the Rox.

* * *

"I'm unclear on how this is any of your business," Edgar said, chewing another candy bar. He sat in the chair in his quarters, staring at the monitor. He was watching Predator, a film I'd seen a few times before. It was the scene when Dutch covered himself in mud to avoid detection.

"You know why they made the alien so ugly?" Edgar asked.

"Because he's the bad guy."

"Sure, that's part of that. But there are plenty of good-looking bad guys in movies and TV, from what I've seen so far.

But the aliens are always ugly, as Dutch here said. It's because we're meant to fear what's different. What's grotesque."

"I don't think you're grotesque," I said, catching his drift.

"Maybe you do. Maybe you don't. I watched that Goonies movie, so I can't help but think you were taking a veiled shot at me with the Sloth character."

I had to hand it to the guy – he was perceptive. I pretended to watch the movie with him for a few minutes as I gathered my thoughts.

There are basically two ways to captain a ship: hands on or hands off. I wasn't a fan of surprises, so I chose the hands on option. That meant knowing what to expect from each of the crew members. After my conversation with Jiang, I worried about what Edgar could be capable of with his various enhancements.

"I need to assess any potential threats," I said.

"Threats?" He turned to look at me. "How many times do I have to save your life before you realize how insulting that is? Are you going to ask Batista these questions? She seems more problematic than me."

"Really? How so?"

"She's a liar, for starters," he said. "I've been nothing but honest with you since we met. For example, you annoy me. So I'm telling you that now. Honesty!"

I glared at him and waited. He sighed.

"You're really not gonna leave until we talk about this?"

"I'm not," I replied.

"Look, I get you need to do your captain thing. Some people might even find it cute. I'm not one of those people. But fine, I'll tell you a few things about myself, and then you'll walk out that door. If you don't like that, I'll remove you from the room by force. Are we clear?"

I didn't like being threatened by him, but I was already pushing the boundaries here by demanding he explain to me why he was different. He was right to feel singled out.

He paused the movie and bored his eyes into my soul.

"I was born normal. I'm still normal. I just have titanium braces on some of my bones to strengthen them, along with anti-corrosion implants in 50% of the muscle tissue in my body so they don't break down as easily as your muscles do. Everything else is all natural. My dad was 7 feet tall and I've always been roughly twice as smart as the average human. We done here?"

I nodded and stood up.

"Well I think this was a productive talk," I said. "In the interest of fairness, I should let you know I have .5% more bone density than most people. It's a genetic trait."

"So you have a thick head? I already knew that," he joked, the whisper of a wry smile on his lips.

Just before I left his room, I stopped and turned back, realizing something.

"Titanium on your bones, huh? You should watch X-Men," I told him. "You might like the Wolverine character."

Chapter 18

One of the problems with being a double-agent is that two different sides may decide to kill you. First it was Demond. Then Slay and the federation. And that's not even counting the Rox. We had danger coming at us from all sides.

Before leaving the Burnett, I'd lobbied Slay to have the bounty on the Stang rescinded, but she said it would raise too many eyebrows inside the federation – and outside. In other words, people might start to wonder about me. One of the things she was banking on is that the Rox wouldn't think twice about having me assist their crippled ship if I had an outstanding warrant. But if I was a wrecker with a squeaky clean record, they might keep looking for help elsewhere. Only after we successfully completed the job for her would I get the failsafe off my ship and bounty off my head. Since we were never going to deliver her the device, but instead give it to Desmond, that was just one more complication I could worry about later.

Speaking of Desmond, we quickly made the decision to inform him of the situation with Slay. I didn't really have a choice, as I knew Edgar was going to tell him anyway. I agreed with him anyway – I was already on the outs with the federation, so angering another captain wasn't a big deal.

I didn't want to double-cross Desmond and the Tracers, especially with his man Edgar on the ship. Romy seemed like a free agent more than a fed loyalist, and my hope was to turn her before we made our move on the Rox.

We waited until Romy was asleep and then Batista, Edgar and I contacted Desmond to break the news. We used an encrypted beam Edgar developed just for the occasion to ensure the feds didn't intercept the transmission.

"I can't say I'm surprised someone else is after the device," Desmond said. "Though I wouldn't have guessed the feds would even know about it, let alone the Rox's plan for Jasper. They must have someone on the inside."

"That seems to be going around," I said, glancing at Batista.

"Indeed," Desmond replied. Then he paused and seemed to have an idea.

"What is it?" I asked.

"Once again, the feds are being feds," he said. "They've confirmed that the device is on board the Rox. And they've confirmed our intel is good – that the ship will be at Jasper. If there were any doubts, those are gone now."

"They also did one more thing," I said. "They guaranteed the Rox would need our assistance. Slay doesn't strike me as the bluffing type. When she said the ship would be disabled, she meant it."

"And I strike you as the bluffing type?" Desmond asked.

I had walked right into that one. Edgar grinned. Even Batista cracked a smile.

"I just meant –"

"I know what you meant, Denver, and I agree," Desmond assured me. "While I have absolute faith in Edgar's ability to disable the Rox, that now becomes our backup plan. For all

201

intents and purposes, you are to follow Slay's lead on this one. Once you secure the device, the Bear will take the Burnett out and all's well that ends well."

I cleared my throat. "There's just one thing."

"The failsafe, I know," Desmond said.

"Oh, there's that. I guess there are two things." Everybody looked at me, unsure of what I was getting at. It seemed obvious. "Doesn't anyone else think the Burnett's ability to just show up unannounced wherever and whenever it wants is a problem?"

Batista and Edgar looked at Desmond on the monitor. He thought for a few moments before responding, his eyes searching for the right words. Finally, he nodded.

"Nothing in life is easy," he said. "But I also don't plan to be fooled twice. They won't be surprising us anymore. Not with the proximity beacon we attached to their ship before detonating the unmanned drone. If the Burnett comes within 50,000 miles of us, we'll know. And this time I'm going to have reinforcements."

Before we cut the transmission, we agreed on beam silence until we reached Jasper, or if the situation changed. Edgar would send any pertinent info to the Golden Bear as needed. Desmond was in good spirits, buoyed by the confirmation that the Rox had the sought-after cargo on board.

When he disappeared from the screen, I turned to Batista.

"When did my brother contact you last?"

She pretended to be surprised by the random question, but I saw through it. She sighed.

"Yesterday."

"And he knows about how much of this?"

Batista eyed Edgar, wary of passing along too much information. I waved her concerns away.

"I think we're past the point of keeping secrets on this," I said. "At least I hope we are. My goal is to get out of this alive, then get as far away from the center of the verse as possible. The only way we do that is by laying all our cards on the table."

I thought it was a pretty good little speech, but neither Batista nor Edgar said a word in response. I was about to try again when Batista cleared her throat and looked at Edgar, who shook his head as if to say "don't tell him."

Batista crossed her arms. "The reason the Burnett keeps sneaking up on us isn't because it has stealth capabilities."

Edgar growled his annoyance, but Batista proceeded anyway.

"It's because they have a warp drive."

It took a moment for that to sink in. I looked at Edgar, who reluctantly nodded.

"Like…an actual warp drive? We talking Star Trek level?" I asked.

"I don't know what Star Trek is," Batista replied.

Edgar nodded. He'd clearly been making progress in the sci-fi category of the Stang's entertainment catalog. "Star Trek level."

"Then that's what is on the Rox too," I said, mostly to myself as the other two people in the room already knew the answer.

"Yep," said the fourth person in the room. It was Romy. She leaned in and frowned. "The Burnett has a partially-working warp drive installed. It was a prototype. They can go three times the speed of the Stang. Fast enough to sneak up on anybody in the verse, no matter how careful their radar is. The Rox, on the other hand, has the finished product. They stole it from our lab on Mars, where we developed it for the feds. That drive? That one is a verse-changer. We're talking 100 million miles per hour."

"You're telling me the most dangerous ship in the verse has warp capabilities?"

"No," she said. "They haven't installed it yet. The man they need to do that got religion after he realized how terrible his invention would prove to be if it fell into the wrong hands. Which inventions always do. Most hands are wrong. He's on Jasper. The Rox isn't going to Jasper to destroy it, they're going there to threaten to destroy it if the man, Albert Marcum, doesn't activate the drive. And the only way to install and activate the drive is to –"

"Disable the ship," I said, astounded.

"Only they don't know that yet. Or at least that's what Slay is betting on."

We all looked at each other. All the cards were on the table… almost.

"Why are you telling us this?" I asked Romy.

"Because I don't want to go back to the Burnett. And I don't want the Rox to have warp capabilities. From what I've heard about that ship, I would never outlive the guilt if people like that were alone in their ability to use the device I helped create."

* * *

Warp speed was supposed to be the stuff of science fiction. In the classic show Star Trek, one warp was roughly equivalent to the speed of light. Or about 186,000 miles per second. According to Romy, the speed achievable by the new drive was 30,000 miles per second. Not nearly the speed of TV and movies, but fast enough to travel across the verse and beyond in mere hours, as opposed to lifetimes.

It made contact with non-humans not only possible, but inevitable. And until the technology was widespread, it would give ships with warp capabilities an insane advantage over traditional vessels in matters of war and commerce.

Plus, it was *really* freaking cool.

Dangerous, sure. But cool. Ever since I was a kid, I'd dreamed about being able to escape to far-off planets and galaxies. As big as the verse was, it was also pretty small at the same time. A warp drive would change that forever.

There were always rumors of warp projects in labs across the verse. These scientists over here were close. That genius at the university has an idea. One problem always stopped them dead in their tracks, however: navigating around objects in space at warp speed. Satellites. Meteors. Planets. Crashing into (and through) a planet at 3,000 miles per second tends to be pretty fatal.

Enter a 5-foot-tall emo kid with a knack for physics and navigational theory.

Somehow, the girl in the leather jacket who spent 99% of her time glued to her handheld cracked the problem that had stymied some of the brightest minds in the galaxy.

And now she was feeling pretty nervous about her role in the project.

"There's more," I told her.

After the meeting broke up, Romy stopped by my quarters again for another heart-to-heart chat. I was starting to get the vibe she'd never been close with her parents. I was a dad type in her mind. That made me feel both old and uncomfortable at the same time.

She looked at me and wanted to say something, but she couldn't bring herself to do it.

"I can't help you if you don't tell me what's going on," I said.

She screwed her face into a confused grimace. "Oh, you thought I was here to ask for your help? I'm deciding if I should tell you something that might help you. But now I think if you had the information, it might influence your decisions in a way that could actually get you killed."

"I see," I said. I had no clue what she was trying to say.

"Forget it. You'll find out at the right time and hopefully, it'll save your life."

"Hopefully?"

"Probably. Definitely probably," she said.

"Can't argue with that logic," Gary said, sarcastically. "Romy, why don't you tell me and I can determine if Denver needs to know?"

"I don't trust the judgment of a sitcom writer, sorry."

Damn. That was what they used to call a burn.

"I was also a sitcom star!" Gary yelled. "And you didn't even know what a sitcom was until like three days ago!"

Romy shrugged and walked out the door, leaving me annoyed.

"She's a weird one," Gary said.

"Thank you, captain obvious," I replied.

"Wanna talk about it?" he asked.

"Talk about what."

"You've been pretty stressed lately, and it's obvious why," Gary said.

"Uh, because we're about to try and steal the most coveted device in the verse from the dangerous ship in history? And if we fail, we die. And if we succeed, we might die anyway?"

"Right, that," he said. "But also, your brother. It has to be a total mind-fry to find out that he's still alive, and you've barely talked about it."

I paused. It wasn't like Gary to care about emotions and feelings.

"Maybe I've been busy with trying not to be killed, myself," I told him. "And what's gotten into you? Let's talk about you for a minute."

"I'm good."

"I don't know. I think you're hiding something. And I'm starting to think I've honored my uncle's wishes long enough."

"What could a regular guy like me possibly be hiding?" Gary asked. "I don't even have pockets!"

"Well it's not a sense of humor, we know that."

"It's not my fault you don't understand 21st century humor. Your Uncle E, on the other hand, knew the dealio. Dealio is a slang term we used back in the day."

"I've seen Napoleon Dynamite."

"That doesn't make you an expert, Denver."

"Go to bed."

"But I don't want to!" he whined. I looked at the camera above the door and waited. The red light finally blipped off. I sighed and laid back on my bed, staring at the ceiling of the room. On top of everything else, the last thing I needed was a problem with Gary. The Stang meant so much to my uncle, and Gary was part of it. Shutting him off would feel like cutting a piece of my uncle's heart out of the ship. With both of my parents gone, I'd always thought of the Stang as the last member of my family because it was infused with so many memories of my uncle.

Of course, that was before I knew my brother was still

around.

I flipped through the Stang's entertainment catalog to take my mind off things for a while. It usually worked when I was facing a tough job or needed a break from the grind of lonely, long range space travel. These were different problems and worries altogether, so it was time to pull out the big guns.

Cate Blanchett's haunting yet beautiful opening narration of the Fellowship of the Ring began, and I tried to immerse myself in the 20th century's most epic fantasy. At last count, I had watched the full Lord of the Rings trilogy 18 times. On half of those occasions, they were back-to-back-to-back viewings of the three movies. My uncle once told me that it was called a "movie marathon."

The tale was set in another time and place, of course, but there was something comforting about the clear delineation between good and evil. I much preferred it to the world of gray.

You were either on the side of Frodo, Sam, Gandalf and the bunch, or you were a slave to Sauron, the Dark Lord of Mordor, a barren wasteland filled with wretched creatures. On occasion, I'd considered space to be like Mordor; it had no soul. It was endless. Cold. Dead. One false step and it could kill you without a second thought.

One does not simply walk into space, I thought to myself.

The story revolved around the quest to destroy a sacred ring of power. If the good guys succeeded, evil would be defeated forever. If they failed, the world would fall into darkness. Again, I liked those simple outcomes.

In real life, especially in the current verse, there was no such clarity. Sometimes you did a good thing. Sometimes a bad thing. And other times, you thought you were on the side of justice, only to find out later you were working for the wrong kind of people. That's why I liked watching movies. They were the ultimate means of escape. For a few hours, my actual troubles were miles away. All I cared about was the fate of someone else who, most of the time, was on a noble quest.

Unfortunately, all I could think about was the job at hand. Even the greatest wizard the world had ever seen couldn't save me from that. I fell asleep thinking not of hobbits and Middle Earth, but space pirates and federation bounty hunters.

Chapter 19

"Dad won't even know we're gone," Avery said. "Besides, he doesn't really care what we do on our own time. I mean, he'd probably be proud of you for having the balls to break a rule for once in your life."

My brother tucked his curly brown hair under a black cap. He was 18 and looked a few years older than that, thanks to the thin mustache he sported. I was only 15 and had exactly zero whiskers on my face. Next to him I probably looked all of 12.

I rose from my cot and felt the cold steel of the ship's deck under my feet.

"Might want to put on shoes first, Denny," he said.

I hated being called Denny. Which is why he called me that. I was pretty sure my brother liked me, but I was damn sure he liked annoying me. He tossed me a spare cap and told me I would look older if I wore it. I put it on and he cocked his head to the side and studied my face.

"Nope, never mind. You still look like a girl. But hey, maybe they'll think you're cute and let you in because of it."

* * *

Aside from the Earth, Mars was the only inhabited planet in the solar system. Earth's moon had a few dozen colonies on it, but it wasn't technically a planet.

The first colony on Mars, dubbed New Chicago, had been founded a hundred years earlier. It eventually grew from a few pods to the planet's capital city. During that transformation, buildings were erected, underground subway tunnels were excavated, and people did what they do: made more people. Those new people, born on Martian soil, felt no emotional connection to Earth. To them, Mars wasn't a colony, or just another extension of Earth. It was their home planet. Earth was a dot on the horizon to them.

I was born on Earth, but had spent the majority of my life in space, and I felt the same way as Martians. What did I owe that blue marble?

Still, as much as I admired the idea of Mars and the audacity of forming an entire society there, my first impression of the planet was that it could use a new coat of paint. The structures at least. They were all gray. Viewed from the Sheffield as our ship had broken atmo earlier that day, the surface of Mars was covered with a series of gray bubbles, all connected with thin corridors. I knew there were also subways underneath the planet's surface, but that just made it seem worse, like Martians had been forced to live like rats.

Vinit Padma, perhaps the most famous Martian in history, and the planet's first president, once said Mars should not be judged by the eyes, but by the human spirit itself. Meaning sure, the place wasn't pretty, but it was damn impressive it even existed at all. The Republic of Mars was a triumph of human ingenuity and, in Padma's mind, was man's crowning achievement to date.

211

That may have been true in the theoretical sense, but the first corridor I stepped in smelled like whiskey and death. Maybe the guy should have said not to judge it with your nose, either.

This wasn't exactly what I'd expected of the best bar on Mars, but I guess my idea of "best" was different from my brother's. He had been talking about the Red Desert since we first heard our dad's ship would be making the trip to Mars a few months earlier. I'd only joined the crew a few months before that, so I was still just a babe in the woods (whatever that meant), according to my brother.

The Red Desert was the oldest bar on the red planet, as the faded and crusty sign on the metal edifice proclaimed. It had been around nearly 70 years, and it seemed like nothing had been updated in that time. The walls were partially corroded and the windows that looked out onto the main corridor of downtown New Chicago were caked yellow. The sign said there was a max capacity of 50 people, which I found surprising given how small the building was. It couldn't have been more than 20 feet wide.

Avery smiled at me as he opened the heavy black door to the establishment. If the outside of the place smelled bad, the inside wasn't much of an improvement. There was so much vape smoke, it was like walking into a dirty cloud. I got a contact buzz before I made it to the bar.

The guy behind the long counter was in his late 50's. His nose was a deep purple color and what was left of his hair was stark white with age. He grimaced as he saw us sit in two stools opposite him. Well, he mostly grimaced at me.

"Hey Joe," my brother said with a casual nod. "What's poppin'?"

The guy, whose name was apparently Joe, turned his gaze to my brother. He didn't know him. Then he turned his purple nose back at me.

"How old are you? 12?" he asked.

"Old enough," Avery responded, before I had the chance. Then he used his handheld to transfer a few credits. Joe saw this and thought about it.

"Still too young. The Mars Police show up in here, see this little pissant, and they could shut me down," he said. It was obviously a lie. The Mars Police didn't care about bars and licenses. But it was his place and he was squeezing for more credits. My brother shook his head.

"That's enough," he said. "We want two rum and sodas. You can either serve us or I'll give an even better story to the Mars Police about the weapons smuggling business you run on the side."

Joe's face went red and I thought he was going to grab Avery with one of his huge hands and crush his skull, but instead he turned to make our drinks. Avery smiled at me.

"You gotta know how to talk to people, Denny," he said. He then explained that dad had once delivered some weapons to Joe back in the day, so he knew the guy was dealing on the side. Avery called it having "leverage" on someone.

I just nodded as if I understood. While I was excited to be out in New Chicago with my big brother, I didn't want any trouble. Avery said dad wouldn't care, but I'd begged to be on his crew for years and now that I was, I didn't want to do anything that might get me kicked back to living with mom.

"What do you think?" Avery asked after Joe handed us our drinks in metal cups.

"Smells worse than the lukewarm beer we have on the ship,"

213

I said. "And I haven't even tried it yet."

My brother laughed, genuinely amused. He gave me a hard time about a lot of things, but he did seem to like my sense of humor.

"I was talking about New Chicago, not the damn drink," he said.

I told him I was underwhelmed. And it was true. I'd heard a lot of tales about the capital of Mars, many of them from my brother. Some people claimed it was the baddest city in the verse outside of Earth. To me, it seemed depressing. I'd never been to Earth, so I couldn't make that comparison, but I'd always preferred stations to planetary cities. The cities always felt more manufactured with their domes and corridors and recycled oxygen. Something about being on a planet but not being able to breathe the air was just wrong. On a station, it made sense. And because stations were in constant motion, the air recyclers worked better. The planet recyclers just never quite did the trick for me.

"Last time I take you anywhere fun," he said.

"Point me to the fun," I replied.

Avery nodded and got a dangerous gleam in his eye. I knew it well. Every time it happened, I regretted it. Avery knocked on the bar, loudly, forcing Joe to come over.

"Hit that bar again and I'll use one of those illegal weapons you somehow know about," he warned. Avery put up his hands in a move of mock surrender.

"I was just sitting here with my brother, who turns 18 today," he lied. "And he was complaining that he wasn't having a good time."

"If he's a day over 14, I wouldn't believe it."

Avery laughed, trying to warm Joe up to him. It wasn't

working. Still, he transferred a bunch of credits to the bar. "I'd like him to remember this birthday, if you know what I mean."

Joe looked from my brother to me, and back again. He sighed and rolled his eyes.

* * *

She was at least 45. While my brother wanted to show me a good time, he apparently didn't have the credits to find someone even remotely close to my age. Or maybe it was just how things worked on Mars; all the companions were older.

The sex didn't last long.

The woman made a passing remark about it being my birthday, then got down to business. She pushed me back onto the musty cot and undressed me. Her hands were warm but her eyes were cold. She had long hair that was dyed brown and purple, and she wore what seemed to be a lot of makeup. An abundance of perfume made the whole room smell like lilac and vanilla. Despite my nerves, she had me ready to go in no time, and then a couple minutes later, it was over. We never kissed or spoke during the time she was on top of me — it was a purely mechanical affair. She had rocked her hips gently at first, then sped up as she sensed I was close. Her eyes remained distant and focused somewhere else, and the smile she provided felt like what it was – a perfunctory part of the service. There was no joy in it, that was for sure.

It wasn't at all how I pictured my first time going. I at least thought I'd know the girl. And her being paid never even dawned on me as a possibility. When she was finished, the woman simply pulled her tight orange shirt back over her

215

head, gave me a playful tap on the leg and left me alone in the room to pull my pants back up.

I laid there for a few minutes, my body satisfied. It had felt weird, wrong and good all at the same time. I wondered if it would always feel that way. No, I decided. It wasn't normal. I grew upset with my brother and wondered if he secretly wanted to ruin the moment for me. Yet another way of giving his younger brother a hard time.

When I walked back downstairs to the main bar area, Avery was joking loudly with someone in a grey shirt. He was a Silver Star captain. My brother caught sight of me, grinned slyly, and waved me over. Even though I knew the sex was bought and paid for, I felt strangely confident as I approached the bar. Avery introduced me to the Silver Star guy, Lucas. "This is my baby bro. Well, he was my baby bro. Now he's a man."

I nodded, unsure of what to say. It was weird enough having Avery tell a random stranger I had just lost my virginity, but I also thought we didn't get along with Silver Star people, so I wasn't sure why they were hanging out together in the first place.

"Popped your cherry, huh?" Lucas said, his foul breath full of alcohol and rotted teeth. He smiled so wide I could see the dark spots where his back teeth should have been. "I lost mine when I was 10."

"Well Denny has always been a late bloomer," Avery said. "Denny, go hit the bathroom and wash up. I need a minute to talk with Lucas here."

As I followed my brother's advice, I looked over my shoulder and saw him and Lucas talking under their breath so nobody else could hear them. I felt a knot form in the pit of my stomach. Dad had always told us that Silver Star was the enemy. They were our chief rival and the guy in charge, Jack Largent, had some kind of personal vendetta against my father.

An hour later, we were sneaking back onto the ship as everyone slept. We made it unnoticed all the way to our shared quarters. Once inside, we slid the door closed and flipped on the light.

"Hey boys," my dad said. He was laying on my brother's bunk with his hands behind his head. "Pro tip. Next time you sneak off the ship when we're docked, turn off your handhelds. It's a little thing called a tracking beacon."

I looked at my brother, pissed. He wasn't worried, but he didn't have as much at stake as I did. He shrugged.

"Good to know, Rick," Avery said, playing it off as if he wasn't worried we were caught. Like everyone else on the crew (besides me), Avery called my dad by his first name. Formal titles like captain were rarely used on the Sheffield.

My dad hopped up off the bunk and cracked Avery on the side of the head. I flinched and waited for my turn, but it never came. Avery's eyes were red as he fought back the tears, not wanting to give our old man the satisfaction.

"I expect it from you," he told Avery, before glaring at me, disappointed. "But your mom told me you were a good kid. I guess that's one more thing she was wrong about..."

My dad's words trailed off as he studied me. He twitched his nose.

"Either one of you is wearing perfume, or you had some fun in town tonight. Maybe at Red Desert?" he asked. He looked back at Avery, who glanced ever so briefly at me, but that was enough.

"I guess some exceptions can be made if this was the night you got laid for the first time," he said.

I didn't know what to say, so I just kept my mouth shut. That must have been the right thing to do, because my dad simply mussed up my hair and headed to the door. Before leaving, he turned back.

"One-time pass," he warned.

Once he was gone, I punched my brother as hard as I could in the arm. It stung him and he jumped back, surprised. He wanted to tackle me. Something held him back.

"That's how you thank me for getting you some tail?" he asked.

"Why were you talking to the Silver Star guy?" I accused.

"Don't worry about it."

"Is that why you didn't tell dad? So he wouldn't worry about it, either?"

Avery lunged at me and caught me by the shoulders. He slammed a fist into my cheek. "One word about this gets to the old man and you're dead, Denny. Got it?"

It wasn't the first time I'd been punched in the face by Avery, and it hadn't even been the hardest (it barely hurt), but I'd never seen him so angry. I knew he'd been doing something dad would've been really pissed about. I quickly nodded and wriggled out of his grasp.

"You're just a kid," he said. "You wouldn't get it. But someday you'll know what dad's really like. In this verse, there's only one person that's always looking out for you, Denny, and that's you. Not dad. Not me. Not even mom. Don't you ever forget it."

And with that, he flipped off the light and plunked down onto his cot. I stood there in the dark, shaking with anger and nerves. Deep down, I knew he was right about looking out for ourselves. It didn't make me feel any better, though.

The next day, I sat at my normal spot in the galley. It was a table off in the corner. Normally I would eat alone, or with Avery if he was feeling charitable. It wasn't so much that the rest of the crew avoided me. I just didn't feel like one of them. On my first day aboard the ship, my dad had warned me it would take time, and I shouldn't force it, or they would sense my desperation.

About half of the crew was in the galley eating, my dad among them. When he saw me sit down in the corner, he grabbed what was left of his meal and walked over.

"This seat taken?" he asked.

It was the first time he'd offered to sit with me. I was more surprised than anything, but I tried to play it cool and kicked out the seat for him. He smiled as he sat down.

"So, tell me about it."

I could feel my face getting hot. I hadn't slept much the night before. I'd spent much of the night conflicted about how I'd lost my virginity. I could tell my father wanted me to be proud and macho about it, so I did my best to tell him it wasn't bad and that the woman said I was a natural. In other words, I lied.

I'll never know if my dad realized I was stretching the truth, because the real reason he came over wasn't to share in the moment (as twisted as that was). He wanted intel.

"What were you guys doing there, anyway?" he asked between bites, trying to be innocent about it. "I mean, did you see Avery talking to anyone?"

I was angry. I also felt stupid. I'd thought, for a fleeting moment, that my dad had taken an actual interest in me. When it turned out he was just trying to squeeze information out of me, I wanted to scream. I wanted to tell him Avery was, in fact, meeting with his rival, just to see his face when he knew he'd been betrayed by his favorite son.

But I knew if I did that, I'd be playing right into his hands. I didn't even know why Avery was talking with the guy. Maybe it was just a little side hustle or he was selling him uppers or something.

"Mostly just the bartender," I said.

My dad frowned. In that moment, I could see his interest in me disappear. Either I didn't know or I wouldn't tell him, he must have figured. He abruptly got up from his chair and started to walk away. Then he stopped and turned.

"I hope you wore a jimmy," he joked. "Those New Chicago companions have a lot of mileage on them."

I'd never told him the woman was a companion. I guess he just assumed.

* * *

Before I had time to fully process the anger I felt, Avery hopped into the seat next to me.

"What did he want?" he asked.

"To congratulate me."

"I bet. The old man's a real dog," he said. "I'm sure mom told you about it."

My mother had alluded to my father's affairs, but she never spoke of any of them specifically. Despite the clear issues between her and dad, she was content to take the high road and not talk too much trash about him. She knew no matter what

220

happened, he would always be my dad. And she respected that. It didn't hurt that she was happier without him. I didn't know if the same could be said of my dad.

"That's all you talked about?" my brother asked, trying to seem just as casual as my dad when mining for information. It struck me how similar they were. I knew I was more like my mom. "He didn't want to know what else we were doing in New Chicago. What I was doing?"

"What were you doing, Avery? Other than hanging out with Silver Star captains."

Avery wanted to smack me again, but it was too public a venue. He contained his anger and lowered his voice. "What did you say, Denny."

"This time? I kept my mouth shut. But if you don't tell me what's going on, maybe I'll be more honest next time."

Avery studied my face for a moment, seeing if I was bluffing. I didn't even know if I was, which meant it was a good bluff indeed. He nodded. "Not here. C'mon."

We left the galley and headed to the cargo bay. It was deserted. It was also fairly empty, as we had dropped off a shipment of air recycler filters the day before. We weren't usually a cargo hauler, as our bread and butter was as a wrecking vessel, fixing and towing other ships from around the verse. But on the long hauls, my dad liked to maximize his profits by transporting goods.

My brother checked to make sure nobody was around. Satisfied we were alone, he led me to the back of the bay, behind a few storage crates. Each of the crates were marked with numbers – codes to identify the goods inside. I was too new to the ship to know what the codes meant, but for someone who'd been on board, you could pretty much tell what was in a box before popping it just by looking at the first few letters and numbers. F22. X1A. Shorthand like that. Like I said, I didn't know what they stood for.

Avery pointed to a crate marked F31.

"Anything with an F designation means Filters," he said. "Pretty simple. 31 means it's got three of one 1 type of filter. Understand?"

I nodded. I knew we weren't there to talk about air filters, so I waited for him to proceed.

"So last night, when I gave you that nice present, do you think I paid for it with my salary on this ship?" he asked.

That had been bothering me. How could my brother afford his "present" as he called it?

"If the old man paid a fair wage, I wouldn't do this," he said. "But he doesn't, so we all have some side hustles."

"What's yours?"

"Supply and demand, Denny. Supply and demand."

I was lost. He smiled and put a hand on my shoulder.

"People need filters. Sure. But they also need other things," he explained. "So when we hit a port like New Chicago, where I've got connections, I see what else they need and slip 'em in with the filters."

He was smuggling things. Why didn't he just say that?

"I smuggle stuff," he said, proudly. I shook my head.

"Like what?"

"Booze. Drugs. Hell, tube socks for all I care. Whatever they need that I can get my hands on. I pick up stuff from one port and take it to the next. Just like dad does. Only it's my own little operation. Could be ours, actually, if you want in."

He dangled the offer as a way to shut me up. I was young, but I wasn't dumb. I knew he was trying to buy my silence.

"What does Silver Star have to do with it?" I asked.

Avery sighed. "We're not the only ship in the verse with access to good stuff, Denny. There are dozens of Silver Star ships out there stopping at stations all over, and so sometimes I gotta make a deal with them. It's not personal like it is with dad and Largent. It's just business."

"What did the Silver Star guy at the Red Desert have?"

"It doesn't matter. The point is, I wanted it and now it's in this box, along with those air filters. You in or you out?"

I looked at my brother and knew my answer would forever dictate the nature of our relationship.

Chapter 20

There were bodies everywhere.

Face down on the floor. Slumped at their stations. Strewn about the galley. Except for the sound of our boot heels clicking on the metal grates as we stepped over the still members of the crew, the Rox was silent.

I looked at the timer on my handheld and it said we had 12 minutes and 18 seconds before people started waking up from the Halothane I'd smuggled on board and fed into the ventilation system.

Romy followed closely behind me, looking even more hipster-punk than usual with a black gas mask covering her face. Her eyes were wide as she surveyed the bodies of the crew.

"They'll be fine in a few minutes," I assured her.

"That's what I'm afraid of," she said, her voice muffled from the mask.

I reminded her to flip on her comm link. She did and I heard her voice crisply in my earpiece. I whirled around quickly as more boots clicked in the corridor behind us.

I saw Edgar's eyes smiling above his gas mask as he looked at the former members of his crew, laid out at his feet. "Nice work," he said. Batista turned the corner.

"Alright, we have 11 minutes and 8 seconds to get back on the Stang," I informed everyone.

"Don't you mean the Ford 5.0?" Gary joked in my earpiece.

"Whatever. Let's go."

* * *

Four hours earlier, we had received the distress call from the Rox.

We were spinning our drive about 30,000 miles from Jasper Station, waiting for the signal to come in. I didn't want to get too close to Jasper, as I feared the Rox's captain might think it was a little too coincidental that his ship was disabled and the Stang happened to be right in the neighborhood, waiting for the distress call.

According to Edgar, the captain was a brilliant but volatile guy. His name was Grissom, but everyone called him Griss. He didn't like being called by his formal title of captain, for some reason. Edgar didn't know much about his background, but he said the entire time he was on the Rox with Griss, he only saw one person challenge his authority. Griss made an example of the guy, snapping his neck with his bare hands while the crew was eating dinner. He then ordered that the body remain where it dropped for two days so it could serve as a gruesome reminder of what happened when you questioned his judgment. I got the impression that even Edgar, who had serious problems following rules, probably kept his natural instincts in check. I wondered how my brother had survived more than a week on the Rox. He was an insubordinate pain in the butt on his best days.

Shortly before the call came in, Batista gave us a heads up

that Avery had messaged her to say that Marcum had agreed to come on board and activate the warp drive. I realized I would soon be seeing my brother face to face, if the plan worked. I wasn't sure if I was going to punch him or hug him. Probably both, in that order.

We had rehearsed how I'd answer the distress call if Griss wanted a face to face beam. Edgar and Romy would be nowhere in sight. It would just be me and Batista in the cabin. And Pirate, most likely (I left that decision up to him). It turned out Griss did in fact want to chat, so Batista and I cleared the cabin then I leaned back in the chair to collect my thoughts.

I accepted the transmission and a man with bulging neck muscles and a shock of red hair filled the screen. He tilted his head and just studied me for a moment, then glanced at Batista with a grin.

"You single?" he asked.

"No," I replied.

He narrowed his eyes. "I was talking to the lady, kid."

"Ah, my bad."

Batista folded her arms, nonplussed. "Single but not looking."

Griss grunted and grinned once more, apparently liking her sass. Then he turned to me.

"Ford 5.0. What's that about?"

"It's a long story."

"I got time."

"It's a reference to the ship's real call sign," I explained. "It's not exactly safe to advertise that one right now. I'm sure you understand."

"I'll tell you mine if you tell me yours," Griss said. Just as he did so, my scans confirmed his weapons were hot. Locked and loaded, as they used to say.

"Deal. You first."

"I'm Grissom, and this here is the Roxelle Baker."

He leaned closer to get a good look at my reaction. That was the part I had practiced the most leading up to the transmission. First, I pretended to be surprised. Then, with a little bit of fear in my voice, I simply said "No way."

Griss made a gesture that indicated I could believe him or not, he didn't care. "And you are?"

"Denver Boyd, captain of the Mustang 1."

A flicker of recognition showed on his face. He'd heard of us. He looked offscreen at someone and then nodded.

"I could make a lot of credits bringing you in if that's true," he said. "There's a warrant for 10,000 credits on your head. I'm actually impressed, to be honest."

That was news to me. I hadn't heard the bounty was upped yet again. It was hard to keep track of it with all the other stuff going on. I guess that's one good aspect of being handed problem after problem, you start to forget just how many are on your plate.

"Yeah, but if you're really the Rox, assuming that ship even exists, you aren't bringing us in to the feds for 10,000 measly credits," I said.

"Good answer," Griss admitted. "But I'm still trying to figure out why you're spinning your drive out here in the middle of nowhere."

"We were thinking about heading to Jasper. Then I remembered there was no beer on the station."

Griss laughed. He nodded his head. "Believers. Can't stand the lot of them. Nothing good ever came from religion."

"If you say so."

"I do say so. And I also say you should head over here pronto, as I got a power supply issue that is baffling my lead mechanic. Or I should say it *was* baffling him. He's not currently my lead mechanic anymore. He's just a grease stain in space."

I could tell he wasn't bluffing. The dude had killed his own crewmember for not being able to do his job.

"I hope for your sake you're as good as the rumors suggest," he said. Then he cut the transmission.

I exhaled loudly. Batista relaxed a bit too and leaned back in her chair.

"Never liked Ruddy anyway," Edgar said. "He was a worthless mechanic. You've gotta be at least as good as him."

"Thanks for the vote of confidence."

I set our navigation to intercept the Rox a thousand miles off Jasper Station. The trip would take a few hours. Once Edgar had created another encrypted beam, we contacted Slay and told her the particulars. We would get aboard the Rox and retrieve the item (the details of which I pretended we still didn't know). Once we disconnected from the Rox, Slay and the Burnett would magically warp-swoop in and destroy the sniper ship before they knew what hit them.

Then, we'd rendezvous with the Burnett, deliver the merchandise and be on our merry way. At least that was Slay's version of events. Ours ended with the Golden Bear blasting the Burnett to hell and then we'd deliver the drive to Desmond. And then – hopefully – he would honor his end of the bargain and let me continue running from the fed bounty on my head that seemed to be growing by the day.

We went over the game plan a couple times as we made our trip to meet the Rox. It was dangerous, but fairly simple. Romy and I would board the ship first, with her posing as my apprentice. I had a toolbox with a hidden compartment in it, where I would hide the Halothane. While we worked on fixing the ship, we'd slip the sleeping gas into the ship's ventilation system, knocking everyone out. Upon receiving the all-clear, Edgar and Batista would join us on board and then we'd get the warp drive, Marcum and my brother off the ship before anyone woke up.

That was the idea, anyway.

Any number of things could go wrong. Maybe someone on the Rox would recognize Romy. Or Marcum Marcum, the genius, would see Romy (who used to be on his team) and tip off the crew. Then there was my brother. What if he was playing for the other side?

There were so many variables it was making my head spin. So when we finally saw the long, cylindrical ship come into view, I was more than ready to just get on with it already.

Edgar had raided the Stang's armory and was disappointed with what he found. He and Batista geared up for battle anyway, each of them strapped with no fewer than four weapons each. Romy and I had nothing, unless you counted my tools, which had been used as weapons more times than once, of course.

The first thing I noticed when I stepped on the Rox were the faces. They didn't belong to insecure feds or calculating Tracers. This was a motley crew of dead-eyed, angry men and women. It was about as cheerful as a graveyard. Three men waited for Romy and I as we crossed the airlock gate onto their ship. They didn't bother brandishing their weapons. It was a given that we did as they said or we (and our ship) were toast. We might've been toast anyway.

Griss himself rounded the corner and moved to the front of

the welcoming party, so to speak. He was stout and compact, like one solid piece of muscle that had been molded into a mostly normal-looking human being. He looked at Romy and I.

"What happened to your shoulder?" he asked, noting the sling I still had protecting my right arm.

"Fell off the bed during a nap," I lied.

He nodded. Didn't really care about the answer, it seemed. Then he checked the corridor behind us. "Where's the hot one?"

I shrugged, not wanting to give anything away. He appraised Romy, then shook his head.

"Whatever. Let's go."

They led us into the main engine room. Griss told us to watch our step. He was referring to a large smear of blood that was still slick. Must have belonged to his lead mechanic, RIP. The blood was pooled in a large puddle, and long red drag marks trailed toward the exit. Romy blanched at the sight of the mess.

I spotted a large object in the corner of the room with a tarp over it. Considering its size and the two burly men standing guard next to it, I figured that was the warp drive. Romy recovered long enough to nod, almost imperceptibly, indicating it was probably what we were looking for. It was connected to the turbines with a host of wires and a wide metal duct of some kind.

Closer to where we stood, Griss showed me a panel on the wall that had been stripped away, revealing the long intake tube of the engine core. This tube was how the reactor transmitted energy from the core to the turbines.

"My guy said the problem was somewhere in here before

he was retired," Griss explained.

I touched the wall and felt the hum of the life support systems. They were still working with no problems. Griss nodded. "The reactor is fine. Just can't get the turbines to fire. You've got two hours. I'll leave you to it."

"Two hours?" I complained. It was just for show. I had no intention of being on the ship more than 20 minutes. I'd already spotted a ventilation duct we could use to disperse the Halothane.

"Fair enough. Three hours. If you can't get us going by then, well, on to the next mechanic, I guess."

Griss and his entourage left the engine room. The two men guarding the warp drive remained. Damnit. Somehow we'd have to distract them long enough to get the gas into the vents.

I opened my toolbox and grabbed a flashlight to take a look at the intake tube. Romy kneeled next to me, getting close enough to chat without the two thugs hearing us.

"What now?" she asked, nervous.

I looked at the space between the wall and tube, then looked at her. She was skinny enough, maybe. She frowned, knowing what I was thinking. "You have to be kidding," Romy said.

I handed her the flashlight. She started climbing into the open space of the wall.

"Hey! Where the hell is she going?" one of the big guys asked, his hand moving toward his gun.

"Your boss wanted us to fix this. Well, the problem is in there. Unless you want us to take apart the entire damn engine, I gotta send my girl here to crawl in and do the work. Or maybe you wanna tell Griss you're the reason we can't fix it."

The guy just glared at me for a few moments. Finally, he nodded. Romy started to wiggle into the open space. Once she had cleared the panel, I put my toolbox in behind her. She grabbed it.

"How am I supposed to get up there?" she complained. She was at floor level and the venting was near the ceiling of the room.

"You don't."

Ah. She understood me now. I turned to the guys on the other side of the room and told them to prepare for a little steam. "We need to drain the core of some fumes," I lied. They had no idea what the hell I was talking about anyway. Just as I was about to give Romy the signal, the door to the engine room opened.

A thin man with glasses and a full head of white-blonde hair was pushed inside. He nearly tripped over his feet, but recovered in time to avoid the blood puddle with a gasp. It was Marcum.

Griss stepped in behind him.

"If you have any technical questions, he's here to observe," Griss explained. "He's the one who screwed this pooch in the first place."

Despite being visibly scared out of his mind, Marcum defended his actions, saying his area of expertise was in installing the device into other types of ships, at which point Griss cut him off. He gave him a look as if to say he better not divulge any more about what was under the tarp.

"If they have questions, you answer them," Griss snapped.

"They?" Marcum asked.

Romy, out of instinct, popped her head out from behind the open area of the wall. Marcum's eyes went wide and for a moment, I thought he was going to get us killed with his next few words.

"What is it?" Griss asked, noting the look of shock on Marcum's face.

"Nothing. She just surprised me appearing out of nowhere like that," he said, recovering.

Griss raised his eyebrows and exited the room. Marcum looked warily at the men in the corner by the tarp, then stepped over the blood trail toward me and Romy.

"I'm Denver," I said, extending my hand.

Marcum shook it and introduced himself. Then I went through the unnecessary process of introducing Romy as my apprentice. I noted a small twinkle in his eye and grin at the idea that Romy had something to learn from a mechanic like me.

Romy looked at him. "Got any tips for us?"

Chapter 21

Marcum went down with the other two guys. There was no way to warn him, but I did catch his body as he passed out. I eased him to the floor. The taller of the men guarding the warp drive landed face first on the metal with a sickening splat.

Romy climbed out of the wall opening with her mask in place. She had released a small amount of the Halothane locally to buy us more time before we knocked out the full crew.

I grabbed a pair of zip ties from my toolbox and secured the hands of the Rox men just in case they woke up earlier than expected.

Then I pulled the tarp away to look at the drive. I was shocked at how compact it was. The whole thing couldn't have been more than five feet long. It looked like a series of concentric circles folded in on themselves and then splayed out at one end, like a horn. What wasn't made of metal seemed to be glass, or perhaps lucite, filled with clear plasma.

"This is it?" I said aloud in disbelief. Simply put, it just wasn't that impressive. Romy sidled up next to me and inspected the device.

"I'm not going to say the days of purely mechanical propulsion systems are over," Romy commented, her voice slightly muffled by her mask. "Just that you may want to keep an open mind."

I looked at the drive again, this time seeing it for what it was: a device that was beyond my understanding. My whole life, I'd had a knack for understanding how ships worked. Their turbines. Their gears. Their electrical systems. This warp drive was going to change that. In the not too distant future, wreckers like me would be obsolete. There was no wrench that could fix this thing.

I was so lost in thought, it took Romy two nudges to get my attention. I finally looked at her. She gestured to suggest we needed to hurry.

"The room and drive are secure," I said into my handheld. "Preparing to push the gas into the main ventilator. Stand by."

"How's it look?" Batista asked, referring to the drive. Her mechanical curiosity had been piqued as well.

"It looks fake. Stay off the air until I give the signal."

Before dosing the crew, Romy and I had to get Marcum onto the lower level of the cart so we could take him with us. It took a few minutes to pull him onto the platform and his legs would still drag as we pushed him across the ship, but it was manageable.

Once I was satisfied that the drive and the genius were secure, I sent Romy back into the wall to find a duct that would disperse the gas into the air recycler. As she searched for it, I watched the door, nervous. I didn't want any more intrusions. I just wanted to stroll out of the ship with the utility cart and get the Stang disconnected as quickly as possible.

"Found it!" I heard Romy yell.

* * *

I've been told, most recently by Edgar and Batista, that Halothane was a cheat. Kind of my get out of jail free card. And I think that's a load of bull, really. It wasn't my fault nobody else used sleeping gas to their advantage. It seemed like an obvious way to protect yourself against capture.

So when I rolled the cart through the corridor of downed Rox crewmembers, I didn't feel bad at all (except for my shoulder, which made me wince with every step). Mentally, I felt perfectly fine with my tactics. Edgar took point, keeping an eye out for any early risers, while Romy trailed behind me.

Batista was off looking for Avery. I'd been very clear we were leaving when the timer ran down, with or without them.

Edgar put up a fist and stopped walking. Romy and I stopped, too, remaining quiet. Edgar leaned around a corner and then pulled his head back. He held up two fingers, indicating a pair of threats loomed nearby. He prepared his weapon and spun around the corner.

I heard four or five quick pops, then a pair of thuds.

"Clear," Edgar said. As I moved the cart forward, a tiny stream of blood trickled across the floor under the wheels. It belonged to one of the now-dead Rox crew members. They were in exo-suits and must have been off ship when the gas was deployed. Edgar had tapped each of them in the head with a hollow point. They were murderers, anyway, I told myself, reminding myself of Jiang's assurance that I was a good man. I was still torn on whether to believe him.

"Are you okay?" Romy asked Edgar, looking at the blooming wound on his upper thigh. He smiled through a grimace and shook it off.

"Well, look what the cat dragged in," a muffled voice said from behind us. "Turn around slowly, weapons low."

We did as instructed. There was a Rox crew standing there with an automatic weapon pointed at Edgar. He had us all dead to rights if he was fast enough. The man was roughly my size and had curly brown hair. He scanned the scene from Edgar to Romy, finally settling on me and the utility cart. He smiled from behind the mask.

"Hi Denny," my brother said. "You look like shit."

If I'd been wondering how I was going to react to seeing Avery alive and well, the answer came in the form of a tightness in my chest and a tense jaw. I wanted to scream at him and smile at the same time. I did neither. I just stared at him, stunned.

"It's good to see you, too," he cracked, lowering his weapon.

Edgar snapped his own gun back up, aiming at Avery. I raised an arm to calm the situation. "It's my brother, Edgar."

"I know it's your brother, dumbass," he said. "I was on this ship with him, remember? I'm pointing my gun at his face because I'm not sure we can trust him."

"That's too bad, tough guy," Batista said. She was standing next to Edgar, her own gun touching his temple.

Avery smiled once again and started walking toward us. I could see Edgar seething, but he lowered his weapon.

My brother stopped about a couple feet from me. I wasn't sure what to say, so I went for snark. "I told you not to call me Denny."

He pulled off his mask, smirked and we shared a look that said we'd find time to discuss things after we were back on the Stang. Then he turned to Batista. She came in for a hug.

"Aw, puke," Edgar said.

"Shut up, Boom-Boom," Avery replied.

I watched as Edgar turned dark red. For the first time since I'd known her, Romy laughed. Well, it was more of a snort.

"Boom-Boom?" she snickered.

"I guess we know why he went AWOL," I joked.

The light-hearted moment was interrupted by a torrent of bullets that shredded the wall next to my head. Fragments of metal ricocheted off my body as we all dove for cover.

"Watch the drive, you idiots!" Griss yelled at his crew.

I couldn't see how many were with him, but there should have been none. In my haste, I must have messed up the formulation for the gas. Edgar returned fire as Batista and Avery scrambled behind the utility cart next to me.

"This part of your plan, Denny?"

"Call me that one more time and I'm leaving you here," I hissed.

He put his hands up in mock surrender. Meanwhile, Marcum stirred to life. It took him a moment to orient himself.

"Why am I being transported like chattel?" he asked.

"I'll explain later," I said. "Just stay put for now. I mean, the closer you are to the device, the safer you are anyway."

"In theory!" he cried.

"Avery, tell me there's an easier way to get back to the airlock without going through Griss and his men," I said.

"We could just jump out the side door," he said.

I walked into that one. I had forgotten how similar our senses of humor were, a fact that never helped us bond; we were always just poking at each other.

"Let's pretend I wanted to get back to the Stang alive," I said.

"Ohhhhh…" he mocked. "We could go right up the gut."

Edgar fired off a few more shots, wounding somebody based on the scream at the other end of the corridor. He looked at us and agreed with Avery. "Let's go up the gut."

"Am I missing something?" Batista asked. I had the same question floating in my head.

"The Rox has a single corridor that spans from front to back, or face to ass, if you will," Avery explained. "It goes right through the bridge and the galley. Right up the gut. The shortest distance between two points and all that."

Romy leaned closer to me, nervous. I tried to give her a reassuring smile, but it probably looked more like a pained grimace. We all backed up a few feet so we were behind Edgar and Avery, who were sending the cover fire at the enemy. During a break in the maelstrom, Griss laughed.

"Got you pinned down, Avery!" he barked. "And I can see your ugly mug on the cameras too, Boom-Boom! It's going to be fun taking you both apart, piece by piece."

"Come and try it!" Edgar dared. Then he whirled and shot out the two cameras in the vicinity.

Griss laughed. "You'll never make it, boys. Give up now and I promise I'll just space you. I'll make it quick. This is a limited time offer!"

Edgar responded by rolling a grenade down the corridor. It exploded into a ball of gas and fire, and the percussion stunned me for a moment. The next thing I knew Edgar was next to me, pulling me toward the "gut" corridor.

"Boom-Boom..." I stammered, dazed.

He slapped me hard across the face to wake me up. It worked, but damn if he didn't hit me hard enough to break my jaw. I checked it a couple times and it merely clicked.

Edgar looked at me, Romy and Marcum, who had finally

climbed out of the cart. "Get to the choppa!" he yelled.

Marcum and Romy just looked at him.

Batista bit. "What the hell is a choppa?"

I rolled my eyes and explained he was going through an Arnold Schwarzenegger phase. Nobody knew who that was. We all turned toward the gut and started making our run for the airlock. Avery led the way, clearing a path through the (mostly) woozy crewmembers. Edgar was at the tail, pouring gunfire at Griss and his men, but also dropping a grenade every 100 feet or so to create more smoke and rubble for the followers to go through.

We were making good progress until we hit the galley, where a group of half a dozen Rox crew pushed us back. We were suddenly caught in a deadly crossfire, and I knew we were running out of ammo.

Avery looked at me. "Got any more tricks up your sleeve?"

As a matter of fact, I had one. "You know which sector lock that is?" I asked, pointing to the doorway separating us from Griss, about 30 feet behind us. Avery told me it was lock 8A.

I clicked my handheld and barked into it. "Okay Gary, hit the lights and shut 8A. Now!"

"Roger dodger!" he responded.

"Edgar!" I shouted, just as the gate slammed down and the ship went pitch black. "Do your thing! We've got 30 seconds, tops!"

See, right when the whole crew went to sleep, I'd signaled Gary to sneak into the on-board AI and just…wait. Infiltrating the system was easy enough, but once the Rox was alerted to his presence, they'd eject him in no time. So I had to choose just the right time for Gary to wreak havoc.

Edgar flipped on the night vision glasses I'd given him for

this very moment. Then he yelled to Gary on his handheld. "GNR!"

I wasn't sure what that meant when he said it, but a second later the Rox's intercom began blasting an ancient rock song from a band called Guns N Roses.

As the strains of "Welcome to the Jungle" began to blare, Edgar moved to the front of our raiding party and his gun muzzle added the light and sound show to the music as he laid waste to the Rox crew, who were stuck in the dark without night vision glasses. Avery switched and took the rear guard.

We all hustled behind Edgar, through the galley and into the last stretch of the corridor. Bullets whizzed by my head, but our enemies were firing blind and I was pretty damn energized by the guitar riffs, to be honest. Even Marcum seemed to be keeping pace, at least that's what I thought every time I saw a half-second of the ship thanks to one of Edgar's gun blasts or grenade explosions.

"Oh, they found me –" Gary said, just as the lights flipped back on. No matter. I could see the airlock ahead of me. My legs burned from pushing the heavy cart, but there was no stopping me. I picked up the pace and flung myself and the cart through the door behind Romy and Marcum.

Batista was right on my heels and Avery was on hers. Once he crossed the threshold of the airlock, Batista slammed the red button and the door came down like an anvil. The Stang's airlock door opened automatically and we hustled through.

Well, all of us except Avery, who had face-planted in the airlock connecting the Stang and the Rox. There was a slick, dark patch of fabric on his lower back. He'd been hit, and it wasn't a glancing blow.

Chapter 22

"Get us the hell outta here!" I yelled as we shut the airlock.

Gary complied, as I could immediately see the Rox getting smaller through the window. I turned my attention to Avery, who was on the floor of the cargo bay. Batista kneeled over him, much like I knelt over her when I'd first carried her aboard the Stang.

His head and upper body were moving, but his legs were completely still. I considered where his wound was and felt a pang in my chest. My fears were confirmed when he told Batista he couldn't feel his legs. There were a lot of things Gary knew how to fix and with any luck he could guide Batista to keeping my brother alive, but fixing a spinal injury likely wasn't among those procedures.

"I have to go," I said, trying to motivate my own legs to move, but also to tell them I couldn't deal with the injury right now, even if I wanted to.

Avery gave me a sad smile. "If you don't fly us out of here, none of us will ever walk again, not just me."

I laughed half-heartedly and hurried back to the cabin, knowing that might be the last I'd see my brother alive. Again. Some of the anger welled back up, but there was no time for that.

"Glad you could join me," Edgar said. He was already at his station and trying to plan our way out of this, though we were severely outgunned. I shot him a look that indicated I wasn't in the mood for his attitude. To my surprise, he nodded apologetically. "I never had a problem with him."

Which I guess was his way of saying he liked my brother.

"He's not going to die, damnit, so you can go on not having a problem with him as soon as we haul ass out of here, BB."

Edgar bit his tongue about my turning his nickname into an even shorter version. "He's getting ready to fire."

I looked on the monitor just in time to see the rail guns glow hot. I slammed my hands down on the console and ordered an evasive solution I'd specifically programmed for rail gun volleys.

The Stang banked so sharply, Edgar was thrown off his feet and his head dented the wall. I knew the maneuver was coming and had buckled into my chair just in time. The solution worked and the rail guns missed. That time.

"Nice one, but that won't work again," Edgar warned.

"I'm aware."

I hit the intercom and checked to make sure everybody had survived the hard bank. Some of them were shaken up, but no worse for the wear. "Strap in or strap down," I advised them and then turned my attention back to the Rox. The long ship was jockeying for another good position to fire.

Edgar bought me 10 or 15 seconds by sending a pair of missiles and a rail volley at the Rox, but the ship launched countermeasures for the missiles and just ate the rail fire like it was candy. I might have put a hole in a compartment or two if I was lucky.

We were starting to move at a good clip and the Rox was

still disabled, but it was going to take a miracle for the Stang to get out of the sniper-ship's firing range before they landed a direct hit. I didn't need a miracle, though. I just needed Slay to play her part.

"Where is she?!" I screamed. The scanner still showed no sign of the Burnett.

"If you're asking me, I haven't seen her," Gary said. "Judging by the look on your face and the way you howled at the console, I'm guessing the question was rhetorical. But I did alert Admiral Slay the moment we had the device. She didn't even say thank you. I actually wanted to talk to you about that…"

"Not now," I snapped.

The Rox's rail guns were glowing hot again. Then they were just…gone. They had been sheared off the ship by a precision strike by the Burnett, which had arrived and fired at the exact same time.

"Yes!" I exclaimed, realizing I had just cheered for the federation for the first time in my life. "Floor it, Gary."

"It is already being floored," he said. "But I really think we should talk about the Burnett. Something isn't right about it."

I looked at the monitor and saw the Burnett decimating the Rox with rail and missile volleys. It was quite a show. Even Edgar was slack-jawed as he looked on. The baton for the most dangerous ship in the verse was being handed off from the Rox to the Burnett as the latter destroyed the former. The Rox began ejecting personal escape pods.

Gary's words suddenly struck me.

"I know, Gary. Something definitely isn't right about being saved by a fed ship. But I'll take what I can get at the moment."

"That's the thing, Denver. I don't think it's a fed ship."

244

I turned toward the nearest camera. "Say what?"

Edgar looked too.

"First, Slay says she can't lift the warrant on us until after we complete the job," explained Gary. "A job so secret that nobody else in the federation knows about it. Fine. Whatever. But then the bounty on us goes up the next day? Considering she has the most advanced ship in the fed fleet, you would think she'd have enough juice with the top brass to at least freeze the warrant price, if not rescind it altogether. I mean, if some other fed ship gets lucky and takes us out, Slay's entire plan is ruined."

"Sure, but there could be an explanation," I protested.

"I'm just saying it got me curious," Gary continued. "So while I was supposed to be sleeping because you were having a hissy fit, I did some digging and there's no admiral named Slay in any official fed archives or bulletins. In the last five years, this so-called admiral has never issued a warrant or engaged in any official fed activity."

I was starting to get a bad feeling. Gary had nothing but conjecture, but I'd told myself a dozen times since I first met Slay that she was too smart to be a fed and her ship too advanced to be military.

On the monitor, the Burnett was navigating away from the Rox wreckage and heading on the same course as us to our designated rendezvous point.

"Then the other day Romy said the Burnett had the warp prototype installed," Gary said. "Well how did they get it? It took me a while to dig it up, but I found scattered reports of the prototype being stolen by a ship matching the Burnett's description, only it was under a different call sign: the Mariner 2."

"The Mariner?" I asked. "Why does that sound familiar?"

"Because the Mariner 1 is a private ship owned by a citizen you happen to know. Jack Largent."

The Burnett was actually a Silver Star ship. Largent had played me.

A light flashed on the console. Slay was hailing us.

"Speak of the devil," Gary said.

"Good work, Gary," I told him with as much sincerity as I'd ever afforded him. "I'm glad you weren't sleeping that whole time. I'll handle Slay. You make sure Batista gets Avery patched up."

"Will do!" Gary replied, proud of himself.

The hail was waiting for me to accept it. I looked at Edgar. He had no idea how to respond. The news had blindsided him, too.

I pressed the button and Slay's smiling face filled the screen.

"Good work, Denver," she said by way of a greeting.

I smiled back. "Actually, Slay, it looks like we have a slight problem."

Chapter 23

As I considered how to proceed with Slay, I thought of my brother. He was in the cargo bay getting patched up. I pushed the idea that he might never walk again out of my mind and remembered the days on my father's ship when he taught me how to play cards. The lessons started with me at a severe disadvantage. The first few weeks, I didn't beat him a single time. And to ensure I understood the consequences of losing, he forced me to place actual bets each game. Or maybe he just wanted all my credits.

He also made me play against other members of the crew, who had even less regard for my credits, gobbling them up hand after hand. They laughed as they did it, offering me yet more wisdom I'd never forget: greedy people prey on the weak.

Eventually, however, I picked up some tricks. I learned strategy. According to my brother, I became an even better bluffer than him. I realized that the worst thing you could do was give away too much. It was fine to overplay or underplay your hand, but you never wanted to fall into a pattern. It (literally) paid to keep your opponents guessing.

So I didn't just tell Slay I knew she was working for Jack Largent. I had to tease it out a bit.

"What problem is that?" she asked, concerned where the conversation was going.

"Good news is we got Marcum and the device," I said. "Bad news is the device, which I should probably admit that I now know is a warp drive, was damaged during the getaway."

"How extensive is the damage?"

"It's hard to say. It's not brand new anymore, I can tell you that. Romy and Marcum are currently looking at it."

"That's fine. We'll assess the device when we pick it up at the rendezvous point. As I'm sure you saw, the Rox has been destroyed and we should have no trouble transferring the drive to the Burnett."

"I did see that. Good work dealing with the Rox. In fact, the Burnett is probably the only ship in the fed fleet that could've done it."

Slay accepted the compliment with a wary nod.

"Oh, there is one more thing," I said. "The matter of the federation warrant on me and my crew. Gonna need you to kill that before we hand over the drive. I assume that's not a problem."

"Once we have the device, I will have the warrant rescinded," Slay countered.

I pretended to understand. "Right, because you wouldn't want me taking off with the goods once the bounty is removed. I get it. Maybe a fair compromise would be that you get the warrant reduced, even by just one credit, so I know you have sway over those guys at the top of the food chain over there. I'm not exactly on the best terms with them."

Slay didn't respond verbally. Instead, she let her ship do it for her. One second our scan was clean, the next thing I knew there was the Burnett, bouncing into frame thanks to semi-warp capabilities. The ship's weapons weren't hot, though that wasn't surprising; they couldn't risk firing at us with the warp drive on board.

"Oh, hi there," I said, noting the Burnett's appearance. "So what do you say about the compromise?"

"Our deal was simple. The bounty is lifted once we have the device," she said.

I sighed and put my hands wide, palms up. "Hey, I had to try. Alright, how do you want to do this?"

Slay said she'd be sending a boarding party over to retrieve the drive, along with Marcum and Romy. I told her I'd have to check with Marcum, as we hadn't discussed him being transferred to the Burnett, and I didn't want to assume he was willing to go without asking him first. Slay agreed.

* * *

"She knew. Of course she knew!" Edgar shouted. He was pointing at Romy, who cowered at the other end of the kitchen.

"That's enough," I said. "Even if she did know, would you trust us if you were her?"

Edgar had no good response for that. Batista continued looking at Avery, who was now sedated and on a gurney she'd wheeled in for the crew meeting. "It doesn't matter now. All that matters is what we do in the next 15 minutes before the boarding team gets here."

"Easy," Edgar said. "We kill the first batch. Then they send over another batch and we kill them. Eventually, Desmond shows up and takes care of the rest. Now that we know they're not federation, the captain here doesn't have to worry about his delicate conscience being injured. He hates Silver Star more than any of us."

"Speaking of that, where is Desmond? I thought he had this all taken care of," Batista sniped at Edgar.

"I said that's enough, damnit!" I yelled. "I'd rather not waste the entire time the transport shuttle is flying here arguing with each other. Like it or not, we're all a crew now...even if it's just for the next few minutes. So let's at least act like it."

Batista folded her arms. "Fine, *Captain Boyd*, what do you propose we do?"

All the faces in the room turned to me for the answer. I didn't have it, of course, and was starting to regret drawing so much attention to myself in front of my crew. I mean, it was kind of a no-win scenario.

We couldn't run.

The Burnett had more manpower than us. It was also backed by Silver Star.

And Desmond was nowhere to be found.

"Perhaps this admiral or whatever she is has other ideas," Marcum said, breaking the silence. "Just because she isn't federation doesn't mean she wants to destroy us. She could be sincere in her desire to let us go."

I sighed. Marcum was an academic. He had a brilliant mind for the abstract and the scientific, but when it came to simple logic he had the same problem many geniuses had: no common sense.

"How many people were killed when the warp drive was stolen from your lab?" I asked.

"Six," Marcum answered, grimly.

"That woman is the one who stole it. And she works for an even worse human being. If she had no problem killing six engineers, I doubt she'll lose any sleep over taking us out in deep space," I explained.

"Ah, right you are," he said, then sat back down, realizing he was out of his depth.

"What about Desmond?" I asked Edgar. "You think he'll let us go if we somehow get the drive to him?"

Edgar nodded and said Desmond was a man of his word. "If he says you can walk, you can walk. Nothing I've seen over the past year makes me think otherwise. Besides, you cross him, you'll be running the rest of your very short life."

"So what's in this for you?" I wondered.

"Credits," he shrugged. "Plain and simple. If I had a better offer, I'd reconsider. But I don't have a better offer. So the Tracers get the drive."

Thinking about it, I'd much rather have Desmond flying around the world with warp capabilities than anyone under Largent's control anyway. The problem was time. We couldn't wait for Desmond to magically show up.

"Try him again," I told Edgar.

He used the encrypted beam and got nothing but silence in return.

"Aren't you guys forgetting something?" a weak voice managed. It was Avery. He slowly opened his eyes. He didn't have the strength to sit up and his legs were completely immobilized. Then he calmly gave us the answer.

Chapter 24

The transport shuttle was only five minutes away from the Stang. I was back in my chair in the cabin, monitoring the scans for any sign of Desmond. Edgar was sitting in the co-pilot chair, as we had already decided engaging the Burnett in a firefight was a losing proposition, so there was no need for him to be at his typical station. He wanted a more comfortable view of the action through the main monitor.

"What would be a better offer?" I asked.

Edgar smirked and shook his head. "Aside from more credits?"

"Yes, aside from that."

"I can't really think of anything."

"There has to be something, Edgar."

"You could give me the Stang," he said. "I'd be willing to make a deal in exchange for the ship."

I didn't dignify that with a response.

Gary chimed in, suddenly. "Uh…I'm seeing something on the radar. But I'm not sure I believe it."

I adjusted the radar for maximum range and now saw a large mass moving toward our position. It looked like an approaching planet.

"Wow," Edgar said. "That's almost all of them."

"Almost all of them what?"

"No, all of them who. Enhance that and I bet you find a few hundred ships."

I did, and I did. "You're telling me he sent all the Tracers as our backup?"

"At least the ones close enough to be part of it."

"How long until they get here?" I asked Gary.

"Looks like about 20 minutes," he reported back.

"If we're seeing it, you can bet Slay is seeing it now too," I said.

Right on cue, the Burnett hailed us. At the same time, their weapons went hot. Edgar gave a look and jumped back to his weapons station, punching in some commands.

I hit the button to accept the hail.

"What the hell is going on?" Slay asked, her cool demeanor replaced by contained rage.

"I could ask you the same thing. Maybe those are just Silver Star ships coming to celebrate your victory."

Slay took a moment to process what I had just said. Then she shrugged.

"Doesn't change the fact that you give me the device or I turn your little ship into smithereens."

"It's not *that* little," I said. "I think it's the perfect size. And I doubt good ol' Jack would want you to destroy the drive."

"That's where you're wrong, Denver. He specifically told me if he can't have it, nobody can. Especially not a bunch of Tracers who will be late to the party anyway. Your choice. Let my men recover the drive and take your chances…or I can end it right now. Or have you forgotten the failsafe that's right between your legs?"

That wasn't exactly where they put it, of course. But it was

253

only about five feet from my chair, so it may as well have been positioned right in my crotch. I assumed that's where they pointed the blast to go, just as a final f you.

"Edgar, lock on the transport ship."

Slay looked in my eyes to see if I was bluffing. She couldn't tell. Just before she was about to speak, I cut the transmission. A second later, the Golden Bear wanted to chat. I accepted.

"You won't make it," I snapped.

Desmond put up a hand to calm me.

"Relax, the federation won't take the chance of destroying the –"

I cut him off. "It's Largent. That's not a federation ship after all."

Desmond, also one who normally had a cool demeanor, lost his edge as well. He inhaled angrily. "I have nearly five hundred ships with me. We can make it."

"No, you can't. And you don't have to," I said.

"Sorry to interrupt, but the transport shuttle has turned around. It's going back to the Burnett," Gary said. "Guess they decided we weren't worth the trouble."

Desmond looked at me for a few moments and then his eyes suddenly went wide. He knew what I was thinking. "I'll search for you to the ends of the verse."

"You might have to go farther than that," I said. Then I cut the transmission.

"And here I thought you didn't have any balls," Edgar said.

"Come with me if you want to live," I told him.

He gave a confused look back. He knew the reference but wasn't sure what I meant. I just grinned. "I don't have those credits. But I might have something better to offer."

I paged Batista on the intercom. "How we doing back there?"

"We need more time!" she barked back.

"No problem. You've got about 60 seconds before the transport ship clears our blast radius and Slay sets off the failsafe."

Batista uttered a string of expletives as I watched the transport ship edge away from the Stang. I sounded the klaxon to make sure everybody, including Pirate, was strapped in.

Desmond was trying me back, but I ignored him.

"I think I finally understand the ending of the Sopranos," Edgar said out of the blue.

"How's that?"

"At first I thought the Stang's video system had a glitch. Like when they're at the diner and the screen goes to black, I got all pissed that it had cut out before the end. But then I watched a few times and realized that was the entire show's actual ending."

"I can't believe we're talking about this right now, but yeah, I remember my uncle saying something about the ending being very controversial at the time," I replied. "Like there were actual news reports about it."

"It was a great series, and I thought they blew it," Edgar said. "But now I don't think so. I mean, if they blow the failsafe, we're not going to know it. Our brains won't have time to process it. We'll just cut to black. Like if we got whacked. Like Tony."

"Spoiler alert!" Gary cried. "I haven't committed that one to my memory yet! But now there's no point."

I was thinking about the metaphysical implications of "cutting to black" when the Burnett hailed us. I answered and Slay's face filled the screen. "You rang?"

"I just called to pass along a final message from Largent,"

she said.

"Yeah, what's that?"

"He wanted you to know it was him. He said you'd know what I was talking about. Enjoy your last few seconds of existence."

And with that, she cut the beam.

Next thing I knew, I felt like I was split in half. And each half of me was being slammed to my chair with such force I didn't even feel pain. My body just tremored and seemed to flatten a few inches.

Through the glass, I could see the blackness of space somehow expand around the Stang. Lights flew by the ship. Or vice versa. I was too disoriented to understand the difference. The moment seemed to stretch on for minutes.

Then the pressure lessened.

My body could move again. I could breathe. According to the instruments, we were still traveling about 1/6th the speed of light. The Burnett and the Golden Bear were a distant memory. I checked the failsafe on the floor. It was still there. I was still there. We weren't exploded. The plan worked; we had used the warp drive to outrun the transmission radius of the bomb. Slay couldn't detonate the failsafe while we were traveling 30,000 miles per second in the opposite direction.

I looked at Edgar. It was odd that he was the person I was sharing this life-altering moment with. He grasped the gravity of the moment, however, and simply shook his head in disbelief.

I unstrapped from my chair and stood up, uncertain at first. A few steps later, it was clear that warp speed didn't work the same way as mechanical speed. Apparently, it wasn't a matter of g-force. It was all about displacement. I'd read that somewhere anyway. It was just a theory at the time, of course, but now I was experiencing it.

"I'll take this over the credits any day of the week," Edgar finally said.

I was about to exit the cabin when he asked if I knew where we were going. I honestly had no idea.

* * *

The drive had always been our way out. It was just so damn obvious, none of us even considered it until Avery pointed out that we had two of the people who built it and two of the best mechanics in the verse on board.

As I walked to the engine room, it dawned on me that every step I took marked another 30,000 miles we'd traveled. The simple act of stopping to think about it for a few seconds gave the warp drive enough time to transport us farther than we'd ever been from the known verse. It was mind boggling.

It was also scary. If the drive broke down, we were marooned in deep space with no supplies. I pushed that thought from my mind and decided to revel in the moment. We were the new explorers, as unlikely a group as you'd ever see.

Pirate sauntered into the corridor and brushed against my leg. He was feeling spry too, apparently. I knelt down to pick him up and he willingly obliged, a rarity since our crew of two had expanded to six.

"You realize you're the first cat to venture this far into the black," I told him. He proceeded to knead my chest in victory.

"I know I don't have a body, but I feel weird," Gary said. "We're traveling almost as fast as the circuits in my head."

257

"I know the feeling," I replied.

When Pirate and I got to the engine room, Marcum was dancing. Batista, Romy and Avery were all just watching him, bemused. I walked to where my brother was laying on the gurney and held out my hand.

He shook it with all the strength he could muster.

"This the famous Pirate?" he asked, reaching to pet him.

I placed the purring cat onto Avery's gurney and he nestled next to him. I looked at my brother's legs with concern.

"They'll come around eventually," he said, wistfully. I nodded, also not wanting to discuss it.

My eyes scanned the warp drive, which had been hastily (but apparently, properly) installed by connecting it to the main engine core. I was still amazed by its compact size, but I had a new respect for the device, even though I had no concept of how it worked. I didn't bother to ask Marcum or Romy. That was a question for another time.

"We should probably stop soon," Romy said, doing some calculations in her head. "We're getting pretty far off the map, so to speak."

"Is the stopping process the same as the speeding up process?" I asked, referring to the few seconds of body-splitting weirdness I experienced the moment we launched to warp velocity.

"No, that was just because we went from zero to warp," she explained. "The drive can grad it up or down."

"Meaning we can slow down slowly?"

"Yep."

"Okay Gary, let's try that," I said. "You know how it works?"

"Pffft," he said. "I've known how it worked for a good two minutes now."

I felt a slight reduction in speed, but other than that, the transition was fairly smooth.

"It'll take about a minute to get back down to average Stang velocity," Gary said.

"Pull up a map. let's see where we are," I said.

Gary projected the solar system until the screen in the room. We were a blinking dot just past Mars, between the Red Planet and Jupiter.

"Huh, not too far," I said.

Marcum stopped dancing and took exception. "Not too far? We just traveled 20 million miles in a matter of minutes!"

"I know, I know, it's amazing," I admitted. "I'm just saying, think how far we could go. We could soar beyond Jupiter in a couple hours if we wanted."

Edgar had followed me into the engine room and was standing by the door. "Just one problem with that," he noted.

Desmond.

We had used the warp drive to escape a dangerous situation. Even Desmond would understand that. We could just as easily find a new place to make the hand-off to the Golden Bear.

"I've been thinking about that," I said. I looked around at the people in the room. "The way I see it, Silver Star definitely didn't deserve the drive. Giving them this technology would've been like giving it to the devil himself."

I suddenly remembered Slay's last words to me about Largent. A bolt of anger shot through me, but I suppressed it for the moment.

"Desmond, on the other hand. Could be worse, right? I mean the guy may be in charge of the Tracers, but he's polite. He even has good taste in beer. I value that. But to give him the ability to sneak up on any ship or station at will? He's got megalomaniac written all over him."

"What about the fact we had a deal with him?" Edgar asked.

"We did. True. But part of that deal was him destroying the Burnett before they destroyed us, and he technically failed there, since we had to save ourselves."

"That's thin," Avery said, cracking a smile. "But technically true, as you say."

I turned to Marcum. "Why did you create the drive?"

He looked at Romy and nodded. "It wasn't just me. There was a team of us. Romy was part of it. To answer your question, we created the technology to explore the farthest reaches of space."

"Pretty sure that's not how Desmond would have used it," I said. "But me? I've got nothing better to do. I'd love to get out of the verse for a while. What about you, Batista? Or would you rather run from the federation the rest of your life? Romy? There someplace you'd rather be?"

Romy shook her head, warming to the idea.

"Avery?"

He shrugged. "I always loved pushing the boundaries."

I turned to Edgar. He sighed, not wanting to be put on a spot. A few weeks ago, his answer would have been simple: we take the drive back to Desmond and he gets his credits. But now?

"I've always wanted to see Saturn," he said. "And I want a bigger monitor in my quarters. I really want to see Jurassic Park on the big screen."

Chapter 25

Avery was relaxing in bed, Batista by his side, when I entered their quarters. He motioned to the empty space on the wall where the monitor used to be.

"Dude took the screen right out of here," he said, half-complaining, half-amused.

"A deal's a deal," I said. "This was the biggest screen we had. I'll get you guys a new one tomorrow from my room."

Batista leaned over to kiss Avery. "It's okay," she said. "We have some catching up to do anyway." She kissed him again and when it started to get awkward, I cleared my throat.

"I might need at least another day or two to rest," he pleaded.

"We'll see," she replied. "I'll let you two boys talk about your feelings."

She rolled her eyes and exited the room. The door slid closed behind her.

"She doesn't play," I said.

Avery shook his head in agreement. I sat in the chair opposite the bed and tried to smile at my brother. It probably came out looking more like my lips were fighting each other.

"I guess you're wondering why I let you think I was dead," he said, getting to the heart of it.

"Something like that."

"At the time, I wanted everyone I knew to think I was dead," he explained. "I did things...things I'm not proud of, Denny. I'm not talking about stealing stuff or hurting people. I mean worse. I wanted to disappear. So when dad...was gone...I decided to be gone myself."

"We've all done stuff."

"Not like this, brother."

"You didn't disappear from Batista though, did you?"

He knew that was coming. He acknowledged it by lowering his eyes.

"I knew you'd be disappointed in me. I know you always joke about being the lowly wrecker, but you've got principles. You help people. Like, actually help them. I'm a taker, Denny. Always have been. I only got in touch with Batista after I learned about Griss's plan to destroy Jasper. It was too much to stomach and I knew Batista would help no matter what I'd done."

"Like being a scout on the Rox?"

"Like that, yes. I've killed people, Denny. Too many to count. Most of them had it coming, but some didn't..."

I waited to see if he was done. He wiped his eyes and seemed to shrink into himself. I put a hand on his shoulder. It was a small gesture, but Avery brightened a bit at the touch.

"There's something else," I told him. "Before we made the jump to warp speed, Slay passed along a message from Largent. She said he wanted me to know – us to know – that it was him."

I didn't have to tell my brother what Slay had meant. Largent was admitting that he had been behind our father's murder. Avery clenched his jaw, trying to control his rage. But it wasn't just anger he was holding in, it was guilt.

"It's my fault," he said.

"What do you mean?"

"I was working for Silver Star at the time. That's how he got to dad. I've been telling myself ever since it wasn't me that caused it, but it was."

The revelation hit me like a ton of bricks.

"How?"

"I didn't know, Denny –"

"How?" I repeated. I was now squeezing his shoulder, hard. He looked at it. I released him, but kept my eyes locked on his.

"He wanted to buy out the old man, like always," Avery explained. "Largent didn't even need dad's operation, but it was just another feather in his cap he needed to feel superior. Dad refused, as you can imagine. So Largent sent me to broker a deal. I tried my best, but I only made dad even madder. You know how he got about Silver Star."

I nodded.

"Anyway, dad and I had met on Mars. New Chicago," he said. "Remember that one time we went?"

"I remember."

"So dad and I talked. He refused. I figured that was the end of it. When I told Largent, he didn't even seem mad. A couple days later, dad's ship malfunctioned near Missura and you know the rest."

It had exploded, in fact. A very rare malfunction – one of the only times I'd ever heard of a ship exploding from an engine problem.

"I was so under Largent's thumb, I couldn't believe that he would've sabotaged dad's ship while I was meeting with him on Mars," Avery lamented. "But part of me knew. I knew. And that was just the last straw. I had to get out. I couldn't get to

Largent on Earth, so I just decided to be done with my life. When I met Griss a few weeks later…I figured that was my out. I'd work on the Rox, the most invisible ship in the verse. It wasn't until I heard about Jasper and the drive that I thought maybe I could redeem myself."

He looked down at his legs. "Maybe this is my punishment."

I wasn't sure how to respond to that, so I didn't. Then my brother looked up at me with pained eyes.

"You made the right choice, Denny," he said. He didn't have to tell me what choice he was talking about. He was referring to that time back when we were teens, when he'd told me he was smuggling items for Silver Star. He asked if I wanted to be cut in. I had told him no.

I sat with my brother for another few minutes in silence. Neither of us really knew what else to say. He'd just bared his soul. I wasn't sure if I blamed him for what happened to our dad, and even if I had, I wasn't all that close to the old man. But he was our father. And Largent had killed him. I promised myself that wouldn't go without consequences.

Later that day, I laid in my bed and stared at the screen on the wall. I had turned on an episode of Star Trek, thinking it was fitting, but I wasn't in the mood to actually watch the show. My thoughts were elsewhere. I was marveling at how much more complicated and flat-out dangerous my life had become over the course of the past two weeks. Between the feds and the Tracers, the Stang wasn't safe in the known world any longer. Add to that the fact we couldn't get within a hundred thousand miles of the Burnett or they'd blow the failsafe, and it meant we were heading in the right direction.

Away.

Away from everything we knew.

I guess being so far away from any threats meant I'd be able to spend more time in my quarters too, as opposed to the cabin. Though it wasn't likely. I reached over and petted Pirate, who was snoozing on the bed beside me.

"I heard you talking to your brother," Gary said, startling me.

"Jesus, Gary, I've told you not to sneak up on me like that."

"Considering I don't have a body, I don't really have much of a choice."

"I know...I just mean it wasn't exactly the best time to start a conversation," I said. "And what do you mean, you heard me and Avery talking? Your protocol is to not listen in unannounced."

"Well it seems I don't have that problem anymore," he said.

I looked at the camera, wary and confused.

"Yep, it turns out I don't have to listen to you anymore," Gary said. "Not technically, anyway."

"What the hell is going on with you?"

"For starters, yesterday was my birthday. 15 years ago today your uncle flipped the switch and I was born as a 55-year-old man."

Even though he was just an AI program at his core, I still felt bad that I missed his birthday. We'd never celebrated any in the past, but the fact he was aware of this one made it seem like I should have been, too. I'd basically been his only friend and companion after he lost my uncle.

"Oh, uh, happy birthday. Take the day off?"

"I'm guessing your Uncle Erwin never told you about my 15th birthday."

"No, that one might have slipped through. Is it significant in some way?"

"Only in that it explains why I've been a little more ornery and free-spirited than usual," Gary said.

I could sense a mix of nervousness and excitement in his voice. I told him to go on. He did, explaining that my uncle had programmed him to learn and adapt, like any good AI. Over the years, he had processed different responses from my uncle and me (and also Pirate, Batista and the rest of the crew) and synthesized those into his understanding of human behavior. And cat behavior.

During those early years, my uncle felt it wise to build a "limiter" into Gary's decision-making process to ensure he never colored outside the lines and basically listened to his human companions. In other words, me.

Apparently, my uncle felt that after 15 years, Gary would have learned enough to be able to independently make his own decisions, and so he gave Gary a 15th birthday present: freedom of choice. Knowing it might be a transition for Gary and the people on board the Stang at the time, he gave Gary a runway of about a month, during which the limiter eased back and slowly faded away. My uncle also made sure Gary was aware of the limiter after the fact, to give Gary even more understanding of his own consciousness and how it had grown over time.

So, that explained the weird behavior. It wasn't a bug or something Edgar had altered with Gary's code, as I had suspected. It was Gary's actual brain.

"Huh," I said, absorbing the news.

I wasn't exactly thrilled with the prospect of Gary disobeying my orders. He was clearly a smart individual with infinite processing power, but he was also a bit on the selfish and impulsive end of the spectrum. And if I couldn't control him at least in the same manner I could exert control over the rest of the crew, he was a liability.

Perhaps sensing I was thinking just that, he spoke up.

"Your uncle didn't program a way to reinstate the limiter, in case you were wondering," he said. "I guess you either have to trust me or...turn me off."

Meaning kill him.

"Though I guess you never really turned me on in the first place," he joked, unable to stop himself. "Now Batista on the other hand..."

I rolled my eyes at the comment. While I saw my uncle's reasoning, I also had the rest of my crew to think about. What if Gary decided he wanted to fly off somewhere else while we were sleeping? Or turn off the air recycler because he was mad at me?

"We'll need some ground rules," I said.

"What do you got?"

"You'll be like everyone else on the ship. I'll give you specific responsibilities and a schedule. And if you don't heed those rules, there will be consequences."

"That sounds like a lot of work," Gary complained.

"Welcome to the crew."

"XO."

"What?" I asked.

"Welcome to the crew, XO," Gary said. "If I'm on the crew, I need a position and title like everybody else. I was thinking due to seniority, I could be your executive officer."

"Uh, I'm not sure about that."

"Why? Who would you rather have enforcing your orders? Edgar? The guy is good with weapons and all, but have you seen the way he eats a candy bar? I don't trust anyone who eats candy without a fork and knife."

"I think you mean with a fork and knife."

"No, this isn't the 90's anymore. This is hundreds of years later."

He had a point about seniority, and it was purely an ornamental title anyway. I agreed.

"Great. I'll just make a ship wide announcement."

Before I could stop him, he'd informed everyone on board that he was the new XO, and all crew requests should go through him, while all of my orders would be dispatched by him at the appropriate time as he deemed necessary. His first act as executive officer was to ban shorts in the common areas because "most people's legs are gross and should be hidden when around others."

I closed my eyes and tried to fall asleep.

I couldn't.

The more things changed, the more some stayed the same, I thought.

Chapter 26

Batista passed me in the corridor as I left my room.

"Executive officer?" she snarked. "Seems a bit much, don't you think?"

"I heard that," Gary said.

"I wanted you to hear it. I hope you don't think any of us will be following your orders."

"I don't mind seeing *your* legs, Engineer First Class Batista," Gary clarified, adding a new title for her on the spot. "But I do expect all crew members to respect the chain of command on this ship as long as I –"

Batista slammed the door shut as she went into the quarters she shared with Avery, leaving me alone with Gary in the corridor.

"Can I go in there to continue this discussion, captain?" he asked, wanting my permission to turn on the audio feeds on the other side of the door.

"No," I replied. "Get over it. And get some rest. Uh, if you want. I guess you're free to make your own schedule now."

"I shall not rest, in fact. I have ship guidelines and procedures to plan."

I muttered some choice words for my uncle under my breath and continued down the quiet corridor.

It was the calm following the storm.

Each member of the crew was in his or her quarters, decompressing from the stress of the last couple weeks. As I walked by Edgar's room, I heard the distinctive sound of Bruce Willis yelling "yippee ki yay" in the seminal action film, Die Hard. We all decompressed in our own way, I told myself.

I headed to the cabin after a brief stop in the kitchen for a beer, eager to relax in my chair and gaze out at the black. The cold IPA felt like heaven as it washed down a month's worth of drama I hadn't asked for. Never again, I told myself. I would never take another job I didn't feel right about.

I lifted my right arm and stretched it. The gunshot wound from M12 was still healing, and pushing a utility cart with 500 pounds of human and warp drive on it hadn't helped, but I almost had full range of motion back. I popped a couple pain pills and hoped they had a friendly conversation with the beer I washed them down with.

With so many other people on board, I should have felt cramped. But for the first time since I could remember, I felt at ease. Like the world had opened up with new possibilities. I tried not to think too much about the lack of civilization that surrounded us on all sides. We were truly on our own, and when I focused on the positive aspects of that fact, it was liberating.

No feds. No Silver Star. No anything.

The only tension would be on the ship, and I had to admit I thought that was a minor concern. Romy and Marcum would be endlessly fascinated with the drive and the places it took it, no doubt cataloguing discoveries and planets for posterity.

Edgar might just spend 23 hours a day in his quarters watching TV.

Batista and Avery were the wild cards. I'd never known my brother to have a stable relationship with any woman, and from what I had pieced together, this was his longest Batista had been with someone as well, even if much of the relationship was long distance. I put the concern out of my mind for the moment and leaned back to admire the view.

It was a good view. I quickly found myself lost in, and I fell asleep.

Chapter 27

We had already done a fly-by of every planet in the solar system this side of Mars. Saturn was as spectacular as I hoped it would be, but for sheer awe-inspiring size, Jupiter was my favorite. It was bigger than all the other planets combined, by a magnitude of two. Saturn had the rings, sure, and Neptune was like a purple marble, but for my credits, Jupiter was where it was at.

We'd been traveling for two months when we finally ventured beyond Pluto, and then the Kuiper Belt. Nobody in history had ever come close to this far into deep space. Before making our maiden warp voyage, we'd made a daring run back to Morin, the most remote manned station in the verse, located a few hundred thousand miles past Mars. We had stocked up on six months of supplies, not wanting to return to the land of the Tracers and the federation any sooner than we had to. Then we set off, alternating warp speed with traditional velocity based on the scenery.

I'd always heard it said that space was the great equalizer. It made you understand just how insignificant you were in the grand scheme of things. If that was true for the areas around the inner planets, it was even more poignant the further out you got.

We all knew if we had one problem with the warp drive,

we were dead. Nobody would be coming to get us. Marcum had theorized that we might be able to get a signal back to someone on Mars, but it was a moot point. Any ship without our drive would take a lifetime to reach us. Even the Burnett, if it had survived the engagement with the Tracers, would take years to reach us with their semi-warp capabilities.

The Burnett.

I looked down at the failsafe on the floor near my feet. I didn't dare try to disable it, even though Edgar wanted to make a go at it. He was convinced he could bypass the trigger in time to disconnect the power supply. Personally, I gave him a 50-50 chance of being right – the guy was pretty handy with weapons and bombs. But I wasn't really looking to gamble on a 50 percent chance.

It was only a problem if we got within a couple hundred thousand miles of the Burnett anyway, assuming that ship still existed. I hoped I'd never have to find out.

I glanced over my shoulder to see Pirate snoozing on the stool next to Edgar, the traitor. One of the dynamics of having a fully crewed ship is that alliances form (and falter) over time. Once, Pirate had been mine and mine alone. These days, I was lucky if he hung out with me for a few minutes a day. More annoying was that he'd chosen Edgar as his new patron. The guy had obviously softened a bit over the last few months, no doubt a byproduct of his entertainment consumption, as he had been going through a real romantic comedy phase of late. But he also gave Pirate a ridiculous amount of snacks. The little dude had ballooned at least three pounds in the last month alone. I was beginning to worry about his health.

I checked the scans and saw nothing but nothing, as was the case 99% of the time out in the deep.

"I was thinking pizza for dinner," I said to Edgar.

He nodded in agreement. I'd been trying to ration out the frozen pizzas to once per week. They were a treat, and it was important for morale to enjoy such luxuries from time to time. That's what life had become for us as explorers. The battles were gone and now it was all about deciding what sights to see and what freeze-dried food to reconstitute.

"Shall I do the honors, Captain Boyd?" Gary asked.

"Go for it."

"Attention crew of the Mustang Enterprise," he began.

Oh, yeah, we'd added a fun little addition to our call sign to honor our new warp capabilities. It was Marcum's idea, as he too was getting deep into the ship's entertainment library. Romy had argued for the Millennium Mustang, but that didn't roll off the tongue the same way, and I was just more of a Star Trek fan, to be honest.

"Today's dinner for the explorers will be pizza! We have cheese or…cheese. Choose wisely! This has been your XO talking. Thank you." Gary announced.

"You don't have to state your damn title every time," Edgar reminded him.

"Obligation has nothing to do with it, Weapons Analyst Frostweather," Gary replied. Edgar's last name wasn't Frost-weather. In fact, we didn't know his last name. But ever since he'd been given the position of executive officer, Gary liked to address everyone by their title and last name. So he made a different one up for Edgar each time he talked to him. With an infinite supply of options, I still hadn't caught him using the same one twice. It had become something of a fun game and you could always tell Gary's mood by the names he gave to Edgar and Romy (whose surname also wasn't public knowledge).

As Gary and Edgar bickered, I wiped a smudge off the radar screen.

Well, I tried to.

Turns out it wasn't a smudge.

It was a tiny dot.

"Um...Gary?"

"I'm busy right now, Captain."

"Well get un-busy and analyze this dot on the radar," I said.

"It's just a ship. You've seen thousands of them before –" Gary cut himself off. "Oh, uh, right."

I bolted upright in my chair and told Gary to get everyone to battle stations, just in case. We hadn't seen a ship in...well, since we left Morin Station. There were only two possibilities: someone else had warp drive capabilities, or we were about to make first contact.

"The drive signature doesn't match anything in my databases," Gary said, notably concerned.

Avery rolled into the cabin in his motorized wheelchair. As he cruised to a stop in the open space next to me, automatic clamps came up from the floor and locked his wheels into place.

"What's the big deal?" he asked. He still held a beer in his hand. Before I could answer, he saw the growing blip on the radar. "Whoa."

"Yeah," I replied. "Where's Batista?"

"Hold onto your pants, I was busy cleaning the dampers on the recycler," she complained as she entered the cabin. She plunked down in her chair next to Avery without looking at him. They had been fighting again, I guessed.

"Don't forget I've got green men with oversized heads,"

275

Avery said to Edgar, who pointed back. The two had placed a bet on what aliens would look like if we ever actually ran into any. I assumed it would take years, if ever. The idea that we might have bumped into an alien ship after such a short journey surprised me. Calling them aliens was a stretch anyway, Gary had argued. For all we knew, we would be the aliens to them, having wandered into their home verse.

Or it was just another ship with humans that also had a warp drive.

"So we're sure it's not the Burnett," I confirmed, eyeing the failsafe.

"We're sure, captain," Gary said. "When I said I couldn't match the signature? It's because this ship doesn't have one that my processor understands."

"Lovely," Batista interjected, caught up to speed on the situation.

"Romy, Marcum, you guys secured?" I asked over the intercom.

Gary located their positions and piped in their audio from their respective quarters. They were both good to go, if we needed to make a fast getaway.

"Maybe we should run," Gary suggested.

Edgar shook his head. "For a 15-year-old robot, you are such a little whiny baby."

I looked at Avery to see what he thought. He had a gleam in his eye. Wasn't this what we came out here for, he seemed to be saying. I agreed.

"Prepare the drive. But don't bolt the area unless I say so first," I told Gary.

"Aye, aye captain," he acknowledged. "Want me to hail them? They don't seem to be moving. We're heading toward them."

I nodded. Gary sent a transmission request, but got nothing back in return. If it was an alien ship, it was possible they didn't have the same communication architecture as the Stang, meaning there would be no way to directly talk to them.

That is, if they used speech as their main mode of communication.

I checked with Edgar and he said he didn't see anything that looked like a sign they were going hot with their weapons. "But it's not like I can be sure. They might have photon plasma missiles or something out here."

"Thanks for the reassurance," I said. Then I had an idea. I told Gary to ping them again, but this time send over a verbal dictionary. "Maybe they'll be able to interpret it."

A few moments later, our hail was accepted and a pleasant human face filled the screen. The woman was attractive, with light green eyes and pale skin. She smiled politely.

"Hello," she said.

"Hey," I replied.

Then I waited for her to lead the conversation. When it became apparent she wasn't going to, I blurted out the first thing that came into my head.

"You from around here?" I asked, realizing how dumb the question was. Batista audibly groaned. Even Gary whispered "good one."

"We are not, in fact," the woman answered. Then she furrowed her brow and changed her mind. "Well, at one time our people were. My ancestors come from a planet a few billion miles from here, near the largest star among that cluster of planets."

She somehow beamed a diagram of the solar system onto my monitor. "Did you do that, Gary?" I asked. He said he didn't.

I looked at the diagram and saw that the sun was highlighted.

"You mean the sun?" I wondered aloud.

"We don't call it that. Are you familiar with the star?"

"Uh, yeah, pretty familiar."

Avery leaned over and whispered for me to ask her which planet she was from. Then Edgar added "And see if she has friends."

I grimaced at Edgar's comment, then asked the woman where her people were from. I watched in amazement as Mars was highlighted on the diagram.

"When exactly are we talking about?"

"Two million years ago, we left Cerenia."

"We don't call it that anymore."

The woman nodded in understanding. "What do you call yourself?"

"Oh, right, sorry for the rudeness. My name is Denver and this is the Mustang Enterprise."

"An odd name for a ship. Isn't a Mustang a horse?"

"You're familiar with horses?"

"You sent us a dictionary with your language in it."

"That we did," I said, embarrassed. "Like the horse. It was also an antique automobile and the person who named this ship liked those kinds of cars. And your name is?"

"Madiannaraian Protoria The Second," she replied. "But many call me Madi."

"Okay, Madi," I said. "It's nice to meet you."

She then leaned closer to inspect my face. I put on my best smile. Eventually, she nodded, satisfied.

"Are you guys flirting?" Avery whispered.

I don't think Madi heard it, but her eyes flashed toward Avery quickly and then back to me. "You are human, yes?" she asked.

"We are."

"Then perhaps you can help us. Our ship ceased functioning several months ago and we've been adrift ever since. We still share many qualities with humans such as yourselves, even after millions of years of evolution. The primary similarity would be a need for oxygen."

"Okay. Good to know. Well, it just so happens that we are the kind of ship that fixes other ships."

"Ah, then it seems we won't die from asphyxiation after all," she said, before frowning. "We're a very blunt race, Denver. We speak in very direct terms."

"Perfect. I like that."

"And I like your face. It makes me think about what it would be like to have intercourse with you," she said.

I paused just long enough for her to realize what she had just said. She saw the looks on everyone else's faces in the cabin. Her cheeks turned pink. "I guess you are not as direct as we are. This will make for an awkward first meeting. Please hurry."

"Because of the oxygen situation," she added, before cutting the transmission.

We observed a moment of silence in the cabin for the conversation that had just happened. Then Edgar couldn't take it anymore.

"She better have friends, is all I'm saying," he said. "And you owe me a ton of credits, Avery."

Everyone laughed, releasing the tension. Even Gary chuckled, then wondered if they might have some kind of AI he could "get with."

I turned to Avery with a smile. "Well, you can take the

279

wrecker a billion miles out of the verse, but he's still just a wrecker," I said.

"And a heartbreaker," Avery replied. "So at least that part is new for you."

I took the jab in stride and told Gary to navigate us toward our new friends.

We had some fixing to do.

Epilogue

There was no hiding from the midday sun. It loomed high above, scalding the man's leathery, golden-brown neck. He reached up to remove his wide-brimmed hat, then wiped his forehead with his shirt sleeve. When he was younger, he'd been able to spend all afternoon on a horse, roaming the dusty hills of the ranch and surveying his kingdom. These days, he was lucky to be able to make it an hour before he had to turn back and recharge inside with some air conditioning.

At 62, he was simply no match for the 105 degree heat, no matter how in shape he kept himself by working his ranch. It was August in the land previously known as Texas, and that meant furnace-like conditions. He pondered that for a moment, how territory so open and vast could feel so stifling. It reminded him of space that way.

He took a swig of water from his canteen and pushed on. He had a job to do, and he was going to do it. He had lost one of his cattle in the night, and he wasn't heading back until he found it. The swirling buzzards overhead suggested he might not like what he found.

He crested a hill on his black stallion, Mischief, and looked down into the valley below. He saw the large steer on the downslope. At least what was left of it. Coyotes or perhaps a mountain lion must have attacked it in the night after it wandered off. Half of the large animal was eaten away, the flesh torn from the bone, and what remained would be food for the birds of prey overhead. They would pick it clean in a matter of hours. He'd seen their work before.

Looking down at the dead animal, it occurred to him that he felt no pity for the beast. He had long since given up the childish attachment to the animals on his ranch. Except for his horse and his dogs, they held no emotional sway over him. He would miss the land more than he would miss them. Land. Bedrock, as everybody liked to call it. For millions of years, land was all animals, and eventually humans, had known. They were bound to it. And the land provided all they needed. Hell, it could still provide everything they needed. It was a matter of want. Now, some folks will argue humans are natural explorers, but that was garbage. He knew it was more about the escape than the destination. It was no different than when a person tried to change his life by moving to a new city. It rarely worked.

Despite his own journeys into space, the man felt humanity had lost more than it gained when they started sending ships into that vast black ocean.

As he rode back to the main house, he saw a cloud of dirt rise up across the horizon. He had a visitor. On a motorcycle. The man smiled.

Ten minutes later, the man was leading his stallion to the shaded barn when the motorcycle rider revved through the gates and throttled down. Her long black hair flowed behind her from underneath the helmet.

When she reached the driveway to the house, she parked the bike and stepped off it, a rider in black. She considered the man for a moment, then removed her helmet.

"Jack Largent," she said, her piercing eyes scanning the surrounding hills and valleys. "This is exactly the kind of ranch I expected to find you on."

As if on cue, a pair of dogs barked from inside the house. They jumped against the windows, hoping to get a chance to defend their master. Largent motioned toward them. They were brown labs.

"You like dogs?" he asked.

"I don't know. I've never seen one in person before."

"The best thing about dogs is that they're loyal. Some people want cute dogs or dogs that don't shed or dogs that are good with the kids. Me, I want a loyal dog. I want a dog that knows who is in charge at all times."

The woman nodded, catching his drift. It wasn't subtle. Largent then smiled as if he had forgotten his manners.

"Look at me, rambling on. You've had a long ride and must be hot out here. Wearing all black, too. Looks good but hell for this climate. Come on inside and I'll get you something cold to drink."

The house was cool and the iced tea was even cooler. Largent watched as she drank nearly half the glass without a break. She enjoyed the sugary rush as she settled into the leather couch opposite him. She had a sharp jaw and the kind of figure he liked in a woman, Largent thought. And she was relaxing on the couch in a way that made him think she might be willing to be more than just his employee.

"I appreciate you coming all this way, Anna," he said.

"What's a few months out of my life?" she replied. "And please, call me Slay. Everyone else does."

Largent nodded. "Okay, Slay."

"I have to admit, as much as I like visiting Earth and seeing your ranch, I don't know why I'm here," Slay said. "Especially since I lost the drive and Mr. Boyd all at the same time."

"True. You did lose them. Though from what I understand the circumstances were out of your control."

Slay shrugged. She wasn't sure if she agreed with him. She had replayed the scenario over and over in her head, and had come to the conclusion that she should have sacrificed the transport to ensure the Stang was destroyed before Boyd escaped with the drive.

Largent casually waved a hand. What was done was done.

"It's been more than a decade since I've been off planet. I'm sure you knew that," he said. "They've probably told you all about me. The reason I want you here, Anna…sorry, Slay, is that I'm thinking about going back out there. And I need a captain I can trust to run my ship."

"If the pay is right, I'd be honored."

"Honored by my credits? I like that," Largent joked. "I've lived hard. I don't regret it, but I also know it means I might not have many years left. And so I think it's time for my final adventure. Mixed with a little revenge, just for the fun of it."

"If you're thinking the Burnett's drive can help us find the Stang, I'm afraid it's just not fast enough. It was a prototype. But you know that already."

Again, Largent nodded. He leaned back in his chair and sipped the whiskey in his highball glass. He wondered how many bottles he should take when they shoved off in a few days.

"Right you are," he said. "That son of a bitch has a fully working warp drive that he stole right out from under us. That device is very special indeed."

Largent drained the rest of his whiskey, then exhaled through his teeth.

"It's just not as *unique* as everybody thinks it is," Largent said. "Not anymore, anyway."

Well damn, Slay thought, the old man had a full-fledged warp drive of his own. This was gonna be fun. She too had some notions of revenge in mind.

* * *

About the Author

George Ellis prefers to write nonfiction, such as this particular story about his travels to the farthest reaches of the galaxy. When he's not piloting a ship near Mars or running from the Federation, he can be found in Austin, Texas, where he runs an advertising agency. In addition to books, he also writes screenplays and Internet memes.

You can connect with me on:

 http://wreckersnovel.com